CULT

OF THE

WYVERN

SEAN E. KELLY

Printed in the United States of America.

ISBN 979-8-9870352-3-8 (paperback)
ISBN 979-8-9870352-4-5 (hardcover)
ISBN 979-8-9870352-2-1 (E-book)

This book is a work of fiction. Names, characters, places, and incidents either are products of the author's imagination or are used fictitiously. Any resemblance to actual persons, living or dead, events, or locales is entirely coincidental.

Cover design and interior formatting by Damonza.

Sean E. Kelly
www.seanekelly.com

"*Once you have tasted flight, you will forever walk the earth with your eyes turned skyward, for there you have been, and there you will always long to return.*"

~ LEONARDO DA VINCI

PROLOGUE

6 November 2026

The knuckleheads had set the sea on fire. *Again.*

The first time a pipe had burst beneath the Gulf of Mexico, sending an inferno of methane gas churning to the surface, the media had gone wild with it; now, a little more than five years later, it seemed they'd gotten used to such blunders happening. It was still making the rounds on social media, no doubt, with posters likening the watery fireball to everything from an undersea volcano to something out of a fantasy-horror movie.

To Lucretia Tang's eyes, it looked like a big ball of orange cotton candy. Hardly worth veering so far from the shallows she and her brother were supposed to be observing, pushing their Pipistrel Velis Electro almost to the limits of its range.

Jeremiah obviously didn't agree. He leaned out from the plane's right seat, hanging halfway out the opening where the large window had been removed so that he could better observe the sea below him, the wind tossing his shoulder-length hair and shaggy beard like so many black ribbons and plastering his sunglasses to his grinning face as he snapped pictures of the boiling waves with his mirrorless camera and telephoto lens. Lucretia chortled under her breath; sometimes, she forgot that her little brother was thirty-three and not thirteen.

She grabbed Jeremiah by his oversized black T-shirt's collar, yanking him back into the cabin. "All right, Maverick," she japed, her soft voice straining against the rushing wind just as was the low hum of the plane's electric motor. "Fun's over; we've got to get turned around now."

"Aw, come on, Lu-Tang," Jeremiah pouted, putting his headset back on as Lucretia replaced her own. They shouldn't have taken them off in the first place, but they both found that the padding on the headphones made their heads sweat, and it pooled annoyingly in their ears. "Just a couple more minutes. You don't get to see something like this every day."

We will if the morons running the energy companies keep playing reckless. "In case you haven't noticed, this isn't exactly a seaplane. If we don't turn back soon, we'll end up swimming back to Scholes. Remember, we're flying into the wind going back. Although, if you call me 'Lu-Tang' again, I'm gonna throw your ass out that window. The substantial savings in weight will surely help in getting me home."

"Hey, don't pretend you don't like it." He yanked on one of her pigtails, knocking her headset off her ear.

Lucretia rolled her eyes as she adjusted the headset. "You're a dork." She nudged Jeremiah's shoulder as she put the plane into a gentle bank, turning east from their southbound heading so that Jeremiah could have one last look at the inferno.

But before she could turn northwest and set a course for Galveston, her eyes were drawn further east. On the horizon, the sky was darkening to an unnatural shade of gray, almost black, the clouds' curling rind afflicted with a febrile green.

"That wasn't in the forecast," Lucretia noted. She knew that the weather over the Gulf could be mercurial; she wasn't overly concerned. They'd be back on solid ground before the storm. With a shrug that brushed against Jeremiah's shoulder in the cramped cabin, she continued the gentle bank toward the Texas coastline.

Suddenly, Jeremiah grasped her hand, and his palm was sweating. "Uh, Lu?" He drew her eyes eastward. The cloud was hurtling toward them with the ferocity of an ethereal freight train, clawing through the azure sky with a rocket's speed, swirling like a horizontal tornado. There seemed a conscious malice in its misty maw. "Are we in the Bermuda Triangle?"

"Nowhere close," Lucretia gasped, her hands shaking at the control stick. She tried to swallow her terror, but her throat was swollen. She banked hard to the left, pushing the nose down slightly to gather as much speed as she could. But the little electric plane only shuddered as the airspeed indicator approached the never-exceed mark of one hundred eight knots.

"Might want to haul ass here, sis!" Jeremiah squealed.

"I'm trying! This thing isn't exactly the Concorde."

Lucretia risked a glance over her shoulder, cursing the plane's lack of rearward visibility as much as she was thankful. In that moment, ignorance was bliss.

A bliss that lasted all of three seconds. The cloud was upon them with a murderous fury. It had overtaken the plane, which was now being tossed this way and that like a toy boat caught between Scylla and Charybdis. The storm had devoured them.

"I don't want to die!" Jeremiah wailed, grabbing the control stick on his side without thinking, pulling it into his chest even as Lucretia struggled to push it forward. If he kept pulling back, lifting the plane's nose, they'd soon stall. The camera hanging from his neck by its frayed strap was flapping against his chest, the long three-pound lens pounding his round belly.

Lucretia could barely read the instruments through the hellish buffeting, but she could see that the airspeed was falling dangerously low. She reached over to knock Jeremiah's hand off the control stick, leaning into him as she did.

The camera bounced again. The lens struck Lucretia's head, and the gray vortex gave way to sudden, silent darkness.

Lucretia awoke outside, on the ground. The storm must have passed or dissipated; she could see no swirling clouds in the strangely colored sky above her, could feel no wind on her cheeks. Jeremiah was hovering over her, shouting. She thought he was calling her name, though she couldn't discern his words over the ringing in her ears.

She must've been out a while, for the sky was dark. Something must've been wrong with her eyes, because there was something incredibly unnatural about its color. There were no clouds, but the heavens were a purplish shade, almost pure violet at their deepest, lightening to a pleasant amethyst hue at the horizon. The stars followed no pattern she could recognize, and there was no moon where it should have been. *I must've taken one hell of a bump on the noggin*, she knew. The sharp pain in her right temple, like someone had whacked her with the butt of a screwdriver, was proof enough of that. She shook her head, which only exacerbated her vertigo, then pressed her hand into the ground to push herself up. The bare soil was warm and soft, almost therapeutic to the touch, and seemed to glow yellow around her hand, as if she'd just squashed a whole family of fireflies.

Jeremiah cupped her face in his hands. "Lu! Are you okay, sis?"

Lucretia blinked to recalibrate her vision, for Jeremiah's face was painted a soft, lambent blue, as if by the glow of a lava lamp. "Uh...yeah. Head hurts a little." Suddenly, she raised her eyebrow, peering just over his right shoulder, where the Velis was sitting blissfully, pristine, bathed in whatever strange blue glow was messing with her head. "Jay...did you land the plane?"

"Landed itself, really," Jeremiah said with a nervous grin. "It's very intuitive."

"Way to go, little bro!" For as much as she'd tried to teach Jeremiah basic piloting skills, he'd taken to it like a fish to the middle of the Sahara Desert. "You saved both of our lives."

"Uh...I'm not so sure." He waved his arms outward, drawing Lucretia's gaze into the strange new world around them. "I don't think we're in Kansas anymore, Dorothy."

Lucretia's eyes grew wide, her mouth falling open as if her lower jaw were the blade of a guillotine. *What the...?* She pressed her hands to her face, covering her eyes, squeezing them shut for a moment as if to wake herself from a fever dream, shaking her head to clear out whatever glitch had momentarily afflicted her brain. But when she looked upon the world once more, the alien scenery was the same. Beautiful. Lustrous. Horrifying.

Only now, the pain in her head was mysteriously gone, as was the spinning, as if the luminescent mud on her hands contained some kind of healing property. Or magic.

She gazed first into the night sky. Or was it daytime? Nothing was as it should've been here. The ether above was indeed a vibrant purple, full of twinkling lanterns far in the distance, like the stars she was used to seeing, albeit out of place, dancing around strange celestial bodies: a white prolate spheroid with dark spots in the shape of a face, like a smiling sidereal football, peering down from high above; a large red sphere just above the horizon behind the plane's tail, halfway obscured by shadows, bearing rings like those of Saturn in pastel green; a shimmering nebula splitting the heavens high to her right.

Beneath the regal empyrean, trees with boles of pure white rose like towers reaching for the laughing stars, their lobed leaves of a deep red, their smooth bark seeming to glow in the light of the bioluminescent plants growing beneath them that reminded Lucretia of sea urchins, their myriad soft spines emitting soothing blues and greens and yellows and fluttering in the still air as if waving to the newcomers in welcome. Lucretia risked a smile; whatever this place was, it was more beautiful than she could have imagined in her most blissful dreams, an enchanted land straight out of fantasy that could've been the cover art for an early Nightwish album.

Still, she couldn't be sure of anything. This was a strange place, and that beauty may have been a façade. It probably *was* a façade.

"Are we dead?" Jeremiah asked, his voice quavering.

Lucretia drew a deep breath; the air was warm and refreshingly clean, tinged with the faint trace of a savory scent that reminded her of cinnamon. "I don't think so." *If we are, then it looks like we didn't go to Hell.* "Let's find out. Hit me. But not hard."

Jeremiah's open palm met her cheek. It was little more than a tap, but she was still wroth.

"I didn't mean my face, asshole!" she snapped. "No, this is definitely real. We're not dead. Hooray." She exhaled deeply. "I don't know what happened, Jay."

"Was it the vortex?"

The cloud flashed through Lucretia's mind, making her shiver even amid the profound serenity that ensconced her. "It must have been; some kind of wormhole, maybe. Some portal into an alternate universe."

"You mean we're in the multiverse?"

She wanted to roll her eyes and chide him for watching too many movies, but maybe he was on to something. What would have seemed nonsensical when they took off was now firmly within the realm of sensibility. "Might be. Or maybe it's a different part of our universe. If the universe is truly endless, then maybe we've just been taken to a part of it that lies beyond human exploration."

"Taken…by who?"

"I don't know, Jeremiah Tang Jia! And I don't care. All I care about is getting back to *our* world. That should be your main concern too; you need your medication."

Jeremiah bit his lip. "But…how?"

Lucretia sighed aloud. "It may surprise you to learn that I've not given much thought to contingencies for finding myself stranded on an alien planet! Give me a minute." She sucked in a deep breath of the disturbingly clean air, swilling the sweet scent through her lungs. "We need to find that cloud. How far did you fly before you landed?"

"Not long. A few minutes at most. I landed as soon as I could find a place. The vortex was gone when I got out of the plane."

"Well, I guess we won't be taking that way back to Texas." She blew some air through pursed lips. "I suppose our predicament could be worse. At least we can breathe the air here. Gravity seems to work the same as on Earth. Did the plane handle any differently once we passed through the vortex?"

Jeremiah shrugged. "It didn't fall out of the sky, if that's what you mean. You're the pilot, not me."

"All right. We have some battery left; we could fly around a little, see if we can find a way back through the wormhole or whatever—"

"Uh, Lu?" Jeremiah squealed, grasping her shoulder clumsily. "We've got bigger problems right now."

Lucretia followed her brother's terrified gaze to the movement behind the trees. Slowly, a creature emerged, waltzing between the lucent flora. Its body was not unlike that of a praying mantis, albeit wingless so far as Lucretia could tell. Rainbow colors danced upon its shimmering thorax and abdomen, and seemed to emanate from the enlarged tibial spines on its long forelegs. But where a mantis would have had middle and hind legs, some sort of tentacles sprouted from this creature's pod-shaped abdomen, at least eight of them, thin and seemingly flimsy, slithering across the ground like so many noodles. Yet those bluish appendages allowed the creature to move with surprising elegance. The head was almost a perfect sphere, clouds of iridescence to match the rest of the body flashing upon the featureless sheen in a manner as expressive as any face. Lucretia could see nothing that looked like eyes, ears, a nose or a mouth. It was the strangest mantis she'd ever seen.

Especially since, as it drew closer, she could see that it was the size of a grizzly bear.

The creature halted a few paces from the trembling siblings. A slit opened in the lower portion of its head, perhaps its mouth, and a tubelike limb slithered forth that Lucretia assumed was something like a proboscis.

As the proboscis drew close to Lucretia's face, a star-shaped opening formed at its bulb, and the single appendage split into five, fanning out like the petals of a lily. The two that flared upward were thicker than the other three, flashing bright green lights from their ends. The other three curled around with the dexterity of ivy coils, reaching out like gaunt fingers.

Fingers reaching for Lucretia and her brother.

CHAPTER I

6 November 1956

PROPELLER BLADES SPUN like the arms of some medieval torture device. Plumes of smoke rose as if every starter cartridge were its own little volcano, marring the otherwise cloudless azure sky over the Mediterranean Sea an ominous black. Men scurried about the cramped flight deck of HMS *Eagle*, half of them shirtless, deftly dodging the churning propellers and avoiding getting sucked into jet engine intakes as they prepped the aircraft carrier's complement of warplanes to bomb the Egyptians into oblivion.

Lieutenant Sidney Daventry of the Royal Canadian Navy hadn't expected to go to war when he'd volunteered to be an exchange officer with the Fleet Air Arm of Britain's Royal Navy. His own country's Parliament had been vociferous in its condemnation of the Anglo-French military action, to the Queen's great chagrin. He still wasn't entirely sure what they were doing there; Prime Minister Eden had told everyone that Britain was playing the part of peacemaker between Egypt and Israel, but everyone with half a brain knew that he and the French were miffed that President Nasser had nationalized the Suez Canal, wresting control of the vital waterway away from the European powers.

Sid had never been particularly political. He was a naval aviator; he flew warplanes and followed orders. And, as he nudged the Westland Wyvern S4 strike fighter he'd been given the privilege to fly, bearing the serial number Victor Whiskey Triple-Eight, from its parking spot on *Eagle*'s port deck, he wasn't thinking about what was happening in Whitehall or Cairo. The mission was all that mattered—and, more importantly, coming back from it in one piece.

Today's tasking was simple: support British forces advancing on Port Said. Each of 1776 Naval Air Squadron's five Wyverns was fitted out with a pair of thousand-pound glide bombs, eight sixty-pound rocket projectiles under each wing, and two hundred rounds of ammunition for each of the four twenty-millimeter cannons. By now, the Egyptians were all but licked, so the scuttlebutt said. British and French forces had been pounding them since the end of October and were now simply attacking targets of opportunity. Still, Sid wasn't foolish enough to get too cocky. This wasn't his first rodeo. The Egyptians might've been reeling, but they were still dangerous. Two Wyverns had already been brought down by Egyptian ground fire, though both pilots ejected safely and were rescued by friendly forces. And there was still the threat of the vaunted MiG-15 jet fighters; Nasser had been mostly using them against the Israelis so far, but Sid wasn't about to let his guard down.

He kissed the nondescript pewter cross pendant he kept in his flight suit's pocket for good luck. Faith had never been one of his virtues, and neither was superstition one of his vices, but the cross was a gift from his wife, and Marie had both qualities in spades. "Bring home some good English tea," she had besought him in that charming Irish accent that a generation of living in Canada hadn't erased as he'd boarded the plane for London. He remembered the radiance of her smile as he'd embraced her and their two young daughters, Emily and Rhiannon, never imagining that his eight-month stint in the Fleet Air Arm would involve getting shot at. He wondered if Marie knew of his perils, if she was exaggerating them in her mind, as was her wont, or if she was putting her trust in God's providence, as was equally her wont. *My love*, he thought in a flood of warm nostalgia. He'd dreamed all his life about flying; now, he longed for nothing more than that tiny, musty cottage just outside Windsor, Ontario, holding Marie in his arms, running his fingers through her thick auburn mane as she read from her vast collection of books, desperate to ignore the girls pestering the two of them with early suggestions for Christmas presents.

He shoved the thought from his mind, as much as it pained him. Operating in the narrow confines of an aircraft carrier deck was not for the faint of heart and required a pilot to be locked in. The scream of the Armstrong-Siddeley Python 3 turboprop and the throaty growl of the twin contra-rotating propellers swirling from the Wyvern's obnoxiously long spinner had almost become a lullaby, helping him to focus on his checklists. Upon verifying the wheel brake pressure and functionality, he set his throttle to the GROUND IDLE position on its quadrant, smiling smugly as he maneuvered past the De Havilland Sea Venom and Hawker Sea Hawk jet fighters parked in regiments toward the bow. The jet jockeys might've laughed at the hulking Wyvern, but now, Sid was the one sneering. On the ground, the Wyvern dwarfed the diminutive jets, especially the Sea Venoms; its diabolical propellers could've chewed the little fighters into smithereens.

Sid thought back to the first time he'd seen a Wyvern. It'd been a sight to behold, all right—for better and for worse.

Some more generous souls had remarked that, when viewed from beneath, the Wyvern's elliptical wings gave it the look of a Spitfire. If that were so, then it must've been Pinocchio's Spitfire, what with its enormous nose, most of which was taken up by the long, pointy spinner. Viewing it from the side was another matter. It was more awkward than ugly; the underside of the fuselage was almost totally flat, the top rising like a small mountain with its apex at the cockpit, which admittedly gave as good a view over the huge nose as could be expected. Then, there was the towering vertical stabilizer, which looked a bit like a racing dinghy's sail turned the wrong way and was positively impossible for even the most adept artist to draw accurately. Sid's mates joked that Teddy Petter had made a mistake when sketching the design for that fin, or he'd had a mite too much to drink, and the assembly line had dutifully churned out the erroneous part. The turbine-powered beast had seemed a step up from the Hawker Sea Fury that Sid had flown back in Canada before going on exchange—though the piston-pounding Sea Fury was actually faster than the Wyvern—and a definite step down from the Banshee jets he'd be flying when he got home. Even after half a year of flying it, his feelings for the plane were mixed; on the one hand, it handled reasonably well for an aircraft of its size, and the view from the cockpit was outstanding.

On the other, he just couldn't get the type's reputation for being accident-prone out of his head. When the Wyvern entered service three years earlier, pilots and engineers alike found out the hard way that the high g-forces of a catapult launch overwhelmed the pumps that carried fuel from the tanks in the aircraft's wings and mid-fuselage to the engine, causing the turboprop to flame out and sending many a Wyvern into the sea, where it made for an extremely poor boat. The Admiralty insisted that the problem had been fixed, and even if a problem should arise, Sid had plenty of faith in his Martin-Baker ejection seat, the components of which he'd checked thoroughly before plopping his posterior onto its cushion. And, of course, the Admiralty would never lie about matters related to aircrew safety. Nay, not a chance.

There was no time to worry about the possibilities. Sid was third in line for the catapult that launched *Eagle*'s air wing, at the waist of a flight deck angled five and a half degrees to port to significantly lessen the likelihood of a landing aircraft missing the arresting cables and, as a result, going careening into the mass of parked machines at the bow, turning the carrier into something resembling a Viking funeral boat. Leading the flight was Lieutenant-Commander Gene Faintary, the head of the squadron, in the aircraft numbered Whiskey Lima Eight-Niner-One. At forty-one, Faintary was a seasoned veteran, his hard-ass demeanor forged flying Fairey Barracudas and Grumman Avengers in the Battle of the Atlantic and in operations over Sumatra. To say that he was by-the-book would've been an understatement of epic proportions; the rules and regulations were practically his Bible, which Sid supposed made him a great commanding officer as much as it clearly made him a pain in the ass. Yet Sid couldn't help but respect his brand of tough love and even had to admit that he liked the man. Faintary's equals called him Fanny, as his surname was rightly pronounced "fan tree," which he utterly hated for reasons that became obvious to Sid the more familiar he became with the British vernacular, though he'd never taken any appreciable action to quell the practice.

A plume of steam shot across the deck as the catapult released its tension, chucking WL891 into the sky as if it were a chunk of rock being flung at the curtain walls of a Norman fortress. Lieutenant James Wellington was next to take the cat. At twenty-eight, Wimpy—as his mates affectionately called him—was seven years Sid's junior, but he'd been in the squadron ever since coming out of flight training and had just been made executive officer. He had also been the first and most enthusiastic in welcoming Sid to the family—not only the squadron's family but inviting Sid to the Cotswolds his first weekend in-country to spend with Jim, his lovely wife, and that dapper five-year-old son who was the spitting image of his old man.

As Wimpy maneuvered Whiskey Papa Three-Three-Five into position, Sid pulled on the knobs next to his right thigh to spread his plane's wings, which had been folded to save space on the crowded flight deck, more than doubling the amount of lateral space the Wyvern took up from twenty feet to forty-four. He went through his final preflight checklist. Trimmers all set to neutral. Throttle friction tight for catapult launch. Air brakes closed. Then he checked the fuel system: High-pressure cock fully on. Tank selector set to draw from the outer wing tanks. Pressure warning light out.

Now, to verify that the aircraft was actually ready to fly. Flaps set for takeoff? Check. Wings spread and locked? Affirmative. *That one's particularly important.* Master control lever fully forward. All warning lights out and indicators flush with the wings. He checked the ailerons to ensure the full range of movement.

Last few items. Instruments set, inverter indicators blank. Oxygen set to high. Chart board and hood locked. Harness tight and locked in the rear position to keep him from being flung from the cockpit. *That's also rather vital.* Tail wheel locked so that the Wyvern wouldn't go swerving off the side of the ship and into the drink. *All set. Time to fly!*

He stole a quick glance over his right shoulder as the deckhands attached VW888's main wheel struts to the catapult. Behind him, the two younger men in the squadron, Lieutenants Tom Wickler and D.B. Barluck, were deftly maneuvering Victor Zulu Eight-Zero-Three and Whiskey November

Three-Three-Eight into position. Sid smiled a little, then shoved the throttle forward, pressed his back to the seat cushion to absorb the impact of acceleration, and signaled to the deckhand that he was ready for takeoff. The deckhand gave the launch signal, and Sid was instantly sucked into the bowels of his seat as if his body had been grabbed by the world's strongest magnet as Triple-Eight went from zero to seventy knots in a split second. He tensed his muscles to keep the blood flowing. The Wyvern lunged off the deck as if to flee the suffocating confines of that floating steel prison.

When he'd first earned his wings, the prospect of flying off an aircraft carrier had enamored him. That was where all the fun was. He'd fantasized about doing barrel rolls straight off the bow as the deckhands cheered him on, reliving the joy and daring of it over a round of rum with his squadron mates after the sortie as if they were a bunch of pirates who'd just bagged the biggest prize in all the Seven Seas. *Ah, the romantic fancies of a green kid!* Even if he could perform such a maneuver without stalling and splashing into the Med, Fanny would have his head on a plate for risking an expensive and vital piece of Her Majesty's arsenal.

The wide-eyed musings of that neophyte had long been beaten out of him. Instead of showboating, he simply raised Triple-Eight's landing gear and pointed the nose to intercept his commanding officer.

"Spoke Flight, form up," came the command from Fanny in his typical brusque formality. "Right echelon formation."

Sid carefully massaged the throttle lever, adjusting his position in the formation until WP335's numbers were just inside his peripheral vision. The brilliant midday sun glimmered on the Wyvern's sky-gray paint and glossy black-and-yellow identification stripes just as she shone upon the tranquil Mediterranean. A humid mist settled on the horizon. *Perfect flying weather.*

Sid only lamented that such an idyllic day would soon be marred with bomb blasts and rocket fire.

Tom Wickler closed in on Sid's left wing. The twenty-five-year-old Scotsman was called Hags by the rest of the squadron, supposedly short for "haggis" as that was all the others seemed to know of Scotland, just as they'd taken to dubbing Sid "Moose," for they knew nothing about Canada besides moose and maple leaves. *As if I've ever seen a moose, or a bear, or even an elk, or any wildlife bigger than the raccoons I sometimes find clattering around the attic.* Hags was a nice enough fellow, though short-fused, and there was something in his strangely blue eyes that unnerved Sid. Barluck, the youngest of the five at a fresh twenty-four, slid in under Hags' wing.

Forty-eight minutes into the flight, Fanny's command crackled over the radio: "Left turn, heading one-one-zero." As if a single organism whose limbs moved in perfect harmony by the will of the brain inside WL891, the five Wyverns jettisoned their centerline fuel tanks, now depleted, and entered a gentle left turn toward Port Said. The coast of Egypt appeared as a pallid crust to starboard. Sid's right hand flew to the armament control panel beside his right knee, the thumb of his left caressing the selector switch atop the control column between his legs, hoping, praying even, that he wouldn't have to use them. He'd killed enough Egyptians.

At that moment, a panicked voice cried out over the radio: "Bandits! Ten o'clock high!"

Sid glanced up and to his left, catching a glint of sunlight against the deep blue heavens—no, *two* glints. *Shit!* Peering closer at the disturbances in the perfect azure, he discerned two terrifying shapes, pairs of sharply swept wings and massive fins bolted to metal beer kegs. The unmistakable shape of the Mikoyan-Gurevich MiG-15 jet fighter.

The two Egyptian jets banked into a downward turn, pointing their blunt open noses at the invading Wyverns. At that moment, Sid discerned another gleam that seemed to be coming from beneath the leading MiG.

But this time, he knew, the flash wasn't sunlight glittering upon polished metal. It was the barrel flash of a cannon.

&

"Evasive maneuvers!" Gene Faintary commanded, as if that weren't the first—nay, the *only*—thing on the other four pilots' minds. Even in the chaos of air combat, the old man was as unflappable, as surgical with his orders as ever. "Spoke Two, break left with me. Spoke Three, Four, and Five, break right."

"Aye, sir," Jim Wellington replied. "Watch your six, Moose!"

Sid threw the control stick hard to the right, standing on the rudder pedal to keep his turn steady. The horizon spun around until the Mediterranean Sea was a deep blue wall against his right cheek, the sun searing his left eye. The two other Wyverns in Sid's section had drifted far away, juking wildly and zipping about whither they would, as if the green pilots had forgotten every bit of the extensive training the Fleet Air Arm had drilled into their heads.

"Where the hell are our fighters?" someone blurted; by the voice's timbre, Sid knew it was young D.B. Barluck.

Sid scanned the sky as he yanked Triple-Eight into a hard downward bank, four and a half times the force of gravity squeezing him into the seat. No sign of the Sea Venom jets that would've otherwise taken on the Egyptian MiGs. *We're on our own. Bloody swell.*

On paper, the odds would have seemed to favor the British. Five against two. But in this instance, it was the equivalent of two mounted knights against five plump peasants with pitchforks.

The Wyvern's intended quarry was warships, later expanded to include anything on the ground when it was given the "Strike" designation. The MiG-15's prey was other aircraft. And, as it had proven over Korea a few short years earlier, it was a dreadfully efficient predator.

"Lose the bombs," Tom Wickler said, voicing Sid's thoughts. Dropping the excess ton of weight and drag might just be enough to let the Wyverns get clear of the fracas, at least long enough for the Venoms to show up. *If they're even in our vicinity.*

"Negative!" Fanny bellowed, his voice revealing nary a hint of exhaustion or strain. "You will not jettison your armaments, that's an order. We still have a mission to complete."

Bugger that. Sid slammed the buttons on the left console, gritting his teeth as Triple-Eight seemed to spring forward and up as if a great burden had been lifted off her shoulders. But even two thousand pounds lighter, the Wyvern flew like a bread lorry; it rolled decently enough, but its high wing loading meant that its turning circle was painfully broad. The MiG-15s could fly circles around him.

Sid had lost sight of his pursuers. *Shit.* They must've been on his six o'clock—directly behind him. But his cockpit afforded an excellent view of all directions except straight down, and the MiGs couldn't have gotten that low that quickly. Even as he glanced around, never so long as to lose his bearings, he saw no sight of them. That was the worst position to be in. If he could see the fighters, he at least had the chance to evade them; if not, he was all but dead. The MiG-15's primary armament, its thirty-seven-millimeter cannon, could blow an enemy's wing off with a single burst. The twin twenty-three-millimeter guns that augmented it may have packed a lesser punch, but they fired at a faster rate and were plenty devastating if they found their mark.

And it was not long before they did.

"I'm hit!" someone shouted. Again, it was Barluck. In his periphery, Sid could see flames shooting from WN338's left side, the plane veering sharply to that side and plummeting toward the waves.

Before Sid could check to see if Barluck had ejected, another flash caught his attention. It was coming from three o'clock high. He shoved the control column forward, his shoulders straining against his seat's harness as the negative g-forces tried to rip him out of the cockpit. Triple-Eight plunged into a steep dive as the bullets whirred past the canopy, the tracers drawing infernal lines terrifyingly close to Sid's head. Pulling level just inches above the Med, being thrust into his seat as if a mountain had been dropped on his abdomen, he glanced up and behind him. No sign of the enemy.

Then, another flash. The MiG had overshot trying to pursue him and was now less than five hundred meters off Triple-Eight's nose. But the MiG was at least a thousand feet above, and Sid had already bled much of his airspeed off maneuvering; if he pulled up to take a shot with his wing-mounted cannons, he risked stalling and crashing into the sea.

"I have a good chute," Fanny announced. Startled, Sid let himself smile for a second and offer a swift word of thanks to the Almighty. That meant Barluck had made it out. *Eagle*'s Westland Whirlwind helicopter would be along in good time to pick him up.

As for Tom Wickler...where the hell was he?

"He's on my six!" Wimpy wailed. "I can't shake him!"

Snapping out of his ephemeral relief, Sid glanced frantically around the sky for his friend, all the while keeping the MiG-15 in his peripheral vision, cursing his impotence at that moment. James Wellington was on his own...and quite probably a goner.

"Come left, Spoke Two," Fanny said, his tone at ease as if

he were directing his butler to pour a little more wine into his chalice. "I almost have the shot."

"You'll never get him, Skipper!" Hags lamented, his transmission weak and fraught with static. He must've been far from the engagement.

"Just you watch me." Sid noted a sliver of haughty laughter, ever so slight, penetrating the professional monotony of Fanny's voice. "You chaps ever heard of Swede Vejtasa?"

"Sir, this isn't a good time for a history lesson!" Wimpy cried, his voice quavering and winded from the labors of maneuvering. "Get this bastard off me!"

Ignoring his second-in-command, Fanny explained: "He was an American dive bomber pilot in the War. Over the Coral Sea, he and his mates were jumped by Japanese fighters. So, Swede turned his lumbering old Dauntless into a fighter and shot down three Zeros. Hell of a pilot."

And not the only one! Sid couldn't believe what he was witnessing. In the distance, he could discern the shape of a Wyvern banking hard in his direction, rolling and jinking, and a MiG-15 closing quickly until the air intake in its nose was almost devouring the British aircraft's tail, firing wildly but missing its mark. Then, almost out of nowhere, a second Wyvern soared up from behind and beneath the MiG, white streaks carving the sky behind its wingtips as flowers of fire blossomed from the leading edge of the wings. The MiG jolted to the left as twenty-millimeter vengeance tore through its rear fuselage. An inferno quickly engulfed the fighter's empennage, and it entered a violent downward spin. The pilot ejected only seconds before the flaming wreck struck the water's surface.

"Splash one, Skip!" Wimpy said, the crackling of the radio matching that in his voice. "I owe you one."

"That won't be necessary, Lieutenant," Fanny shot back, the

strain in his voice at last apparent as WL891 pitched forward sharply to regain all the airspeed the maneuver had bled off, the violent negative g-forces trying to tear the skipper out of his cockpit as if they were giant invisible hands reaching down from the abode of malignant gods. Even from a distance, Sid could see Fanny's aircraft shuddering a little. The commander had taken his aircraft to the very brink of stalling.

The whole affair had lasted only a second or two. When Sid turned his attention forward, the MiG that had been chasing him was almost out of firing range, and would have been had it not started to turn back for dry land. With adrenaline surging through his veins, and the sanguine delight of knowing that victory over one of the nimble jets was within his grasp, he yanked hard on the control column, climbing and turning toward the MiG, squeezing the button to fire the cannons. The burst tore through his eardrums like a mechanical saw. It was the most blissful sound he'd ever heard. *That's for D.B., you rotten bastard!*

"Spoke Three, knock it off," Fanny commanded. "He's bugging out. Let him go."

Indeed, the MiG was rocketing toward home. Sid's heart sank a little; was Fanny trying to be compassionate by letting the Egyptian live, or did he simply want to ensure that he'd be the only one who could claim an air-to-air kill—as far as anyone knew, the first for a Wyvern? Sid couldn't even tell if he'd hit his MiG. Though for a moment, he thought he'd seen a white cloud streaming from the wing, meaning that something—one of Sid's bullets—had punctured it, and the MiG was losing fuel.

Panting like a hound in midsummer, Sid wiped away the sweat that he only now noticed pouring down his face from the sea of it pooling under his flight helmet. *Skipper's right.* He glanced one more time at the fleeing MiG, offering a salute. The Egyptian pilots had clearly been inexperienced, or else the whole flight of Wyverns would be sinking next to the wreck of Whiskey November, but they'd fought bravely. *I hope the magnificent bastard lives to be a hundred.*

"Form up," Fanny ordered, his voice once more tranquil as if nothing out of the ordinary had happened.

"You all right, Wimpy?" Sid asked as he brought Triple-Eight into position in what was now the penultimate slot of the echelon.

"Tip-top," Jim shot back amid his frenzied panting. "That's about enough excitement for one day, if you ask me."

"Indeed, sir. I could use a stiff drink after that little encounter."

"We'll pour one out for Barluck too," Wimpy said, his carefree laugh breaking through the nerves still ravaging his voice.

"Ah, he might just beat us back to the boat."

"In one of those bloody whirlybirds?" Hags snorted. "I'd trust the enemy more than that contraption."

"That kind of disdain for the valiant men of *Eagle*'s search and rescue unit, and the nonpareil equipment bestowed upon them by the distinguished leadership of Her Majesty's Royal Navy, will not be tolerated, Lieutenant," Wimpy said with a chortle.

"As you say, sir," the Scotsman sneered. "Should've let the Canuck blast that camel jockey, skipper. Or, better still, let me do it. Oily-eyed bastard deserved it after what they did to poor Barluck."

Have some respect for your enemy, Sid wanted to say. "Knock it off, kids," he muttered instead. "We're not out of the woods yet."

"And a damned shame, that," Wimpy said. "I never did care much for the forest. Give me good English countryside any day. Especially when the trees are shooting at you." He uttered a chortle through his radio. "Whaddya say, boss? Call it an afternoon?"

"Negative," the commander said firmly, seemingly more irritated by his underlings' utter disregard for propriety and radio decorum than by the fact that the lot of them had damned nearly gotten killed. "We still have our rockets, and we have our orders. We will complete our mission."

Sid's eyes rolled even as he laughed, noting that Gene Faintary had indeed jettisoned his bombs.

"Well done, chaps," Fanny added. For all his rigorous adherence to codes and procedures, the skipper had never hesitated to commend his pilots for their efforts. Sid knew that, by midnight, everyone on board *Eagle* would hear the squadron's accolades. "But your libations will have to wait."

"Yes, sir," Sid japed, suddenly bristling with the confidence that only a strike pilot who'd just fended off an attack by jet fighters could experience.

But as he spoke, a shadow swept across his left. When he turned his head, he froze in his seat. The sky, once pristine, had darkened as if night itself had risen up from the sea. The storm had come out of nowhere—if the abomination hurtling toward them was indeed a storm. Whatever it was, it was not the weather of the world; the swirling vortex appeared as some kind of demon, some monster of cloud spawned in the bowels of the underworld. And it was coming for them, faster than any jet fighter, fierce as the hand of God.

"So much for getting back to the ship," Wimpy said, his voice quavering.

Even if Sid wanted to tuck tail and run for home, he couldn't. His arms hung like lead at his sides, his hands like clay that had hardened around the control stick, stricken catatonic by a fear worlds greater than that which any enemy among man or mortal beast could summon.

"Maintain present heading," Faintary ordered, his tone nonchalant as if the otherworldly weather were but a minor inconvenience. "We'll land at Port Said. Our boys hold the airport. We'll wait out the storm there."

But long before Port Said, or even a branch of the River Nile, was within sight, the cloud engulfed the four Wyverns. Sid's plane was tossed to the right. A sudden impact jolted him in his seat, and with it, the clangor of metal striking metal. He glanced right; his wingtip had struck the cowling of VZ803. Had Hags been a foot further in trail, his propeller blades would have cut right through Sid's ailerons.

The maelstrom grew to ravenous fury. Sid lost sight of Fanny and Wimpy. His hands shook, his fingers throttling the control column. With a sudden paroxysm, his left hand flew to his chest without a conscious thought. His fingers fumbled at the pocket where he kept Marie's cross.

And at that moment, he prayed. He prayed like hell.

CHAPTER II

THE GLOWING VINES from the creature's tongue probed Lucretia's body like the noses of little kittens who couldn't figure out why the large, soft mass they were so ardently prodding wouldn't fall over like it was supposed to. The sensation was strange; warm and smooth, ticklish even, but not as moist as she might have expected. In fact, it wasn't moist at all. It was as if there were no liquid inside the creature's body. The supple appendage felt her from feet to face, yet she didn't feel threatened by it.

Not even when one of the tendrils curled around her neck.

"Hey!" Jeremiah bellowed, his hands flailing as he tried to grab hold of the retreating limbs. "Let her go!"

"It's okay, Jay," Lucretia whispered. "It's not constricting. I don't think it means to hurt us. But we shouldn't frighten it."

Good thing he left his camera in the plane, she thought—at least she assumed he had, or else it had fallen out amid the storm. The alien might have assumed it was some kind of weapon.

The creature looked at Jeremiah—at least, that's what Lucretia thought it was doing. It reached for him with another tendril, though it seemed to be hesitating, as if nervous or intimidated.

At last, the lithe limb flew to Jeremiah's side, coiling around his wrist. Then it drew back slowly, retracting the tendrils that ensnared Lucretia and Jeremiah.

"It wants us to come with it," Lucretia deduced.

"Why?" Jeremiah's voice floundered like a rowboat in a hurricane. "So it can lead us back to its nest, liquefy our bodies, and eat us?"

"I told you, Jay. I don't think it means to hurt us."

"And what if you're wrong?"

"Let's just see where it's taking us, and try not to make it anxious. I'm not overly keen on being strangled by an alien."

"But, if you're so sure it's not going to kill us, why are you so worried?"

Lucretia sighed aloud. "I don't want to piss it off! Right now, it doesn't see us as threats, or else it would have attacked us and, yeah, probably killed us. But it hasn't. It seems pretty docile to me. But if it feels threatened, it's going to defend itself, and you're not the one with the tentacle thingy around your neck." She screwed up her face. "Why am I the only one being dragged by the neck, anyway?"

"It probably can't see mine through my beard," Jeremiah japed, and Lucretia could hear in his tone that he was calming down.

"Or because you've got no neck, fat ass." Lucretia stopped for a moment, grabbing at the tendril. The creature halted, momentarily coiling the limb until it was uncomfortably snug. *It's startled*, Lucretia knew—or rather, hoped. She held up her hands, then pressed the palms together and stretched her arms out in front of her.

The creature's head tilted left, not unlike the way a puppy's does when it's perplexed. The tendril slowly eased, then slid from Lucretia's neck and curled around her wrists. The colors in the creature's head seemed to brighten a little. *Almost as if it's contrite.*

"Thank you," Lucretia said softly. "You know, you don't have to hold on to us. We'll follow you, if that's what you want."

What am I doing? This thing can't understand a word I'm saying.

Yet the creature seemed to comprehend something; if not Lucretia's words, then the fact that she was trying to communicate with it. Its head moved a little.

But even if it did understand her, it was leaving nothing to chance. As it backed away, its tendrils still encircled the siblings' wrists, and for a while, Lucretia knew what it was like to be a dog on a leash.

The creature pulled Lucretia and Jeremiah through the glowing, swaying forest for what felt like an hour, though it was probably only fifteen minutes or so, still ambulating backwards upon its swirling tentacles, seeming to move with equal adeptness as if it were moving forward, as if it had no conception of forward and backward. Lucretia felt secure in the creature's embrace, though she couldn't help but wish that she could communicate with it, kindly asking it to release one of her arms so that she could scratch her armpit where the edge of the tear in her shirt's sleeve always seemed to chafe her.

She gazed upon the placid beauty of her strange new world, still not entirely convinced that she wasn't dreaming. *If I am, I'm not sure I want to wake.* The sky hadn't changed from its ataraxic purple, and Lucretia wondered if this world existed in a kind of perpetual twilight, with neither searing midday sun nor terrifying moonless darkness to mar the tranquility. The ambient sound pervading the landscape was like that of crickets, but sweeter and gentler, and it danced in Lucretia's ears like a Mendelssohn symphony.

The trees grew taller and brighter—though never so bright as to scald the eyes—as they ventured deeper and deeper into the iridescent wilderness, sometimes set amid pools of liquid that glimmered with the same vibrant yellow that beamed from the soil around the newcomers' feet. Their trunks flared out at the bottom, like bell-bottom trousers, reminding Lucretia of the cypress trees that surrounded her cabin in the bayou beside Caddo Lake. There were even beards of silver hanging from their branches like Spanish moss, yet aglow like everything else. If ever an alien world could feel like home, then Lucretia Tang had found it.

Yet a part of her wished it *didn't* feel so much like home. Her mind inexorably wandered back to the world she left behind, even as she tried to barricade her thoughts against the ugliness of that reality, lest it break through and mar the perfection ensconcing her. Those trees were suddenly a reminder of a home she hadn't chosen—though she'd come to love it—but to which she'd fled to escape the scorn of Silicon Valley.

Their slander had cost her everything: her career, her reputation, her marriage, her joy. One day, she'd been a biotech wunderkind; the next, she was the scum of the earth. The headline was still seared into her memory, as if etched into her eyelids, boring into her as she slept, as she tried to escape it:

PLAYING GOD WITH NATURE'S TREASURES

Richard Daniken, that sanctimonious turd. He'd called himself a "bioethicist" but in reality he was little more than an outspoken asshole who refused to believe that those who didn't see things his way could possibly be decent and virtuous human beings. But his words carried weight, bolstered by the hordes of braindead celebrities and social media influencers who took his vitriol as the Gospel. Lucretia didn't care about climate change or the integrity of coral reefs as a result of it, Daniken had written; no, she only wanted her name in the papers so that she could line her pockets by committing sacrilege against nature with the evil of genetic engineering. "Researchers Jeremiah and Lucretia Tang…," the hit piece had begun, as if Jeremiah was any more than a biologist observing the changing behaviors of marine invertebrates, who hadn't taken a scalpel to a DNA sequence any more than he'd taken a pair of scissors to the brambly black forest growing from his face.

And then the rest piled on, with pundits and peewits alike hurling all manner of insults and accusations at the two of them, usually tossing in some casual racism to boot. More than one influential voice had even accused them of being agents of the Chinese Communist Party; the evidence was nonexistent, the argument being along the lines of "they're of Chinese ancestry, so you've got to wonder," but so often do lies take root in soil too callow to cultivate the truth.

Jeremiah had taken it all in good humor, as was his wont, even as the universities and institutes that would have otherwise benefited from his surplus of knowledge and enthusiasm were suddenly reluctant to hire him. *He wasn't the one who had the person he loved walk out on him*, she thought with a bitterness that startled her. The pain of the divorce still lingered in Lucretia's heart. When Mark had kissed her at the altar, she'd truly believed the vows they'd exchanged would endure, until death did them part. Neither of them had wanted it. Lucretia's rational mind understood that she'd become a toxic asset, and Mark couldn't jeopardize his law career by being associated with her. They still kept in touch, albeit on the downlow. But three years after the Daniken piece, with most of the furor having been long forgotten, the pieces of Lucretia's past remained scattered and shredded like so many mementos left in the wake of a tornado.

All she had left now was her work, and her brother. The one who'd been by her side through it all. He could've jumped ship like the others, salvaging his reputation. But he hadn't. He *wouldn't*.

She glanced at Jeremiah, shooting him a slight smile that he couldn't actually see as he marveled at the fantastical milieu around him. Lucretia had a sneaking suspicion that he was imagining himself a character in a video game. *If only that were true.* Sublime as the world they'd been whisked off to was, they couldn't leave the one they'd come from entirely behind. Jeremiah still needed the medications he took to control his type 2 diabetes. She often scolded him for giving himself the disease with his fondness for sugary drinks and junk food, but she still hated that he had to suffer for his mistakes.

He's all I have, she mused. *And now he's stuck here, worlds away from home. Because of me.*

But her worries could wait a while. After all, the soil seemed to have healed the pain in Lucretia's head; maybe it could fix Jeremiah's pancreas just as effectively. She looked at him again, rolling her eyes with a jovial smile as she observed his carefree demeanor, relieved that he now seemed fully at ease. Now and then, he'd start rapping under his breath, and Lucretia could only sigh at his choice of music for the occasion. *This place is totally symphonic metal. Or maybe prog rock, if one can stomach that.*

When the creature halted, Lucretia's eyes and mouth opened like caverns. Two of the pallid trees stood astride the road, their lowest branches arching together to form something like an arboreal gate hung with lucent blue strings aglow in a way that made Lucretia think of the glowworm caves she'd seen in New Zealand, close together and perfectly straight like pickets in a fence, another single row arranged horizontally across the base. Lights surrounded the trees in ascending regiments—not the natural lights emanating from the flora all around them but lambent glimmers in what looked like sconces woven in lithe vines around the trunks—and beneath them, jutting out from the impossibly smooth boles, what appeared to be spiraling stairs leading up to the scarlet canopy. Lucretia couldn't help but be reminded of Lothlórien from *The Lord of the Rings*.

Should've brought my elf ears, she thought with a surreptitious grin. Long before they were married, or even dating, back when they were high school kids nerding out on comic books and video games, Mark had always remarked that she had the cutest ears, and that they were even cuter when pointy. *Eat your heart out, Galadriel.*

The gate opened, and another alien glided out, a mere speck between the towering trees. The gate must have been much farther away than Lucretia had first assumed. By her calculations, which were in fact wild guesses, the trees must have been at least fifty feet wide at their bases. The creature approached and halted beside its ilk; it was slightly smaller and had a slightly different color pattern on its abdomen, with more purple than any other color.

The creature that had been leading Lucretia and Jeremiah emitted a strange sound by rubbing together the bristles on its forelegs, a call of sorts: three distinct syllables, with emphasis on the second, uttered in a soft, surprisingly high-pitched voice, warm—comical even—in timbre, holding the final syllable like the last note of an eighties rock song.

"What are they saying?" Jeremiah asked, seemingly perfunctorily.

"Well," Lucretia sneered, "this language is quite foreign to me, but it sounds like *racosku*. Actually, I think that's what I'm gonna call them from now on: Racosku." She turned to the alien that had accosted them. "You good with that, Noodles? You're a Racosku now."

Noodles rubbed out another *racosku*. Whether that was "yes," "no," or "I have no damned clue what that noise coming out of the big hole in your face is," she couldn't be entirely certain.

She turned to the other creature. "Same for you, Violet. You're a Racosku."

"Is that singular or plural?" Jeremiah japed.

"It's both. It's like 'moose.' Except they're not as ugly as moose."

Violet glanced at the newcomers—as far as Lucretia could tell—but, where Lucretia would have expected it to search them, or probe them, or perform some kind of interrogation, examination, or violation, it simply backed away. Nothing about its actions suggested that it was frightened, or suspicious, or in any way uncomfortable. It was as if Violet had seen human beings before, or knew something about them. Lucretia wasn't sure if that was a good thing or a bad thing.

Noodles' proboscis released the siblings, and only then did Lucretia realize just how much that tattered and faded old Kamelot shirt that she stubbornly refused to dispose of had chafed her underarm. Violet turned away, making swiftly for the mammoth trees, and Noodles followed close behind.

I guess we'd better go with them, Lucretia thought with a shrug as she took her brother's hand and set her feet upon the road to the fantastically—and perhaps deceivingly—beautiful arboreal abode of the Racosku.

The maelstrom had seemed to last a lifetime. Yet, as suddenly as it began, the vortex vanished.

But there was no blue sky on the other side, no beige coastline on the far horizon, no unblemished sun beating down on the four Wyverns that were now scattered about the strange purple sky. *And no enemy fighters. That's a positive, at least.*

Sidney Daventry scanned the sky around him. It seemed to be late twilight, yet he could see the other aircraft in his flight in the distance as clearly as if it had been midday, their sky-gray fuselages now a glossy bluish yellow, as if each had absorbed a bolt of lightning. The glow, he saw as he glanced over his wing, was coming from below: a scenery unlike anything he'd ever seen or even imagined, for which no word in the English language—and probably not in Marie's old Irish Gaelic, either—could describe. The forest below was glowing as if the trees and hedges had lightbulbs inside them. Only they burned much too steadily to have been lit by electricity. Was this real? Was he hallucinating? Had his collision with Tom Wickler's plane jarred something loose in his head? Had he died in the storm and flown Triple-Eight off to Aviator Heaven? Or had he just lost his bloody mind?

"What the bleedin' hell?" Hags bellowed over the radio. "Where the holy hell are we?"

I guess this means it's not just me. Sid wasn't sure if that was a good thing or a bad thing.

"Spoke Flight, return to formation," Commander Faintary said nonchalantly, as if they were still over the Mediterranean and nothing out of the ordinary had just happened. "We will assess our situation and proceed as the circumstances dictate."

"The *circumstances* dictate that we get the fuck out of here!"

"That'll be all from you, Lieutenant," Fanny snapped. "Rest assured that your insubordination will be dealt with when we return to the ship."

If we ever get back, Sid had a mind to say. But, like Jim Wellington, now half a mile off his port wing and slightly above, making no maneuver to rejoin with WL891, he kept his mouth shut. He nudged his control column to the left...

Nothing.

"Sir," he said as calmly as a man who'd found himself in unfamiliar airspace in an unresponsive aircraft could, "I've got no aileron control." *Must've jarred something loose when I hit Hags.*

"Say again, Spoke Three?"

"Ailerons are not responding, sir." Sid tried the stick again. This time VW888 shuddered a little but stubbornly refused to bank left.

Only when he glanced at the artificial horizon dial in the center of his cockpit did he notice that he was banking indeed— to the right.

And his nose was dropping.

"Shit!" Sid yelped. "Sir, I think I'm going down!"

"Oh hell!" Wellington interjected. "Eject, Moose! Eject!"

"Silence!" Fanny barked. "Spoke Three, what is your condition? Do you have positive control?"

Sid pulled back on the column. Triple-Eight's nose slowly lifted. Sid breathed a sigh of relief. "I have elevator control." He pushed gently on the rudder pedals; first the left, then the right. The Wyvern responded as it should have. "Positive rudder control." The collision must've damaged the aileron rod; the force of the storm had done the rest.

I can manage this. Getting Triple-Eight back on dry ground— if the strange ground beneath him was indeed dry—would be no easy feat. But he had lateral and pitch control. *As long as I don't need to make many sharp banks, I'll be fine.*

"Look!" Wimpy shouted. "Two o'clock low. There's an aeroplane down there!"

It was almost a sign from Heaven. There between the glowing plants and shining trees sat a small single-engine high-wing aircraft, not unlike an Auster or a Piper Cub, but with much more elegant lines and svelte wings that reminded him of a damselfly's. Sid let himself laugh a little. *If he could land here, then so can I.*

I'm going to make it. I'm getting out of this alive.

Marie's prayers weren't for naught.

"I'm going to try to put her down beside that plane," he said.

"Negative, Spoke Three," Fanny ordered. "You have no knowledge of the integrity of the landing surface."

"That plane down there made it," Wellington noted.

"And a Wyvern is a good fifteen times heavier than that thing."

The skipper was right, Sid knew. He reasoned that the surface was not paved; if the mud was too soft, the Wyvern's tires could sink into it until the aircraft nosed over. Too violent a halt could even flip the aircraft onto its back, and Sid was in no mood to be crushed in his cockpit.

The skipper's gruff voice broke through Sid's reverie: "Spoke Three, maintain present heading and altitude. I'll make a survey of the site."

"Aye, sir."

No sooner had the words left Sid's mouth than he felt a jolt forward, accompanied by a sharp shudder to the left.

"I'm losing power, sir," Sid noted, panting as he reminded himself that the Westland Wyvern was not a particularly useful glider. He made a quick glance at his fuel gauges. All three showed normal levels. *Damn it, the pumps are damaged.* "I've got to take her down now, or else punch out."

"Understood." There was no apparent worry in Fanny's voice. "Save your aircraft if able. Good luck, Lieutenant."

Save the aircraft. Sure, it'll be a cakewalk. No roll control, power cutting out, and I don't know where on God's green earth I am. No problem at all.

"I'm praying for you, Sidney," Jim Wellington said, his voice crackling. "Whatever happens, I want you to know that it's been an honor flying with you."

"Don't talk like that, Wimpy," Sid shot back. "In a couple hours, we're going to be laughing about this over a round of good Canadian beer. We'll even save one for you, Skipper."

"Focus on your landing, Lieutenant," the droll voice commanded.

"Aye, sir."

The open ground where they'd seen the other plane was now well behind Sid's wing. He glanced right; there appeared a large cluster of those majestic trees with the silvery trunks and red leaves, much taller than the ones he'd first seen. With Triple-Eight slowly descending, the branches were almost level with his wings. About a quarter mile to his left, the glowing flora ceased, giving way to a broad, flat expanse of silvery ripples. *Almost like water.* If all else failed, he could ditch there.

If his guesses were correct. Could he really know *anything* about this weird new world?

Sid pressed the push button on his left to lower the landing gear but felt no jolt, no shudder, no deceleration. "Spoke Four, do you see my wheels?"

"Nay, mate," Hags announced.

Damn it. Sid was sweating now, his breathing ragged.

At that moment, the engine failed.

Thoughts of death flashed through Sid's mind, visions of Marie and the girls crying interspersed with reminders from his training. *Focus, Sid. There's no time to waste.*

Without hesitation, he feathered the propeller blades, then stomped on the undercarriage emergency release pedal. A sudden thump. *That's not good.* The wheels had released but hadn't come down. The doors must have jammed somehow. All the while,

Sid cycled the high-pressure cock in an attempt to restart the fuel flow.

Nothing.

This is it. He jettisoned his canopy's hood, grabbing hold of the ejection seat's firing handle behind his head with his left hand as his right trembled at the control stick, easing the nose back as the glimmering surface drew nearer, as the Wyvern dropped lower and lower. Had he bothered to lower the flaps, Triple-Eight would've now been wrapped around one of those beautifully imposing trees.

Leaning hard on the left rudder pedal, Sid brought his Wyvern over the silvery sheen that he hoped was water. He pulled back on the stick...

Too hard. Triple-Eight's tail struck the surface with a violent thud, suddenly jolting forward. Splashing waves and creaking metal were the last sounds Sid heard before his head slammed against the control panel.

CHAPTER III

VIOLET LED THE humans to the base of the tree on the right. The planks that Lucretia had assumed were stairs were actually the struts supporting a ramp made of a strange material clear as glass yet with the friction of rubber. And a good thing about that friction, for the ramp was steep, rising at an angle of at least twenty degrees, maybe twenty-five. Lucretia followed closely behind her alien host, Jeremiah behind her. She'd thought about letting him walk in front of her, being as he was heavier and in worse physical shape, but she figured Noodles was back there, either to make sure the unwitting bipedal visitors didn't try to run away or to catch one if they should tumble over. *Nice Racosku.*

The light fixtures in the trunk, reaching out in elegant whorls around translucent vases in which steady bluish light burned, were at least twelve feet above Lucretia's head and appeared to be lit by some kind of electricity. She was about to inquire about the source of the light before reminding herself that Violet's response would either be silence or *racosku*. She really hoped that the Racosku weren't taking her and Jeremiah in for interrogation;

they might well get frustrated by their inability to communicate and, as Jay had so dourly predicted, liquefy the humans' bodies and eat them.

No, they wouldn't do that. Would they?

Lucretia was winded when she reached an embrasure in the trunk, but she found that the comfortably cool breeze trickling through the forest had swiftly dried the sweat on her forehead. Jeremiah and Noodles were still a ways behind. Violet stretched out a foreleg toward the arched doorway leading into an opening from which another steady light beamed, stronger and a little darker this time, like the glow from an LED computer or television screen—or a roomful of them.

When Jeremiah reached the doorway, he was panting like an overweight dog on a hot summer day.

"Gonna be okay there, Jay?" Lucretia asked.

Jeremiah said nothing, giving only a slight nod.

Returning the gesture, Lucretia quickly turned and followed Violet through the tall, narrow entryway. What Lucretia saw inside took her breath away. If it hadn't been made abundantly clear by their ornate lighting sconces, impeccably engineered ramp, and elegant arches that the Racosku were no primitive insects living in hives of rotted wood, then the room that Lucretia entered, full of translucent plates that emitted three-dimensional images in myriad colors, almost like highly advanced computer graphics, or even holograms, had certainly confirmed it.

"Whoa!" Jeremiah said, echoing Lucretia's sentiments. "This is amazing!"

"Yeah," Lucretia gasped. "Just a bit."

Two more Racosku were ambulating around the room. The one with the reddish hue seemed to be working the razor-thin screens while the other moved a series of objects around the room without any apparent intent. Some of the materials that the paler Racosku was dithering with looked vaguely familiar, even intimately so—such as a few cardboard boxes—while others were of the strangest shapes, and Lucretia wasn't about to even venture a guess as to what they were or what they contained.

As Lucretia gazed about the room, mouth agape, she felt Violet's tentacle tickling her arm. She followed the Racosku's foreleg to a flat space on the wall, which was coated in a white reflective material. Upon that surface appeared, in vivid blue lettering, in clear Latin script, the word: WELCOME!

Lucretia gasped aloud. She turned to the red Racosku, propped up on its forelegs as its first set of tentacles plied at the holographic screen.

Her eyes returned to the display board, which now read: DO YOU UNDERSTAND?

"Yes!" Lucretia exclaimed. "Yes, I understand! Wow! You… you know who we are? I mean…*what* we are? You know our language?"

YOU ARE *HOMO SAPIENS SAPIENS*, ALSO KNOWN AS ANATOMI-CALLY MODERN HUMANS, COLLOQUIALLY REFERRED TO AS HUMAN BEINGS, AND ALSO AS MEATBAGS. BASED ON YOUR PRIOR VOCAL-IZATIONS, THIS LANGUAGE APPEARS TO BE THE ONE YOU PREFER TO COMMUNICATE IN.

"That's…right! English. It's called English." Lucretia bowed slightly; she wasn't sure how to communicate respect to the Racosku, but that was her best guess. Either the Racosku indeed understood what she was saying or, more likely, some program inside the screen was translating her speech into something the creature could comprehend. Either way, she could finally communicate with her hosts. *And ask that very most important of questions.* Folding her hands, she began: "Listen, this planet of yours is beautiful, and we're very honored to be your guests. But we must return to our home. Do you know how we can get back to Earth?"

Quickly, the red creature scrawled out: THE PASSAGE THROUGH WHICH YOU ARRIVED WILL ALSO RETURN YOU TO YOUR ORIGIN. IN THREE MOTIONS OF THE STARS IT WILL REAPPEAR. YOU WILL ARRIVE AT YOUR ORIGIN AT THE DATE AND TIME AT WHICH YOU DEPARTED.

Lucretia breathed the most heavenly sigh of relief she'd ever breathed. She could've kissed the magnificently noodly mantis-like marvel right on its lips, if only it'd had lips to kiss. "Thank you! Thank you, thank you, *thank you!*"

"Wait," Jeremiah said, "what does it mean by 'motions of the stars'?"

"I'm guessing that's their equivalent of days." She hoped that was what it was, anyway, and not the equivalent of years. Or millennia.

THE MOTIONS OF THE STARS ARE MEASURED BY OUR INSTRUMENTS. THIS IS INCORRECT; THE STARS DO NOT MOVE. OUR PLANET MOVES. OUR INSTRUMENTS MEASURE HOW OUR PLANET MOVES RELATIVE TO THE STARS.

"So, like a sextant," Lucretia said under her breath. Turning to the Racosku, she added: "How long is one motion of the stars?"

BY YOUR MEASURING, ONE MOTION IS APPROXIMATELY THIRTY HOURS.

"Sweet! So, ninety hours until the wormhole returns, then. Give or take." Ecstatic, she slapped Jeremiah's back harder than she'd meant to. "I can hang out here for four days."

"What happens if we miss the vortex?" Jeremiah asked.

YOU MUST ENTER THE PORTAL AT THE COORDINATES THROUGH WHICH YOU EXITED. IF YOU ENTER THE INCORRECT PORTAL, YOU WILL NOT BE RETURNED TO YOUR ORIGINAL LOCATION, DATE, AND TIME.

"Well, that would suck," Lucretia said. "Wouldn't want to end up in North Korea or something. So, you mean there are other wormholes? These passages you speak of, there are other ones?"

YES. MANY PASSAGES OPEN. TRAVELERS SELDOM PASS THROUGH THEM.

"And you can point us to the right one when it's time for us to leave?"

WE WILL DIRECT YOU TO THE PROPER PASSAGE. YOU ARE WELCOME TO REMAIN WITH US UNTIL THEN.

"Thanks, Brain! I'm gonna call you Brain, if that's okay." She gestured to the paler Racosku. "I guess that one's Pinky, even though it's not pink." She nudged Jeremiah's shoulder. "Remember that old cartoon *Pinky and the Brain*? These guys kinda remind me of that. I honestly have no idea why. Remember how Mom always had us watch cartoons from, like, ten years before, because she thought all the new ones sucked?"

Jeremiah chortled as he shook his head. "I'm just glad Mom and Dad didn't let you name me."

Lucretia couldn't help but share in his newfound joviality. She turned to Brain. "So, is this your home?"

OUR DWELLINGS ARE IN THE HIGHER ELEVATIONS. WE WILL LEAD YOU THERE PRESENTLY. YOU ARE STANDING INSIDE OUR CREMATORY.

Lucretia jolted back. "Uh…crematory?"

The Racosku's head flashed a deeper shade of red. FORGIVE ME, I MADE AN ERROR. THIS IS NOT A CREMATORY. THE CORRECT TERM IS LABORATORY. I AM SORRY.

"No, it's all good. I mean, you're forgiven." Lucretia uttered a theatrical *whew*. "Had me worried there for a minute!"

PLEASE, ACCEPT MY DEEPEST APOLOGIES. I ASSURE YOU, YOUR BODY WILL NOT BE INCINERATED. YOU WILL BE TREATED AS OUR GUEST. WE DO NOT INCINERATE OUR GUESTS. THAT WOULD BE VERY IMPOLITE.

"Oh, I was just messing with you."

The creature's head cocked to the side. YOU HAVE MADE A MESS? THAT IS INCORRECT. I DETECT NO MESS IN YOUR VICINITY.

Lucretia's mouth opened, but no words came out.

Jeremiah nudged her shoulder. "Might want to keep things formal, Lu."

"Thank you, Jeremiah," she said with a roll of her eyes. Then she turned to Brain. "So, do you have a name? Your species, I mean. What do you call yourselves? Just so I don't have to keep calling you guys Racosku."

The transliterated gobbledygook that appeared on the screen would've tied even the most gifted wordsmith's tongue, and would've been at least eleven syllables if Lucretia had tried to pronounce it logically. *I guess I'm sticking with Racosku.* Making a series of silly faces, she muttered: "That's a mouthful."

So IS MY LOWER ABDOMINAL APPENDAGE. HA, HA, HA.

Lucretia screwed up her face. "Your 'lower abdominal appendage?' But…you've got, like, eight of them."

"Uh, Lu?" Jeremiah chortled. "I think it means a specific kind of appendage, if you know what I mean."

"Wait…did this thing just make a dick joke?" She turned venomous eyes upon the Racosku. "Did you just make a dick joke at me?"

Nonchalantly, Brain noodled: PLEASE EXPLAIN, WHAT IS A DICK JOKE?

Lucretia raised an eyebrow. "It's…a joke about your dick. You know all this stuff about humans and their language; don't you know what a joke is?"

I AM FAMILIAR WITH A JOKE. PLEASE EXPLAIN, WHAT IS A DICK?

She sighed aloud. "Please, tell me you're joking. Do I really have to explain this? The dick! The penis, the cock, the phallus, the wiener, the man sausage, the fleshy ramrod. The male reproductive organ. How do you…I'm confused." She drew a deep breath. "How did you know to make that joke? Where did you learn that?"

Brain gestured to Pinky, who brought a cardboard box and laid it at Lucretia's feet. Shuffling through the contents of the box, she was overcome with despair. There were a bunch of DVDs, including all the *Sharknado* films, plus some with titles that she'd never heard before and wasn't overly keen on finding out what they were about, though she had her suspicions.

"Wow," Jeremiah said. "B movies and loads of porn." The latter confirmed Lucretia's suspicions. "They must think the world of us. I wonder how they even got this stuff."

"Probably one of those space capsules," Lucretia guessed. "Every once in a while, nerds and rich people get together and crowd-fund campaigns to send elements of human culture into space, hoping that some aliens will find it. The American government did it a long time ago, back when the Space Race was the big thing. Usually, they put the best parts of our culture in it: classical music, great literature, poetry, photographs of famous people and inventions." She shook her head. "These guys got the stuff sent up by a bunch of celestial trolls."

"But, if they've got all this porn, then how the hell do they not know what a dick is?"

Lucretia turned to Brain. "Yeah, how do you not understand what a dick is, after you've been exposed to this nonstop sausage party?"

Brain's tentacles flew to the screen. I DO NOT COMPREHEND THE FUNCTION OF A DICK.

Lucretia squeezed her eyes shut. *My brain hurts.* "Okay, let's start from the beginning. How does your species reproduce? How do you make baby Racosku?"

POLLEN.

Lucretia's mouth twisted. "Pollen? You mean you…pollinate each other?"

An image appeared on the substrate where the text had

been—a video, or perhaps a window to another part of Racosku World. There were hundreds of the creatures gathering near what looked to be some kind of liquid with an argent glimmer upon its gentle waves. The Racosku all folded their serpentine legs beneath them, extending their forelegs until their bodies pointed skyward at forty-five-degree angles. They sat in circles of twenty or so creatures, all spread out along the shoreline.

Then, the creatures extended their proboscises, the top folds waving in the air like ribbons, the green lights flickering like the lanterns of so many fireflies.

Like moths to flame, a swarm of large insectoid creatures descended upon the lights. The plump insects looked a little like giant bumblebees, except their abdomens were striped iridescent green and magenta. As they descended, probing at the green lights with thin appendages of their own, puffs of yellow particles rose from the Racosku's forelegs, swirling around and catching in the folds beneath the bees' wings. As the insects flew from one stationary Racosku to another, the pollen fell from the bees, twinkling in the air like flecks of snow in subzero air as it blanketed the creatures.

"Incredible!" Lucretia said. "You really do pollinate each other!" *I guess they don't have to worry about paternity tests around here. No one knows who their daddy is. And I'm guessing they don't care, either.*

Brain backed away from the panel, and something in its movements, suddenly hunched and sluggish, suggested a deep sorrow affecting the creature.

"Brain?" Lucretia prodded. "What's the matter?"

Another moving image appeared on the panel, this time showing the beelike creatures that had acted as the Racosku's pollinators settling over a pond glowing green…and dying.

"What's happening to them?" Lucretia asked.

We do not know. That is where they go to breed. This has been happening for one thousand turns of the stars.

"It's almost like something's poisoning the water." Lucretia gestured to the pond. "What is that green stuff? Is that the bees' food?"

It is excreted by organisms beneath the surface. The video disappeared, replaced by a schematic of what looked somewhat like a sea anemone. These are the source of the detritus that the pollinators feed upon.

"Must be some kind of defense mechanism," Jeremiah noted. "Some marine invertebrates secrete a mucous layer that contains cytolytic proteins that are toxic to predators. Maybe that's what's happening here; the lake creatures might be injecting similar toxins into that sheen."

"That makes no sense," Lucretia said. "I could understand if the alien bees were eating the crawly water-thingies, but they're basically eating their shit."

Jeremiah shrugged. "Evolution has a mind of its own."

"No, Jay, evolution doesn't have a mind at all. It doesn't always work out for the best, and you know that as well as I do." Lucretia turned back to Brain. "What will happen if the bees keep dying like this?"

We fear that, if we cannot pollinate enough of our species in the next cycle, no new offspring will hatch again.

Lucretia gasped. "You mean…you'll go extinct?"

Brain's proboscis extended and opened, the thinnest tentacle wrapping around Lucretia's wrist as the desperate words appeared on the wall: Can you help us?

"Uh," Lucretia stuttered, blinking the tears from her eyes, "oh my God, I wish I could. But—"

The panel flashed, and the text was replaced by professional portraits of Lucretia and Jeremiah, along with snippets from their résumés.

Lucretia chuckled even over the ache in her heart. "Yeah, we're scientists. But we know nothing about you guys, or this world."

The images disappeared, yielding to more text: PLEASE, HELP US.

This could be the chance I've been waiting my whole life for, Lucretia knew: a chance to put her skills and knowledge to use for something good, something bigger than herself.

Without thinking, she gently caressed the appendage clinging to her. "We'll try. We can't make any promises, but you have my word, my brother and I will do everything we can for you."

"Lu!" Jeremiah whispered sharply. "We need to be thinking about how we're going to get out of here."

"We know how we're getting out," Lucretia reminded him. "We have almost four days, and we've got nothing better to do. Best get to work—"

As she spoke, a strange sound drew the Racosku's attention. The four of them scurried to the doorway, Lucretia and Jeremiah following closely behind. The sound was a high, caustic drone, as if every bee, wasp, and hornet on Planet Earth decided to take wing all at once around the same megaphone. It was a mechanical sound—the sound, Lucretia was almost certain, of aircraft propellers. *More Earthlings?*

And not just any propellers. That racket that hung in the air like a strange form of ambient music was unique to the violent air disturbance caused by tandem sets of contrarotating blades. The only aircraft type Lucretia knew of that still featured such an arrangement was a Russian strategic bomber. *Just what we need.*

Suddenly, four shapes appeared in the sky in the direction from which the sound was coming. Sure enough, they were aircraft, but they were not the bombers that Lucretia had feared. They were much too small. Three of the planes held a tight echelon formation, but the fourth seemed to be descending.

"Aren't those Spitfires?" Jeremiah asked, apparently noting the planes' elliptical wings, or more likely just spouting off the name of the first propeller-driven warplane that came to mind. His tone was a mixture of bewilderment and cautious excitement, as if the planes had come to rescue the two hapless humans.

"No," Lucretia observed, squinting at the four aircraft, for she must've been seeing things. She recognized them, all right: a relatively obscure carrier-borne strike aircraft used by the British for a brief spell in the fifties. None of that type remained airworthy; hell, only one was even still intact. "This can't be right. Those are…Westland Wyverns!"

"Never heard of that one. But then, you're the aviation expert."

Lucretia peered closely at the four aircraft. There were bumblebee stripes around the rear fuselages—the identification markings, she knew, that had been used by British and French forces in Operation Musketeer, the military action in the Suez Canal Crisis of 1956. *What the…?*

The fourth Wyvern nosed down sharply, and Lucretia could see that the propellers had stopped. *He's going to crash!* She made a quick study of the land around her. About half a mile beyond the arboreal gate was a flat, glimmering expanse that looked like a river. She flew down the ramp as fast as she could, through the glittery gate and into the swaying luminescent forest.

She reached the riverbank well after the plane struck the surface. The pilot had pulled up before impact, but the tail had hit the water hard, causing the plane to halt violently and nose over. If the pilot had even survived the crash, then he'd surely been knocked unconscious, even with a helmet to protect his head. The canopy appeared to be open. *If I can reach him…*

The Wyvern was sinking quickly. Lucretia threw off her T-shirt and pants, drawing a deep breath as she made ready to plunge into the river, even over Jeremiah's protests. The water could have been noxious, it could have been acidic enough to melt the flesh off her bones, could have been nearly frozen or almost boiling. There could have been any number of sharks or stingrays or piranhas or poisonous jellyfish or strange and deadly creatures out of her worst nightmares lurking beneath that deceptively tranquil surface. But she didn't care about that, only about the hapless airman who was sure to drown if she didn't reach him.

When she was waist-deep in the water, the surface fell away from her feet. The river was surprisingly warm, brushing against her skin like a fine silk. She swam as hard and as fast as she could, but the plane was sinking too quickly. The pilot hadn't moved from his seat. Lucretia could see him slumped over, his flight helmet knocked off his head a little.

The large vertical stabilizer disappeared when she was a hundred feet from the plane. Holding her breath, she dove beneath the surface, swimming toward where she estimated the plane's depth would be when she reached it. She couldn't see a damned thing.

Until a bright flash seared her eyes, and a burst of bubbles tossed her about like a paper boat in a typhoon.

Come to me, Marie's serene voice called out. *Come home to me.*

Don't forget to bring some good English tea.

When Sid awoke, he was drowning. The water was in his nose, in his mouth, in his eyes. He'd nearly swallowed it. He was trapped.

Frantically, he reached behind him, grasping only water— no, not water. It was heavier than water. Why was he sinking so quickly?

He squeezed his eyes shut, pinching his face. *Don't swallow. Don't breathe.*

Consciousness was slipping away.

With one final effort, he reached behind him, grasping the handle on the back of his ejection seat. He yanked hard. A muffled roar broke through the waves' gurgling drone, and a flurry of bubbles raced past him, as if he were looking at a waterfall from the inside. The seat shot skyward, slowed by the water pushing down upon it.

Sid had barely managed to unbuckle his harness as the seat halted just beneath the surface. He raised his hand, clawing at the water to reach the precious surface as his vision darkened. But at that moment, he was pulled back as if by the tentacles of some sea monster. *The parachute*, he knew.

He clawed at the strings, at the pack's straps, all for naught.

I'm sorry, my loves, his mind whispered to Marie and the girls. He closed his eyes, resigning himself to death, praying that God would have mercy on a combat pilot's soul.

The last thing he thought he saw was a hand, distinctly soft and feminine, reaching down for him. *My love.*

CHAPTER IV

SIDNEY DAVENTRY'S MOTHER had always waxed lyrical about how, when she died, there would be an angel there to show her the way to Heaven. Sid had always assumed it was the cancer talking. But, sure enough, there was an angel standing—no, *kneeling*—over him. She was speaking, no doubt in the idyllic language of angels, though he could only hear the deep droning in his ears. Blue light formed a corona around her, and Sid could not see her face, only the smoothness of her long hair, which seemed to be tied into pigtails not unlike a child's and glimmered in the light like Marie's did right after she'd bathed, and the svelte shape of her small body. He'd always expected an angel to look like the love of his life. This angel had the figure and stature of his oldest daughter.

But...why was the angel yelling at him?

And why was she pounding on his chest and slapping his face?

And why was he choking on whatever water he wasn't spitting in the angel's face?

And why was the sky purple?

Suddenly, a storm was raging in Sid's bowels, splashing hot waves into his stomach, exploding into his throat, erupting from his mouth in a torrent of water that had a strange and strong taste, not unlike the salt water of the ocean, but more pleasant, quite like cinnamon.

Coughing as if to expel some evil spirit, Sid sat up, nearly tipping over until the angel caught him in her arms, patting his back as water and puke sluiced over his lips.

Catching his breath, he glanced at the angel's face…only now he saw that she was no angel at all. She was no child but a grown woman who looked to be of an age with him. She was wearing only a bit of cloth to protect her womanhood, a wardrobe even skimpier than the most risqué swimsuits he'd ever seen—such immodesty as only a harlot would display.

Then, he made a study of her face: round, soft features, tan in complexion, narrow eyes. He drew back. *Oh, bloody hell*, he thought. *The Japs must've gotten me!*

"Wait…what?" the woman said, her accent strangely familiar.

Sid shook his head, only now realizing that he'd actually said that aloud.

The woman pinched Sid's chin, turning his eyes to meet hers. They were very beautiful eyes. "Are you all right, Mister"—she glanced at the name tag on Sid's flight suit—"Daventry? Can you hear me?"

"Yes," Sid managed. "Yes, ma'am. Thank you. I must've hit my head."

"Yeah, you were definitely out when your plane sank." She made a fist with her right hand, raising her index and middle fingers. "How many fingers am I holding up?"

"Two?"

"Okay, great, you don't have a concussion. Or maybe you do;

I'm not a doctor. Well, I *am*, but not a medical doctor. Anyway, I think you'll be all right."

You think? He shoved aside the thought. The woman, whoever she was, had saved his life. After taking a moment to catch his breath and calm his nerves, he said: "Ma'am, I owe you a great debt. I suppose it's proper to introduce myself. My name is Sidney Daventry, Lieutenant, Royal Canadian Navy."

She made a dismissive motion with her hand. "Oh, you're good. I was thinking about going for a swim anyway. Never knew Canada flew Wyverns."

A lady who knows aircraft? "I'm on exchange with the Royal Navy."

"A-ha!" she said with a wink. "My name is Lucretia Tang, by the way." She gestured to a man, podgy in stature and looking quite disheveled in his wrinkled trousers and shirt that seemed much too big even for such a fat man, hanging from his broad shoulders as if he were wearing a tent. With his long hair and scruffy beard, he had the look of a caveman. "That's my brother, Jeremiah."

"Hey," Jeremiah said, then he handed Lucretia a shirt not unlike the one Sid wore to sleep in, albeit black in color and tattered beneath the sleeve, bearing a vivid image of what looked like a ghost playing a violin and the word *Camelot* spelled with a *K* for some reason. Lucretia quickly slipped the shirt over her head, then snatched another garment from Jeremiah's hand: a pair of leggings, or near enough to them—they certainly couldn't be called trousers—that extended to her ankles, the glossy material hugging the sculpted contours of her legs. *People around here sure dress strangely.*

Wherever *here* was. As Lucretia Tang dressed, Sid looked past her, regarding the strange world around him with mouth agape.

He must've still been in a daze, because everything around him really *was* glowing!

"Yeah," Lucretia said. "It's a lot to take in. Just take a breather. I'll try to explain everything, at least all I know. I'm still getting a feel for the place too."

They talk rather strangely as well. Lucretia's accent was distinctly American, but…was *this* America? Not even New York, or Miami Beach, or the Las Vegas Strip, or even Hollywood, was so brilliantly bright and beautiful. *Or as terrifying.*

"Hey!" a familiar voice called out, this time in an unmistakably Scottish accent. "Get away from him, you slanty-eyed bitch, or I'll blow your fucking head off!"

Lucretia gasped as Tom Wickler ran toward her and her brother with his Webley Mark IV .38-caliber revolver raised. She held up her hands, trembling, but said nothing.

"Wait, Hags!" Sid called out. "They're not the enemy. Put the gun down. This is Lucretia. She saved my life."

"Lucretia, my sheep-shagging arse," Tom spat. "More like Little Lady Mao, if you ask me. Ain't that right, Tokyo Rose?"

"Lieutenant!" another voice bellowed—this time it was Gene Faintary, approaching with Jim Wellington close behind. "You will lower your weapon at once and stand down."

"No harm taking precautions, sir."

"That's an order, Lieutenant!" Fanny barked.

With a grumble, Tom Wickler complied.

Fanny turned to Lucretia and Jeremiah. "Lieutenant-Commander Eugene Faintary, commanding officer, Number 1776 Naval Air Squadron, Royal Navy. Please, accept my apologies for my man's behavior, ma'am. Rest assured that disciplinary action will be taken."

"No worries," Lucretia said with a nervous shrug.

"You all right, Moose?" Wimpy asked, offering Sid a hand.

"Well, considering that I've got neither a plane nor a damned clue where I'm at, I couldn't be better." He clasped Jim Wellington's hand. His grip was weak, but Wimpy was strong as ever, yanking Sid to his feet and gathering him up in a powerful hug.

"Good to see you still breathing, mate," Wimpy said. "Although, looking at this place, I'm not entirely sure we're not all dead!"

"Where did you land?"

"Ah, we put down on that spit of land where we saw that other little aeroplane. Turns out you could've landed there, mate!"

"That plane would be ours, by the way," Lucretia chimed in.

The phlegmatic grumble of the commander's throat clearing jarred everyone, even the civilians, to attention. Gene Faintary was not a tall man, standing all of five foot seven, but with his impeccably combed black hair, chiseled jawbone, and barrel chest, he cut a commanding figure—one that demanded obedience by his mere presence.

Fanny's stark blue eyes bored into Sid. "Are you all right, Lieutenant Daventry?"

"Yes, sir." *Miraculously all right*, he thought, considering that he should've been killed when he'd first impacted the water, or at best, come out of the whole thing with at least a broken bone or two from the ejection. His helmet had cushioned his head just enough to keep his skull from cracking open like a walnut against the dash panel, and the weight of the water must've dampened the force of his ejection enough that his body was, as far as he could tell, fully intact.

"Very good." The skipper swiftly spun about, and his wrath fell upon Tom Wickler, who could only shrivel. "You'll be lucky if you aren't discharged with dishonor from Her Majesty's Service,

Lieutenant! Where were you during the engagement, when your section leader was in peril?"

"Sir," Hags stammered, "I was…I was attempting to reform—"

"You were nowhere to be found! You disengaged as soon as you saw Lieutenant Barluck's aircraft go down. And now, you draw your firearm on a civilian without cause?"

"I thought they might be enemy agents, sir." Tom's eyes narrowed, a crooked smirk forming upon his broad, mustached face. "Have the 'civilians' been checked for weapons, Commander?"

Faintary stepped into Hags' face. "Perhaps they should be given yours." He held out his hand. "Turn over your service weapon, Lieutenant."

"Sir—"

"*Now*, Lieutenant Wickler!"

With a harrumph, the Scot complied. "Commander."

Fanny nodded brusquely, stuffing the holstered revolver into his belt, then turned to Sid and Jim. "We need to set about the task of returning to the ship. Now, I estimate that the elapsed time between our encounter with the storm and Lieutenant Daventry's forced landing was ten minutes; certainly no more than twelve. For a margin of error, let us assume that the time was twelve and a half minutes; at the Wyvern's cruising speed, that means we traveled approximately sixty-four nautical miles from the funnel."

"Aye, sir," Wimpy said, "but in which direction?"

"In the direction from here to the location of our aircraft."

He has no idea which way's which here, Sid knew. *Not that Gene Faintary would ever confess to such ignorance.* "Sir, I didn't see the funnel cloud after we exited. It was like the storm vanished. I'm afraid…"

The reality of his situation struck Sid harder than his instrument panel had struck his head when he hit the water.

Drawing a deep breath, he said: "I'm afraid we may be stranded here, sir."

Lucretia cleared her throat. "If I may, Commander?"

"Not now, ma'am." Fanny gestured in the general direction of where the Wyverns were parked. "We have three functional Wyverns remaining, plus the small aeroplane we parked next to."

"Uh, sir," Lucretia said firmly, "that's *my* airplane!"

Faintary shot her a look of incredulity. "I'm afraid we'll have to commandeer your aircraft, ma'am. My men and I need to return to our ship. Rest assured that aid will be sent to you once we've reached *Eagle*."

"That's not how things work around here—"

"That will be all, ma'am." Fanny turned back to his men. "Based on our prior fuel consumption, we will have enough fuel to make it back to the phenomenon that led us here and, assuming we return to the same vicinity where we entered, back to *Eagle*—though I must stress that the margin for error will be very thin. We were operating at high power settings during combat and while inside the storm, and burned a great deal of fuel."

"With all due respect, sir," Sid said, "that's a lot of assumptions."

"I know, Lieutenant. But it's the best we can do, given our situation and lack of knowledge."

"Commander," Lucretia attempted again, "if I may, please?"

"You may *not*. This is a Royal Navy matter. I have said that we have heard enough from you."

"Yes, I know what you said! But, one, I don't take orders from you. I'm a civilian, and a United States citizen. Two, doesn't a good commander listen to the advice of people who know what the hell they're talking about? You said you lack knowledge of this place. Well, you guys just got here. Jay and I have been here a little more than an hour. We've learned a thing or two about it—and, more importantly, how to get back to *our* world."

Sid scratched his head. "Our...*world?*"

"Yes, Lieutenant Daventry! In case it's not blatantly apparent, we're on an alien planet!"

Neither Sid nor his squadron mates said a thing. The thought had certainly occurred to Sid; sure, there was a time when he had marveled at the night sky, at the distant stars, imagining what life might be out there in strange new worlds. Just like there was a time when he'd believed in the Tooth Fairy.

"Okay," Lucretia continued. "Now, according to the Racosku—that's the indigenous species here; they look like giant bugs, but they're incredibly intelligent and have technology that allows them to communicate with humans; you'll meet them soon enough, but please, don't shoot them, they're very nice— anyway, according to them, the vortex will reappear in just under four days. It apparently goes two ways."

"So, we can get home that way?" Wimpy asked.

"Whoa, hold up there. That's the vortex that Jay and I came through. It'll apparently spit us out at the time and place where and when we entered. You'd have to ask Brain—he's, like, the chief scientist or whatever—when yours will appear."

"Forgive me," Sid said, "but I'm not sure I follow."

Lucretia folded her hands in front of her mouth, blowing into them. "Okay, here comes the crazy part—I mean, all of this is crazy, but...well, okay, here goes. Now, judging from the stripes on your planes' wings and fuselages, and the fact that you're flying Westland Wyverns, which, if I remember correctly, were in service less than five years, I'm guessing you guys are from 1956."

"That's right," Wimpy said, his right eyebrow raised.

"And, just out of curiosity, what day in 1956?"

"Sixth November."

"Well, Jay and I left Earth in the year 2026—also on November the sixth."

Sid's mouth opened, but no words came forth. The Brits' gaping suggested that they were equally dumbfounded.

"Yeah," Lucretia added. "You know how they say it's fallacious to assume that time is linear?"

I have no idea what you're talking about. Sid was about to voice those very words when a hellion's shriek pierced the purple tranquility.

"Oi! Jesus Christ!" Tom Wickler squealed like a skewered pig. His hand fumbled at his side, as if reaching for the revolver that he'd forgotten he'd surrendered. "What the bloody fucking hell is that thing?"

Sid's eyes followed Hags' frantic gesturing to the glowing, swaying forest of strange vines, between two of which emerged a faceless creature that looked like a giant grasshopper walking on snakes, all manner of colors dancing on its skin, some reflections of the plants around it but others seeming to be coming from inside.

"Blimey!" Jim Wellington gasped.

Lucretia sighed aloud. "That's a Racosku! The native fauna that I was telling you about. For God's sake, man, they're harmless." She waved at the creature. "How's it going, Noodles?"

"Bollocks!" Hags barked. "That thing's going to bloody eat us!"

"It's not going to eat you!" the American snapped. "Jay and I were just in their laboratory. They didn't eat us, did they?"

"*Laboratory*? Christ Almighty! It's some kind of Frankenstein bug out of Hell!"

Sid had to chuckle under his breath. Nothing about the creature suggested that it was in any way dangerous.

"Yeah, laboratory. We're scientists, Jay and me." Lucretia glanced at the rest of the pilots. "The Racosku have asked us to help them. Until the portal opens, that's what we're going to do."

"Help them how?" Sid asked.

"I don't know yet; this was just dropped on me a little bit before we heard you guys flying over. But they face a threat to… well, to their very existence. Without getting into the scientific details, they've lost the ability to reproduce. If we don't do something, they'll all die off within a generation or two." Gingerly, Lucretia approached Faintary, folding her hands as if in prayer. "With all due respect, Commander, we could use your help too. I'm sure we could use your planes."

"I would like to help you, ma'am," the skipper said, and Sid noted a genuine sympathy in his voice, "but it's out of the question. We have our orders and regulations; we cannot use our aircraft for such purposes without authorization from higher up."

"What kind of help would you need?" Sid asked.

Faintary shot him an askance glower but yielded the floor to Lucretia.

The scientist tried to explain the creatures' predicament in layman's terms. Sid heard something about pollen and bees dying off because of some kind of poison, but none of it made a damned bit of sense. At this point, *nothing at all* made a damned bit of sense.

"We could use your planes to survey the breeding ground," Lucretia said, and Sid finally understood what she was trying to convey. "I mean, I guess we could use our Velis, but it's slow, and I'm not even sure it's got any charge left."

"Charge?" Sid asked.

"Yeah, it's electric."

"They make electric aeroplanes?"

Lucretia nodded. "In 2026. But, like I was saying, if one of you could fly over the site, get us some data, even just some video or even still pictures. You have cine cameras in your planes, don't you? For the guns and stuff?"

"You certainly know your aeroplanes, Ms. Tang," Faintary said approvingly. "Quite impressive. But, as I said, it is out of the question."

"Sir," Sid dared, "can we not spare just one Wyvern? One sortie, to get the Tangs the pictures they need?"

"No, Lieutenant, we cannot! We need our aircraft to return to the ship. We cannot waste fuel on pointless errands."

Sid turned to Lucretia. "How many people can fit in your plane?"

She raised an eyebrow. "Two."

"I promise, I'll personally see that you get back to where you came from."

"You're not listening, Lieutenant," Faintary barked. "We will not fly our aircraft until such time as we can make our way back to HMS *Eagle*. That aeroplane does not belong to you, Lieutenant Daventry. It belongs to the United Kingdom, and to Her Majesty the Queen. Now, you will speak no more of this madness; if you do, you will be charged with insubordination. Do I make myself clear?"

Sid bowed his head, exhaling his frustration, his disappointment, his despair. "Yes, sir. Perfectly clear, sir."

He risked a glance at a fuming Lucretia, then to the creature she'd named Noodles, offering a face of sympathy.

What else could he do?

The British pilots and their Canadian pickup had been offered accommodation in the higher levels of the arboreal complex, in a space that Lucretia learned had been left vacant after the Racosku who'd lived there metamorphosed—that was how the Racosku described the death of the body and the freedom of the spirit—without any offspring to take their place. The tight-assed commander was wandering the forest at the base of the ramp, perhaps marveling at the splendor in his time of solitude where no one could see his emotions breaking through his rigorously formal veneer, or perhaps deep in planning for whatever he was going to order his men to do next. *I'm leaning strongly toward the latter.*

Lucretia couldn't have cared less what the rigid old stick was doing down there. She focused on the panels, scrawling through the databases in the manner that Brain had taught her, which, in truth, wasn't much different from scrolling on a tablet or touch-screen computer.

"What are you thinking?" Jeremiah prodded.

"I don't know." Exhaustion and dejection weighed down Lucretia's voice. "I still don't even know where to start. All I have are these static schematics of the urchin thingies. I need more than this, Jay. We don't even know where the breeding ground is, let alone anything about the urchins' behavioral patterns, their genetic makeup, or what's in the sheen they're secreting to make it poisonous to the alien bees. I need DNA samples: the urchins, the bees, the slop…how the hell do we get that?"

She buried her face in her hands, blowing out her cheeks, disturbed by how foul her breath smelled.

Jeremiah's fingers kneading her neck and shoulders took away some of her tension, her frustration. "Did you ever stop to think that, maybe, we're not meant to help these creatures? Did it occur to you that maybe nature selected them for extinction? I know it upsets you, but…"

Lucretia turned sour eyes on him. "Jay, what do I hate more than anything in the world?"

"Onion rings?"

"Well, yes, they're disgusting." She drew a deep breath. "I'm being serious, Jay."

Jeremiah chortled. "When people anthropomorphize nature and attribute the stochasticity of its happenings to conscious processes. When people treat nature as some wholly benevolent deity and assume that everything the great mother does is for the greater good."

"Bingo. 'Natural selection' is a fancy term for 'randomness' and 'occasional fortuity,' Jay. Oh, and don't forget: 'error.' Nature doesn't have a mind. It isn't conscious. It doesn't choose who lives or dies; that stuff just happens according to a set of biochemical algorithms. Stop reading that panpsychism garbage and following all those self-fellating hippies on social media. Nature doesn't always get it right. In fact, it gets it wrong a lot more often than our species likes to think about. If nature always gets it right, then why do mosquitoes exist?"

"Question for the philosophers."

"We don't know how interconnected the Racosku are with the rest of the flora and fauna on this planet. If they go extinct, what impact will it have on the rest of life here?"

Jeremiah shrugged. "Survival of the fittest."

Lucretia spun around, shoving her hands into her hips. "You're the last person alive who ought to be extolling natural law, Jay. Because, if survival of the fittest applied to human society, your diabetic ass would be dead right now. At the very least, you'd be blind. And no one would give a shit, because you're too weak to survive."

Jeremiah bit his lip. "Point taken."

"I need more data, damn it," Lucretia said with a sigh. All she could do with the panel was scroll through images; there was no search function that she could see, and she probably wouldn't have been able to use it anyway. "*Brain!*" she called out.

In a flash, the red Racosku ambulated into the laboratory and halted beside Lucretia. Noodles followed close behind. She hadn't noticed before, but the creatures emitted a slight piquant smell, quite like that of Tunisian spice when frying.

"Sorry if I woke you up," she said with her head bowed slightly.

Brain's tentacles danced across the panel. WE HAVE RECEIVED SUFFICIENT REST. WE WILL ASSIST YOU WITH ALL THAT YOU REQUIRE.

"You're the best, Brain. You know that, right?"

I AM VERY AWESOME. THIS IS FACTUAL.

Lucretia burst into laughter. *I wonder where it learned that one.* "Okay, now, do you happen to have...oh, shit, how do I explain this?" *Don't underestimate their intelligence. They were smart enough to construct this interface.* "Okay, do you guys know what DNA is?"

DEOXYRIBONUCLEIC ACID, A POLYMER THAT DELIVERS GENETIC INSTRUCTIONS FOR THE FUNCTIONING OF ORGANISMS, OFTEN REFERRED TO AS THE BLUEPRINT OF LIFE.

"Yes!" Lucretia squealed. "Now, do you happen to have the DNA sequences for the urchins...I mean, the aquatic creatures that emit the detritus that the pollinators feed upon?"

"Lu," Jeremiah interjected, "just for future reference, sea urchins and sea anemones aren't the same thing, and it annoys me when people use the terms interchangeably. In fact, some anemones eat urchins. These things resemble anemones, so if we're going to associate them with creatures familiar to our world, let's stick with that, okay?"

Lucretia pinched her face as she nodded. "Duly noted. Pedant."

As she spoke, the panel on the wall grew black, and characters appeared in white classic typewriter font—hundreds, nay *thousands*, in short bars of the Latin letters *A*, *C*, *G*, and *T*.

Lucretia gasped aloud, covering her mouth as she giggled like a teenager at a Taylor Swift concert. Jeremiah stood beside her, mouth agape as if he'd been frozen in place.

"Oh my God!" Lucretia yelped. "Oh my God, oh my God, oh my *God!*" She drew deep breaths to calm herself. "Okay," she said to Brain, "can you save this for me, so that I can access it as I need it?"

THE INFORMATION WILL BE MADE EASILY ACCESSIBLE FOR YOU. IS THERE ANY OTHER INFORMATION YOU REQUIRE ME TO FIND?

"Do you have the sequences for the pollinators?"

Another DNA chart.

"Yes! Now all we need is the goop."

"If it's even organic," Jeremiah said.

"Well, if it's made by organisms, and contains organic toxins, then it's a safe bet that it's organic matter, isn't it?"

Sure enough, a third sequence appeared on the panel.

"Yeah," Jeremiah said, "but is that with the toxins or without them?"

"Well, I'm guessing that the Racosku haven't risked taking a sample of the poisonous stuff, lest they get killed by it too, so probably before. Brain?"

THE INFORMATION THAT YOU HAVE BROWSED WAS GATHERED WHEN THE POLLINATORS WERE HEALTHY.

"So," Lucretia mused, "what we need now is a sample of the insalubrious sheen."

"We could take the plane over," Jeremiah suggested. "I mean, yeah, the battery's probably dead, but they've got all this technology here that has to run on some kind of electronics. I'm sure they've got something that could recharge it."

"Yeah, but how far do we have to fly? Even with that upgraded battery, we can only stay up for three hours."

"Three and a half."

"Yeah, that 'and a half' is what's known as an 'emergency reserve.'" Lucretia turned to Brain. "Can you show me a map of the area between here and the pollinators' breeding site? Preferably with topography."

A three-dimensional holographic image appeared on the panel before them, in exquisite detail. Even without any distance references, Lucretia could tell that the distance between the Racosku's abode and the breeding ground was significant, and the terrain was not exactly flat. In this strange world's perpetual twilight, those mountains would be all the harder to see and avoid.

"Could you measure the distance between here and there, please?"

THE DISTANCE IS APPROXIMATELY 475 KILOMETERS.

"Thank you," Lucretia said with a sigh. "That's just under three hundred miles."

Jeremiah scratched his chin. "That seems like a really long distance to travel just to make babies."

"Some birds and bats migrate across continents," she reminded him. "Whales sometimes travel halfway around the world to mate and give birth."

"Yeah, but these are basically bees."

And hardy little buggers too. "We'd barely make it there even if we dipped into the battery reserve, and we'd have no way of getting back here. And that's as the crow flies. This crow ain't flying over any mountains." She blew some air through pursed lips. "Sure wish we had one of those Wyverns."

"Regretting getting an electric plane, Lu?" Jeremiah japed.

"Does it matter? Even if we could make it there and back again, it'd take us at least three hours either way—and again, that's straight-line distance, and those big hills might have something to say about that. The Wyvern's cruising speed is three times our plane's top speed; maxed out, it's almost four times as fast. They could do the whole thing in less than two hours."

"But how would they get the sample?"

"Ever seen those videos of planes skimming the water with

their wheels? I mean, that pond looks big enough; a good pilot might be able to do it. I'm sure at least some of the stuff would cling to the rubber." She shook her head. "Doesn't matter. The commander won't let them do it. I guess that's that."

She sat down on the ground, resting her arms on her knees and hanging her head between them. *All this data, all this knowledge, and I can't do a damned thing with it.*

Lucretia Tang hadn't felt so helpless since the day Mark had handed her the divorce papers.

Aliens. The word played out in Sid Daventry's mind like a mantra, accompanied by alternating waves of wonder and terror. *We're in outer space. At the end of the universe. Maybe even in another dimension.*

Far, far from home. A home I may never see again. I'm sorry, Marie. I'm so sorry, my precious girls.

He thought back to the sensational reports from nine years earlier about an incident in the New Mexico desert, near a town called Roswell, where the newspapers and radio programs told of a flying saucer recovered by the American government and hidden at a secret base. The Yanks denied it, of course, saying that the object was actually a military balloon, but suddenly, the world was in a frenzy over extraterrestrial visitors to Earth. *Now here we are, extraterrestrial visitors on an alien planet.* The irony was almost enough to make him laugh.

At least the native creatures—it would've been wrong to call them *aliens*, for Sid and his mates were the aliens here—seemed friendly, or at least accommodating. They'd offered the Royal Navy pilots a room high in their tree mansion, next to the one where Lucretia and Jeremiah Tang were lodging. There seemed to be hundreds of such hollows in the trees, those beautiful behemoths that now reminded Sid of the medieval towers dotting the English countryside. He chuckled as he recalled seeing Broadway Tower in Worcestershire when he'd gone to visit Jim Wellington's family the first time, for at first glance he'd seen only two of the three turrets, and how disappointed he was when he'd learned that it wasn't a stronghold for the likes of Alfred the Great at all but merely a fancy decoration raised late in the eighteenth century. That was what the arboreal gate reminded him of the most.

The room's walls were perfectly round, as if the whole place were one giant tobacco tin, albeit with walls of smoothed wood. All around the room hung a series of what Sid could only describe as large hammocks, made from a strange rubbery material emitting a faint white glow that seemed to know exactly how firm or how soft Sid wanted it to be. There was a small window carved into the wood, tall like a castle's arrow slit and arched at the top, between the bunks taken by Sid and Jim, and the serene rustle of those bright red leaves and melodious whistle of the wind, like notes on a piccolo, swam through that slight embrasure, serenading the men as if it were coming from a record player. Water trickled down the walls from the side opposite the window and at ninety degrees to either side, adding a tranquil melody of its own, pooling in bowls of whitish leaves supported by baskets of wood woven into impeccable octagonal patterns.

Under different circumstances, Sid would have been hesitant to drink the water. But, parched as his throat had been when he'd entered his new quarters, it was the first thing he'd gone for. It was heavier than the fresh water he was used to, having a texture more like seawater, though not so strong as the water he'd nearly drowned in, and carried a strange but pleasant flavor, different from that of the river. But rather than exacerbating his thirst, it seemed to quench it much more quickly and thoroughly than the water back on Earth. And the food? The food was exquisite, like a banquet thrown by the old gods, as long as one could ignore the fact that it was glowing, and, where Sid came from, that usually meant that it was either illuminated artificially or radioactive. There was no meat, but the myriad fruits and leafy stuff that must have been this planet's form of vegetables were rich in flavor and, unless Sid's mind was playing tricks on him, must have had medicinal qualities, because, even after his ejection, even after slamming his head on his plane's cockpit dash, after the rigors of air combat maneuvering and nearly drowning, he felt better, more refreshed, and clearer in the head than he had when he'd woken up that morning.

Lying on his back, staring up at the slightly domed ceiling illuminated by the glow of his hammock and regiments of tiny lights like the ones he'd seen light up around his feet whenever he stepped in the cool soil down below, he mused on the two Americans who had also gotten stranded here. *People are strange in the future*, he thought, half amused, half despairing. He wouldn't be caught dead looking like the man, Jeremiah. He'd seen hobos and criminals who'd taken greater pride in their appearance. And Lucretia, decent though she seemed…why was she wearing tattered clothes with profane images painted on them? Why did she wear her hair like a little girl? Did everyone in the year 2026 walk around looking like they'd just come out of hibernation?

Sid shoved the thought aside, squeezing his eyes shut. He let out a loud grunt.

"Can't sleep either, Moose?" Jim Wellington asked.

"Not a wink," Sid confessed.

"Don't worry, mate. Pretty soon, we'll be back on the ship, and all this will be behind us."

"Unless we get jumped by MiGs again," Tom Wickler said with an exaggerated sigh. *Way to stay positive, Hags.*

"Ah," Sid said, trying to adopt a cheerful tone, "at least the skipper showed us how to shoot them down."

"Damned right he did, that old laird!" Hags exclaimed with newfound sanguinity. "I still think you should've smoked that bastard." The young Scot sat up in his hammock, flashing Sid a sideways smile. "Meaning no offense, Moose, but sometimes I think you'd rather not be a combat pilot."

Sid rose and turned to meet his gaze. "Is that so?"

"Oh, aye, mate. You're so intent on helping those bugs, those Americans—if they're really Americans, and not commie spies. I seen the way you looked at that little chink. You got eyes for her, sure as sheep shit."

"I'll have you know that I love my wife very much," Sid said firmly.

Tom held up his hands. "Aye, I never said you didn't. I'm not saying you're not a good man, Daventry. She's a bonnie lass, I'll give you that. For an Oriental, I mean. If I was as old as you, I might be trying to court her myself, enemy agent or nay."

Sid lay back down, hoping that Wickler, taking the hint from being ignored, would shut his bloody mouth.

But Tom Wickler did not shut his bloody mouth. "If you ask me," he went on, "what we really ought to be doing right now is seeing what we can get out of this place. What we can do for Queen and Country, if you take my meaning. Then report back to the Admiralty, maybe even the Prime Minister; hell, maybe even to Her Majesty. I'd reckon Lizzy would be right pleased with us."

"Eden would be so proud of you," Jim interjected with a harrumph. He'd never been particularly shy about his firm belief that the current occupant of 10 Downing Street was worthless as goose shit on a well pump.

"Aye, he would," Tom exclaimed as if it'd been a compliment.

"We're combat pilots, mate. We're warriors. Killing the enemy is our job. What right do those sandbags have to that canal?"

"I suppose the small fact that it's in their country," Jim sneered, taking the words right out of Sid's mouth.

"It's in our empire!" Hags blurted. "God made Britain to rule the world. That's what we're doing against those desert rats, and it's what we ought to be doing against these bright shiny cockroaches and those two yellow scoundrels. Fight and win, just like we did in the War."

Sid exploded from his hammock. "The War, eh? Tell me, Hags, what did you do in the great World War Two? Ah, yes, of course. You were in your mother's bedroom playing with your little toy soldiers, tripping over your own feet. I was there, young man. I was fighting the Krauts while you were fetching newspapers off your papa's porch." He sat down, but his eyes remained fixed on the jaded Scotsman. "I knew plenty of guys like you, guys who loved to fight so much that they thought they were invincible, and that God was on their side and wouldn't let them fall. And I saw plenty of them cured of that delusion, usually in a big ball of fire."

Hags slunk in his hammock, hands raised. "Now, no need to get angry, mate—"

"And by the way, Lieutenant Wickler," Sid seethed, a sudden fury rising in his throat as he remembered Hags' disappearing act over the sea, "if you're so committed to 'fighting and winning,' where were you during the engagement? If those 'sandbags' were so pathetic, so much lesser than your glorious British backside, why were you so quick to cut and run and leave me on my own?"

"You calling me a coward?" Tom's paltry defiance crumbled at the tremors in his voice.

"Gentlemen!" Jim bellowed, and when Sid turned to face him, the executive officer was on his feet, silhouetted against the corona of his hammock's glow, and he appeared as an angel of wrath. "You will dispense with this nonsense right now. Is that understood?"

Sid leaned back, all the while keeping his glower fixed upon Tom Wickler. "Yes, sir."

"Aye, sir," Hags said, his voice still quavering. "It's like I say. I meant no disrespect."

"We're all on the same side here," Jim reminded them, kindly but firmly. "Now's not the time or place to be forgetting that."

Sid nodded, fanning his face with his hand to cool the fire still simmering under his skin. He snatched the trousers that he'd laid atop his folded wool serge flight suit, donning them and his boots, knowing that his cotton undershirt would be enough in the mild temperatures. "If it's all the same to you gentlemen, I think I'll take a walk." He nodded to Jim Wellington. "Good night, XO." Then he flashed a glower at Tom Wickler. "Lieutenant."

CHAPTER V

LUCRETIA WONDERED WHAT time it was, even though she didn't actually care. It must've been getting late, though "time" seemed irrelevant here, at least under normal circumstances. She wasn't tired, and even if she were, she wouldn't sleep, partially because she didn't want to sleep, wanted to spend every minute of the fleeting time she had in this world marveling at its beauty, and partially because she couldn't, knowing that the beauty before her would soon be drenched in sorrow, and there wasn't a damned thing she could do about it.

What if Jeremiah was right? What if the Racosku's time has come, and there's nothing we can do to stop it? The creatures were clearly intelligent, brilliant even; why hadn't they taken any action to halt their own extinction? Did they not have the means? Or did they simply not believe in interfering with natural processes? *Do they even have beliefs?*

They must have, or at least been capable of complex thinking and reasoning. Why else would they have asked Lucretia and Jeremiah for help?

Lucretia undid her braids, letting that smooth black mane over which Mark had always crooned so lyrically fall, tucking it behind her ears, and trudged down the spiraling ramp, having no trouble keeping her footing. Jeremiah followed, having nothing better to do, though Lucretia could tell that he'd had enough of the alien world's mystique and was ready to go back to the familiar.

When she reached the bottom of the ramp, movement between the glowing bushes to her right startled her.

"Oh!" she exhaled, placing her hand over her chest. "Commander Faintary. I didn't see you there."

"Good evening, ma'am," the airman said with the rigid formality that seemed to be all he knew. "I hadn't meant to startle you."

"It's all good. Hey, uh, would you mind if I went over and checked out your planes? I won't touch, I promise." She laughed nervously. "I've been to lots of air shows. I know the drill. No touching!"

The commander's face betrayed no emotion. "For reasons of security, I cannot grant you unescorted access to our aircraft."

Lucretia bit her lip. "You think we're spies, don't you? Wish I had a way to prove to you that we're not."

"Be that as it may, you are not military personnel. You have no operational need to be around those aircraft. I'm sorry, ma'am, those are the rules."

Lucretia harrumphed under her breath. *He's stranded on a foreign planet that he knows almost nothing about, surrounded by strange creatures and plants beyond count, and he's still committed to the damned rulebook.* Part of her admired that kind of dedication.

Then, out of the corner of her eye, Lucretia saw Sidney Daventry coming down the ramp, his impeccable service bell-bottoms, somehow neat and dry as if they'd just come out of the dryer, contrasting with his dirty white undershirt. "Could the lieutenant escort us over, then?"

The commander pursed his lips for a moment, then offered a brusque nod. "Lieutenant," he called out.

"Sir?" Daventry said, snapping to attention.

"Would you be so kind as to escort these civilians to the landing site? It would do you good to familiarize yourself with the location for when we depart."

Daventry nodded. "Yes, sir."

"Very well," the commander said to Lucretia. "But keep your distance from the aircraft, and remain with Lieutenant Daventry at all times." He turned to the lieutenant, adding: "Do not let them leave your sight. Is that understood?"

"Yes, sir." Daventry turned to Lucretia and Jeremiah with a smile that was professional yet genuinely warm. "If you'll come with me, please."

Lucretia strode to the pilot's side, straining to match his long, precise strides. He was not an especially tall man, maybe five foot ten at the most, a full two inches shorter than Jeremiah, but most of that height was in his legs. For his part, Jeremiah ambled well behind them, as if he'd expected to be a spectator to some blossoming romance. *Not a chance, bro.* The man came from seventy years before them, which meant he was seventy years older than she. *Right? Isn't that how it works? Oh, who the hell knows anymore?*

She studied Daventry out of the corner of her eye, noting nothing at all special or peculiar about him. He wasn't sharp and dapper like the younger Englishman or even the commander; no, he was as ordinary as ordinary came, an Everyman, an average joe. That was the best word Lucretia could think of to describe him: *average.* Perfectly average. The kind of guy she would've seen on the street and not taken any notice of. His narrow face was that of an insurance salesman or car dealer: far from repulsive, but not so handsome as to be distracting. He was vanilla ice cream. Lucretia's favorite flavor. *Just like Mark.*

"Thanks," Lucretia said to break the silence. "I've never seen a Wyvern before. There's only one left where I'm from…or, I guess, *when* I'm from. It's in a museum over in England; I haven't made it over yet. Plus, I think it's the prototype, so it's not like yours."

Daventry smiled. "It's my pleasure, Ms. Tang. By the way, is it *Missus* Tang or *Miss* Tang?"

Lucretia couldn't help but chuckle. "Well, technically, it's *Doctor* Tang. But, hey, no one likes people who go around flaunting their credentials, right? Why don't we just stick with Lucretia?"

"You can also call her Lu-Tang," Jeremiah spoke up. "She loves it."

"No, she does not. Don't ever call me that."

"I don't follow," Daventry admitted. "Why would I call you that?"

"It's a play on Wu-Tang," Jeremiah noted. "You know, Wu-Tang Clan? The greatest group in the history of rap music?"

"That's a bit after his time, Jay," Lucretia reminded him. She never thought she'd have cause to utter that phrase.

"Oh, yeah. That'd be, like, the Beatles, right?"

"More like Elvis Presley." Lucretia nudged Daventry's arm. "Sorry. My brother loves his music. Me too." She pointed to the logo on her shirt. "This is one of my favorite bands. I guess it's kinda like rock 'n' roll, but ten times louder."

"Louder than Elvis?" Daventry chuckled warmly, and the glow from the swaying plants playing upon the dimples in his cheeks prompted a smile from Lucretia. "I don't think I'm ready for the future, ma'am."

"Please, it's Lucretia."

"Lucretia." Her name flowed from the pilot's lips like a lyric in an old love song, back when love songs were actually about love, and not just sex. "Well, Lucretia, you didn't answer my question: is it *Miss* or *Missus*?"

"Oh, it's Miss. If you'd have asked me three years ago, it would've been Mrs. Leibovitz." She exhaled the sudden bitterness in her mouth. "Yeah, I'm divorced now."

Sid drew back as if in shock. "At so young an age?"

"Yeah. Marriage isn't what it was back in your day." She chuckled a little. "You know, I'll find these movies from the fifties buried on streaming, and it's always like the denouement is the boy and girl getting married. Now—in my time, I mean—they start the movie already divorced or separated. If it's a happy ending, they get back together; if not, they get a good lawyer to figure out the child support payments, I guess. I'm glad Mark and I never had kids, honestly. It'd be awful for them to go through that bullshit."

"I'm sorry," Daventry said as if he'd opened a door that was meant to stay resolutely locked for all eternity.

"Oh, enough about me!" Lucretia said, adopting as jovial a tone as she could. "What about you? I see a ring on your finger there. You have a family?"

"Yes, ma'am," he beamed with a pride and joy that Lucretia could only wish she still knew. "I'm blessed with a lovely wife and two beautiful girls."

"Aw! How old?"

"Rhiannon is nine, and Emily, bless her heart, just turned twelve."

"Sounds to me like you've got your hands full, Lieutenant!"

"I wouldn't have it any other way, ma'am." Daventry smiled. "And please, call me Sidney. Or Sid, your choice."

Lucretia nodded. "As you wish, Sidney."

Sidney returned the gesture. "So, Lucretia, you're a scientist, eh? What kind of scientist?"

"I'm a biochemist," Lucretia said. "Jay is a marine biologist."

"Sounds quite prestigious," Sidney said in a manner that suggested that he was trying to cover up the fact that he had no idea what a biochemist or marine biologist actually did.

"Oh, not quite," she admitted. "We're not exactly looked on favorably in some circles. Big circles. It's why we're working for a small private lab and not some major university or institute. We tend to flirt with controversial ideas."

"We're not *flirting* with controversial ideas, Lu," Jeremiah blurted. "We're balls-deep in controversial ideas. Well, you are, anyway—not literally, obviously, because you don't have balls, but—"

Lucretia spun around. "Jay, please, stop talking."

"Yeah, good idea."

They walked in silence for a few more minutes, watching the flora swaying around them, bathing each other in cool blues and golden yellows. Ever and anon, Lucretia would glance behind her, snickering at how the lights painted Jeremiah's shaggy beard, and how her brother indeed looked like some kind of gnome in a video game.

Then, they came to the clearing where Jeremiah had so deftly landed the Velis. The little electric plane looked like a child's toy parked next to the three Fleet Air Arm strike fighters.

"Whoa!" Lucretia exclaimed as she made for the nearest Wyvern, bearing the number 891 on its forward fuselage. "It's bigger than I expected!"

"That's what she said," Jeremiah whispered.

Lucretia rolled her eyes. "Not to you, she didn't." She quickened her pace until she was standing behind the Wyvern's wing, noting the serial number WL891 in smaller letters on the rear fuselage beneath the words ROYAL NAVY. *That's odd*, she thought; the serial number and squadron code usually didn't match.

"Never thought I'd see one of these with my own eyes, especially one that could fly."

"She's something else," Sidney said with admiration for his mount. "Want to have a look in the cockpit?"

"Oh, I'd better not!" Lucretia said reluctantly. "I promised not to touch. I don't want the wrath of your commanding officer coming down on me."

"I wouldn't worry about Fanny too much," Sidney said with a rebellious grin. "He barks louder than he bites—when it comes to civvies, anyway!"

Lucretia raised an eyebrow. "Fanny?"

"That's what we call him behind his back. I wouldn't recommend saying it where he can hear you. Only his equals and the higher-ups get away with that."

"I can see why! I wouldn't appreciate being likened to someone's butt, either."

"Uh, actually," Jeremiah said, "if I'm not mistaken, in British slang, 'fanny' means 'vagina.'"

Lucretia screwed up her face. "That's way worse."

"Indeed," Sidney said. "You're probably right; better to skip the cockpit tour. Wouldn't want you to fly away on me," he said with a wink.

Fly away. She looked into the pilot's brown eyes, marveling at the way the glow of the forest danced upon their sheen. In that moment, she wanted nothing more than to get in one of the brutish fighters and take off, following Sidney Daventry's lead, cavorting about the purple sky as they looped and rolled over the lustrous world below. To be as free as a bird in Paradise.

Fly away. Not from this place, though she knew she had to. If only she could fly back to 1956 with Sidney, find herself a gentleman—not the gentleman beside her, a gentleman though he verily was; *hell no*. Even if she were remotely interested, she didn't stand a chance. Men of his era honored their wives; "until death do us part" wasn't just a perfunctory utterance but a promise, a vow, a sacred oath. *Except to the ones in Hollywood and Washington*, she thought with a snicker. *Some things never change.* And, sure, that gentlemanly chivalry she'd seen in those movies had always struck her as antiquated, cheesy, even patronizing, as it did when she beheld it in the nondescriptly charming aviator standing at her side. But she *liked* it. Women were treated like prizes, not penis receptacles.

The "old days" had always held a confounding appeal to her. The world was a more orderly place, it seemed. Society had values, flawed though some of them were. People believed in hard work and good character. There wasn't the chaos, the nihilism, the selfishness and rash stupidity that all too often seemed to define her generation. In her rational mind, she knew that she was committing the fallacy of romanticizing the past, that human nature evolves over eons and doesn't change much in a few decades, for better or for worse; even those old movies were probably full of lies, like perfume sprayed in a septic tank, and life "back then" was probably every bit as shitty and every bit as beautiful as it was in 2026, after its own fashion.

Would she really want to live in the fifties, even if they were as idyllic as the construct she'd created in her mind? *Could* she? Did women still wear corsets? If so, then that was a deal-breaker; Lucretia Tang wouldn't be caught dead wearing one of those abominations. Then, there was the whole Cold War thing, living under the constant threat of nuclear annihilation. Lucretia had the benefit of knowing how it would all turn out, but could she endure living in that environment of perpetual paranoia and suspicion? And that was to say nothing of the prejudice. That was still around, alas, and Lucretia feared that there would never truly be a cure for that most hideous disease, but, whatever she faced in 2026, she figured it'd be ten times worse in Sidney's time. Hell, she'd already gotten her fill of it from that idiot Wickler.

And…could she really stand to live in a world devoid of the comforts of the twenty-first century? As much as she hated the banality of it all, she was indeed a woman of her time. The old hats incessantly lamented that humanity had gone soft, but Lucretia didn't want to live in the cutthroat worlds from the olden days that she'd only read about.

No, as much as the dapper, clean-cut avatar of a bygone time allured her, that perfect image, like the man who embodied it, was just that: the romantic fancy of a woman much too old to believe in fairy tales.

That reality was brought home as she walked to the front of the Wyvern, greeted by the two short, tubelike protrusions jutting out from the right wing's leading edge that housed the cannons, and the eight rockets underwing, slender and disturbingly elegant—not the blue inert training rounds, not relics in a museum, but live munitions with high-explosive warheads hidden beneath their broadened tips. The realization struck her with the force of a bomb. The machine before her was an instrument of war, and its pilot, that smooth-skinned, impeccably proper Boy Scout with the perfectly combed hair and trimmed fingernails, was, whether by conscious choice or the demands of his chosen profession, a killer.

No one had talked much on the way back to the tree sanctuary. Sidney was taking in the scenery around him, quite mesmerized by it all—quite in contrast to Jeremiah, who had snatched the backpack that contained their equipment from the Velis while Lucretia was checking out the Wyvern and was now fiddling with his smartphone, as if he'd already grown bored with their new milieu. Lucretia could only sigh.

As for Lucretia? Hell, even Lucretia didn't know what Lucretia was thinking. Her thoughts flew this way and that as if they were in a pinball machine, never staying in one place long enough to become lucid. Seeing the Wyverns had only exacerbated her frustration at her impotence. How could she convince that obstinate commander to spare one of his planes? Could she steal one? Could she even fly it? A complex, high-performance warplane was a far cry from the gossamer Velis, and that particular warplane was not exactly known for having a sterling safety record.

She was jarred from her jumble of thoughts by Sidney calling her name.

"Oh, sorry," she said. "I guess I was daydreaming."

"It's all right." Sidney's hands folded tightly at his waist. "I still feel that I owe you for saving my life."

She couldn't help but smile. "Please, Sidney, stop saying that. I did what I thought was the right thing to do. You were in danger, and I thought I could help you. So, I did. My conscience wouldn't like me very much right now if I hadn't."

"You're a very fine lady, Lucretia Tang."

His words sent flutters through Lucretia's heart. She couldn't remember the last time someone had paid her a compliment that wasn't accompanied by a request for a favor or didn't have an asterisk attached. "Um...wow, thank you, Sidney."

He nodded kindly. "Suppose I could convince the skipper to lend me an aircraft—and I'm not saying I could—you said you needed some pictures?"

That perked Lucretia right up. "Yes! I mean, that's a start. Just some footage so I could make notes about the anemone things' behavior and whatnot." *A lot of good that will do*, she knew. She looked at Sidney, gnawing on her knuckle.

Sidney took the hint. "And?"

Lucretia bit her lip. "Okay, here's another thing—in the hypothetical scenario where you convince Mr. Fanny to let you borrow his plane." She revealed her idea about flying low over the pond, skimming the surface with the undercarriage. To reassure the bewildered pilot, she pulled out her phone and found a video that she'd downloaded and saved, showing a group of vintage trainers performing the maneuver.

Sidney's expression wasn't far off that when he'd first seen the Racosku, whether because of the contents of the video, or the quality of it, or the fact that it fit on a pocket-size screen.

"You think I'm nuts, right?" she prodded.

The airman made that face someone makes when they're trying like hell to be polite when they, indeed, think you're nuts. "Well, you'd need one hell of a pilot."

"Up for the task, Mav?" she asked with a wink.

Sidney looked at her like she had three heads.

"It's a movie reference; you wouldn't get it. You'll have to wait thirty years."

"I'll put it on the list," Sidney said with a chuckle. "Along with Wu-Tang Clan and...what is it, Kamelot?"

"You can listen to some of our music right now," Jeremiah blurted. "We've got lots. No harm in a little entertainment while we wait around, since this talk is all for nothing and the old man clearly isn't going to give us a plane."

Lucretia shot her brother a glower that was both acrid and hopeless. "You may *entertain* yourselves by helping me!" *In my Sisyphean task.*

❦

When Sid and the Americans arrived back at the tree towers, the other pilots were outside. Jim Wellington was talking to Commander Faintary, while Tom Wickler moped this way and that, hands folded before his mouth, his zigzags sharp, his movements alternating between short, light steps and sudden strides in whatever direction his feet would fall. No one seemed eager to get any shut-eye, knackered though they were—or ought to have been. He might've assumed that his mates' sleeplessness was just nerves from being stranded in some far corner of God's creation, though Lucretia Tang had promised that there was indeed a way home. But, Hags notwithstanding, no one seemed nervous. Wimpy and Fanny were chatting as if out behind the church after Sunday services. Sid, too, was as free from dread or uncertainty as he was from the pain that should've been lingering in his head and back. He didn't know how long he'd been awake, but he still felt refreshed. *What is it with this place?*

Wimpy flashed a grin as Sid approached. "Pleasant evening, mate?"

"Pleasant as pleasant can be," Sid said with sincerity. "I thought you'd be sleeping."

"Well, Hags and I decided we'd best keep an eye on you, mate. Make sure you're not out plotting something behind our backs." His carefree mien suddenly vanished, and his face flushed red as he looked at Lucretia, who appeared offended. "Oh, I meant nothing by that, ma'am. I was just taking the piss with Moose here, you see."

"*Yes!*" Lucretia exclaimed as she burst into laughter.

Sid, and everyone else, including Jeremiah Tang, looked at her like she'd lost her mind. Maybe she had; after all, they were standing in a world of giant bugs, glowing food, and tree mansions. Whose mind would be next to leave them?

"Sorry," Lucretia said, pinching her face to constrain the laughter that nonetheless kept spilling out her small, shapely nose. "I really just wanted to hear someone say 'taking the piss.'"

Jim shot her a slick smile. "It wasn't you I was worried

about, ma'am." He shot a wink at Sid. "It's just that Lieutenant Daventry, he's a fast one, if you take my meaning."

Sid landed a playful slap on Jim's back. "He's also happily wed."

The look he got back from Lucretia Tang disturbed him, wrought him. Her smile seemed tainted with envy, the look in her eyes distant and wistful, as if she desired nothing more than the stability of a family that, to hear her tell it, seemed as alien to her time as the world she was standing upon.

Sid shook the thought from his mind. "Anyway, what were the two of you plotting, that you had to be so secretive about?"

Faintary cut off Jim's reply. "Lieutenant Wellington and I were discussing contingencies for our departure," he said bluntly, with a tone that seemed to chide Sid for asking. Then, he turned to Lucretia. "Which brings us to you, Ms. Tang. Now, you stated earlier that the native creatures know how we might return to"—the commander cleared his throat, lowering his eyes as if he foresaw that what was about to come out of his mouth was patently ridiculous—"to our planet."

Lucretia perked up, as if startled to be called upon. "Uh, yeah. I mean, yes, sir—"

"You needn't address me so formally, ma'am," Faintary said in the calmest, tenderest tone Sid had ever heard out of the man. "Please, just relax and tell us what you know."

"Yeah, of course." Lucretia drew a deep breath. "Okay, according to the Racosku—"

"The *what?*" Tom Wickler asked, suddenly snapping out of whatever reverie he'd been trapped in so wholly that he hadn't been paying attention to anything that had been said before.

"Racosku," Lucretia repeated. "That's the indigenous species. It's what I call them; just a bit of onomatopoeia."

"On a what?" Sid asked.

"Ono—just, never mind. It's the sound they make. Their actual name is impossible to say, and I figure it's more polite than calling them Noodly Iridescent Giant Mantis Critters. Anyway, they told us that, in around three and a half days—or what would be days on Earth—the wormhole will appear again, and will spit us out exactly where and when we got sucked in."

"And you are able to communicate with these creatures?" Faintary asked.

Lucretia nodded. "But that's *our* wormhole. Obviously, you guys weren't here yet, so who knows when, or even *if*, that one will come around?"

"Well," Jeremiah chimed in, "they arrived, what, an hour after us? So, logically, their portal should open an hour after ours. Or maybe an hour before, if it all works backwards going the other way."

"That's pretty reductive logic, Jay. We have no evidence that that's how the wormholes work—in fact, I'd argue we've got solid evidence that it *isn't*. The box of movies Pinky showed us, for one. Think about it, Jay: if the wormholes work in a linear temporal fashion like that, in which every hour forward here equals seventy years in reverse on Earth, that capsule would have come from at least some time in our future. Probably more than seventy years, or even twice that; the Racosku would need more than an hour or two to make sense of humanity, let alone how to master not only our language but how to translate their thoughts into it without having the same vocalization techniques, especially with a toolkit that's so...shall we say, lacking? So, by that logic, it would have come from hundreds, probably *thousands* of years from now—I mean, *our* 'now'—and people then will have long forgotten about *Sharknado*."

"Oh, I think you're massively underestimating the staying power of the paragon that is the *Sharknado* franchise, Lu."

Lucretia sighed loudly. "If that's the case, then it's a sad indictment of the human species."

"Pardon me," Sid said, "but what on Earth is a Sharknado?"

"It's a tornado full of sharks," Lucretia said matter-of-factly.

Sid gaped at her, then at Jim Wellington, whose eyes were as wide and bewildered as his own. Tom Wickler looked like he was about to soil his britches. Even the commander's lips were pursed, one thick eyebrow poking above the other like a caterpillar peering over a log.

"It's a movie series that basically trolls itself," Lucretia clarified. "Makes fun of itself, I mean."

"What are you talking about?" Jeremiah said. "The *Sharknado* movies are the pinnacle of cinematic excellence." He turned to face the airmen. "Based on a true story, you know. Yeah, in the future, there are storms that chuck massive sharks down from the sky. Terrifying."

The airmen looked at each other, and no one seemed to know whether to be skeptical or stupefied.

Until the two Americans burst into laughter. *Good one*, Sid thought, and he was sure to put *Sharknado* on his list of things to remember if he lived to be a hundred.

"I'm glad I won't live to see it," Faintary said, and Sid was shocked to see the corner of his mouth curling upward a little.

"Anyway," Lucretia said, "if you guys *really* want to know when you get to go home, you should probably ask the experts." She jerked her head to the ramp spiraling up the pallid bole, causing her shimmering black hair to flutter in the air like a silken banner. "Shall we?"

With a smile, Sid held out his hand to the ramp. "After you, Dr. Tang."

Lucretia gave the aviators a moment to marvel at the laboratory. They wouldn't have seen that kind of technology back on Earth—hell, even Lucretia had only seen things resembling the holographic projections in films or as mock-ups—so seeing a bunch of insectoid creatures wielding such power was clearly a shock to the system. She had grown up reading stories about time travel and space exploration, watching *Star Trek* and *Back to the Future*, trying to imagine herself in a different time, a different world, a different everything. Part of her envied the pilots, living out both of her dreams at the same time.

Although, she supposed, in her own way, she was living out hers too.

The lab had seemed compact to Lucretia when she'd first entered; not small but not too big, the kind of room where a scientist and her small team could work comfortably while leaving no room for the lab director to stand breathing down their necks. Yet, even with four more human bodies and now five Racosku, the space didn't seem claustrophobic at all. The Racosku had taken their places around the periphery of the room, folding their forelegs in, standing like statues in the great hall of a castle.

"All right," Lucretia said, "let's all get acquainted, shall we? Guys, meet our hosts! That one's Brain, there's Pinky, Noodles, and Violet." She waved her hand to the fifth, who looked almost identical to Noodles, though the colors on its abdomen were not so vibrant. "Hi there! We haven't met yet. I'm gonna call you Ramen. Cool?"

"Really, Lu?" Jeremiah sneered. "What's the next one's name going to be? Vermicelli?"

Lucretia shrugged. The Racosku made no sound.

Jeremiah produced his phone from his pocket, setting it on the surface next to the interface screen. He began pressing buttons when Brain ambled forward, nudging him away, then sliding its proboscis around the interface controller. Then the Racosku moved its head in something like a nod. Jeremiah cocked his head like a confused puppy, eyes fixed on the creature as he unlocked the phone, his expression brightening when he saw the contents of the screen appearing on the display substrate. Then he opened his music app, queuing "Triumph" by Wu-Tang Clan. *He'd better put some of my music on the playlist too.* The pilots seemed as bewildered by the rhythms and percussive raps as they were by the laboratory. The commander in particular was clearly appalled by the violent lyrics and liberal use of profanity; Sidney and Jim Wellington seemed more perplexed than disgusted, though the youngest pilot, the jackass who'd pulled the gun on Lucretia back at the riverbank, seemed quite amused. *Damned kids.*

"Now that we've got that important detail out of the way," Lucretia said, "shall we begin?" She turned to Brain. "Our guests would like to know when the wormhole through which they entered will open again."

The words that appeared on the screen caused Lucretia to chuckle: WHY IS EVERYONE SO HASTY TO DEPART? DO YOU FIND THAT WE CATER TO OUR GUESTS IN THE MANNER OF EXCREMENT?

"No, Brain, you're not shitty hosts!" She smiled at the airmen, all of whom were staring at the screen with wide eyes and gaping mouths. "These guys are a riot."

"May we please dispense with all the foul language?" the commander asked in a tone that strongly insinuated that he wasn't asking.

"Sorry," Lucretia said sheepishly. "Brain, please?"

THE PASSAGE USED BY THE MORE SONOROUS VISITORS WILL APPEAR AT THE THIRD TURN OF THE STARS.

The more sonorous visitors gave Lucretia another chuckle. She knew Brain was referring to the noise of the Wyverns and not their crews, but she couldn't help herself. She felt sorry for Brain, knowing that it was doing its very best to communicate with the alien visitors, that it wasn't trying to sound so amusing, and that she'd sound a bazillion times sillier if she tried to emulate Racosku sounds. "Could you be more specific? Isn't that when our portal will reopen?"

That is correct.

"So...they'll open at the same time?"

That is correct.

Lucretia scratched her bottom lip. "Then how will we know which is which?"

A three-dimensional map appeared on the screen showing the general vicinity of their location; Lucretia guesstimated that it covered an area of around fifty square miles. Lines swirled down from the top-right of the hologram, forming something like an inverted traffic cone. *The wormhole.* It was about twenty miles from the tree city.

A curl of Brain's proboscis drew her attention away from the map and to the panel on the wall. This is your hole, the text stated.

Oh, Brain, I do love you.

The map then zoomed out so that the area shown doubled in scope and shifted a little to the left. Another vortex circled down, farther away from the Racosku's abode. It made sense; Lucretia thought she remembered the commander estimating that they'd flown sixty or so miles from the wormhole before landing. *Looks like that's about how far it is, give or take.* She wondered if the wormholes always appeared so close to the Racosku's home, if that was why they had built it there in the first place. By the way gravity worked and the curvature of the maps Brain had showed her, she guessed the planet they were on was around the same size as Earth.

"Easy-peasy!" she exclaimed. "You guys fly left, we go right. Well, that's that!"

"Very well," Commander Faintary said in his typical stoic manner. "We'll plot our course based on this information. In the meantime, get some rest, gentlemen."

"But, Commander," Lucretia cried, gesturing to the panel that now read: PLEASE, HELP US.

She looked hard at the commander's stern face, studying every facet of his countenance for any sign of thought or emotion. But, as he stared at the panel, he betrayed nothing: no intrigue, no bewilderment, no tactical thinking…and no compassion.

"These creatures understand us, yes?" he asked Lucretia.

Lucretia jerked her head at the panel, drawing the squadron leader's eyes back to it.

I COMPREHEND YOUR VOCALIZATIONS, GREAT LEADER OF FLYING HUMAN BEINGS.

Some emotion finally broke through Faintary's stony façade, if only ephemerally: a suppressed chortle.

"Very well." The commander looked at Brain; the fact that he was about to speak to an extraterrestrial lifeform that bore not even the slightest resemblance to any sapient being on Earth seemed not to affect him in the slightest. "Understand that it is my duty to return these men to their homes unharmed. I cannot risk their lives. I'm afraid there is nothing I can do for you and your friends. I am sorry."

"Commander!" Lucretia perfunctorily grasped Faintary's wrist, quickly pulling away. "I'm not asking for the moon here. Please, help me help them. These creatures are giving us food and shelter—"

"And for that, I am grateful. But what I have said stands. Those aeroplanes are not toys, ma'am. We've already lost one aircraft to the enemy, another when Lieutenant Daventry was forced to ditch. As commanding officer of this squadron, it is my duty to return those aircraft—and, more importantly, their pilots—to safety."

Lucretia bowed her head. *At least he's looking out for his men. At least he cares about them.* "I understand."

"Sir, if I may?" Sidney Daventry spoke up.

The sudden coldness in Faintary's eyes could've frozen the blood in a man's veins. *Or a woman's.* "Lieutenant," he said, almost in a hiss.

"Sir, might we hear what Lucretia has to say? She and I discussed some of her ideas while we were walking, and I believe we could fly the sorties she's requested and have enough fuel to get back."

"But, Moose," Jim Wellington said, "we'll barely have enough as things are. Did you check your indicators when you came out of the storm? Between that and dodging the Egyptians, we were using high power settings more than usual."

"Then I'll make for Port Said, assuming that we egress the storm at the same coordinates as where we entered." He turned to Faintary. "That was our intention anyway. You did say that our forces hold the airport there, sir."

"That's beside the point," Faintary said. "The decision to divert was based on factors beyond our control. It was prudent based on the weather conditions. Foolhardy risks taken for selfish purposes do not fall into the category of 'prudence.'"

"Selfish?" Sidney snapped.

"Yes, Lieutenant! With all due respect to our hosts, we owe them nothing. Our allegiance is to the United Kingdom and to the British Commonwealth. We are not authorized to use Her Majesty's aircraft for errands unrelated to the defense of the realm, nor would I approve such a reckless endeavor."

"Sir, please, just listen to what Lucretia has to say before you make your judgment."

Faintary exhaled sharply. "Very well, I will listen."

Lucretia shriveled under the commander's venomous gaze. "Well, uh, like I said before, some video footage from your gun cameras would help Jeremiah and me to observe the anemone thingies' behavior. Then…" She glanced at Sidney, who nodded back at her, as if to say it was okay to reveal the second part.

And she did, watching the infinitesimal variations in the commander's countenance as she proposed having one of his pilots skim the surface of the pond with wheels that were very much *not* designed for landing on water.

"I could do it in one sortie," Sidney said as soon as Lucretia finished, before Faintary could retort. "I could make a recon pass over the area, then make a long teardrop turn, do a touch-and-go on the surface, and fly straight back."

"Are you out of your mind, mate?" Tom Wickler blurted.

"It can be done," Sidney assured him. "Lucretia has found footage of some Harvards performing the maneuver." He glanced at her. "Show them your little telly."

"Telly?" Lucretia wrinkled her nose. "Ah, you mean my phone—"

"No, not your telephone. Your telly. That little television you keep in your pocket. The one that looks like your brother's stereo."

"This?" She produced the Motorola from her pants' back pocket. "Oh, this is my phone."

"*That's* a telephone?"

"Yep. So is Jay's. In the future, your whole life will be contained in this device. It's amazing and ridiculous at the same time." She played the video she'd shown Sidney. "Pretty neat, huh?"

Faintary harrumphed. "Quite the stunt."

"Why would you need to do that?" Wellington asked.

"I need genetic samples," Lucretia said. "And unless you guys have a giant bucket that you could pull under your planes without spilling any of the stuff, it's the only way I can think of to bring some of it back here. If I could get some samples off that pond and compare them to the healthy samples that the Racosku have on file, I might be able to figure out what's going wrong."

"And then what?"

Lucretia's heart sank. "I don't know. Just get more depressed, I guess. Pretty hard to save a species with nothing but guns and bombs."

"Actually, sis," Jeremiah said, "you could totally do it."

Lucretia lifted an eyebrow.

Jeremiah shook his head, laughing. "Come on, Lu. You're an engineer. And you said yourself that you like to flirt with controversial ideas. Now seems like a good time to stop flirting and go balls-deep. Figuratively, of course."

"A gene bomb!" she exclaimed with a thunderous clap of her hands that seemed to startle poor Brain. "Yes! Jay, you're a genius!"

"No shit, Sherlock," he shot back with a self-assured wink.

"I think that will even work! I have the stuff in my bag." She always brought her lab kit with her, just in case.

"Pardon me, Dr. Tang," Sidney said, "but what is this 'gene bomb' you're talking about?"

"It's something that, back in my world, will get you blacklisted from any respectable institution just for mentioning it, which is kinda why I'm where I am right now, professionally speaking. But we're not in that world, and the stakes here are dire, so to Hell with their precautionary approaches. Basically, I would engineer a CRISPR compound in quantity and saturate the area with it, so that my compound would quickly replace whatever errant DNA strain is killing the pollinators."

She looked at the men's faces, almost staring down their throats, for so wide were their mouths open. *I guess you forgot you were talking to airmen from 1956, and not your fellow scientists from your time.* She flashed a guilty smile. *Oops.*

"So, uh," Sidney stammered, "what is this 'crisper' you're talking about?"

"It's the part of the fridge where you keep the veggies," Jeremiah said, managing to keep a straight face.

Lucretia rolled her eyes. "It stands for *clustered regularly interspaced short palindromic repeats.* Snippets of DNA, usually twenty nucleotides—'letters' in the vernacular—but, more and more, even fewer, that, using advanced gene-editing technology, we can manipulate to alter certain genetic outputs. It's actually derived from a naturally occurring defense mechanism found in prokaryotes, whereby they can change their genetic signals to confuse or deter predators. Kinda like a natural cloaking device. Wish I had one of those."

"Doctor," Sidney said, "I don't have a clue what you're talking about."

Lucretia had a sneaking suspicion he was speaking for his squadron mates as well. She blew some air through folded hands. "Okay, DNA is basically the building blocks of life. It's hard to explain succinctly, but, basically, it's the instruction manual for how living things function. What we do—actually, what *I* do; Jay's just a biologist who studies the normal workings of things and how those workings change based on evolving environmental factors—but anyway, what I do is make changes to those instructions. Rewriting the language of life, so to speak."

Sidney jolted back. "You can do that?"

"Yep. There's a lot of debate on whether we *should.* You make a lot of enemies in my profession, and, admittedly, they've got some good points. Genetic engineering is powerful stuff, its effects profound. You can mess up a lot of things if you're not careful—or ethical. And, believe me, there are a lot of scientists out there who are neither careful nor ethical. But, at the end of the day, there are just those who feel like we're messing with stuff that just shouldn't be messed with."

"Understandable," Wellington said.

Lucretia leaned over the hologram, rapping on the surface beside Jeremiah's phone with her palms to the tune of the music. "Look, guys, I know this sounds crazy. I know there's a chance it could blow up in my face. I'm fallible, I know that—and that alone disqualifies me from doing what I do in the eyes of many. I get why they feel that way, why *you* feel that way. But I don't see any other way of helping the Racosku, especially not in the time we've got. I'm not leaving here without at least trying to help them. I owe them that much."

The silence that followed settled over the lab like a mid-summer's heat, so thick that no one wanted to even breathe, let alone speak. The pilots looked at each other—all but the commander, whose thoughts remained impossible to read as though they were computations on the Antikythera mechanism—while Brain's limbs glided over the projector, drawing Lucretia's eyes back to those words that wrought her heart: PLEASE, HELP US.

Don't do this to me, she wanted to plead with the pilots and their obstinate commander. She pleaded with fate, or the universe, or the God she wasn't sure if she even believed in. *Don't give me hope that I can do a good deed, only to rip it out from under me and force me to live with that guilt.*

"I've heard enough," Faintary said at last, and Lucretia could hear in the dark timbre of his voice that her hope was about to be shot to pieces. "There will be no usage of our aircraft for Ms. Tang's purposes. Is that understood?"

"Yes, sir," Jim Wellington and Tom Wickler said in unison.

But Sidney Daventry only glowered at his commander. "No, sir," he said, veins bulging from his neck as his teeth gritted. "I don't understand at all."

Faintary's eyes narrowed. "What did you say, Lieutenant?"

"Dr. Tang is right. These creatures helped us, and we owe it to them to help them back. It isn't right to leave them to die, and you know it."

"That will be all, Lieutenant!" the commander bellowed. "You will fly your aeroplane back to *Eagle*, after which you will not fly again until you've returned to Canada. Is that understood?"

"Understood," Sidney spat, and he stormed out of the laboratory.

Suddenly, the room felt cold. The Racosku scurried away, even Brain, hugging the walls as they sped for the doorway. Lucretia slunk away too, snatching up Jeremiah's phone and silencing the music and shoving it back to him, taking his hand, yanking him out the door, up the ramp, to their quarters, where she would spend the night weeping.

CHAPTER VI

"ANGER IS A burst of sudden flame," Sidney Daventry's father had always told him. "Regret is the ruin it leaves in its wake."

Sid kicked the soft mud, causing little sparks of bright yellow to spread out before his boot. Earlier, the sight of it would've made him chuckle, but now, it irritated him. Irritated him enough to keep doing it, which only irritated him the more. *Damn it, Sid, what the hell were you thinking? Faintary is your commanding officer. You owe him your respect and your compliance, whether you like it or not.*

Sidney Daventry was a combat pilot, and a combat pilot was expected to obey his commander's orders without question, and not give any guff while doing it; he was to say "Yes, sir," saluting if appropriate, and then keep his mouth shut.

Sid had failed on all counts. *And look where it's gotten you.*

And yet, as much as Sid was kicking himself as ardently as he kicked the strange alien soil, obeying this time just felt wrong. He couldn't understand why. Everything Faintary had said made perfect sense. They owed the creatures of this world nothing—those peculiar creatures, those giant bugs, remarkable bugs, strangely adorable, but bugs no less. Who was to say that the bugs' pleas for help weren't some kind of magic, the same dark magic that Lucretia Tang talked of doing in her laboratory? *Rewriting the language of life. The devil's work.*

Maybe everything about this place was the devil's work.

But it wasn't, Sid knew; he didn't know *how* he knew, he just *knew*. A gut feeling, the way God or his conscience had a way of reassuring him when he was doing the right thing and screaming at him when he was about to do something stupid. The voice inside wasn't screaming; it was singing a lullaby. The bugs meant something to Lucretia. He thought of the alley cat that used to come knocking over the rubbish tins outside the cottage, how he was ready to take his old hockey stick and bash the mangy bastard's skull in. But Emily, all of five years old, pleaded with him to spare the pathetic creature. He remembered the tears in her little eyes, the aching squeak in her cries. So, he put the hockey stick away, resigning himself to cleaning up the mess each and every week. Not for the cat; to Hell with the damned cat. For his daughter.

And now, for Lucretia.

He was pacing back and forth when the wet rasp of a man's throat clearing pierced the glowing forest's hymn. "A word, Lieutenant?" Gene Faintary said in a tone that made it abundantly clear that it was an order rather than a request.

Sid turned and came to attention. "Sir."

Faintary approached him, not halting until his breath was hot on Sid's face. "I know you men think that I'm stubborn… rigorous…a real son of a bitch."

"Not at all, sir," Sid muttered. *What am I supposed to say?*

"Cut the shit, Lieutenant. Don't think I can't smell it."

"As you say, sir," Sid said, exhaling as he caught the hint of a grin forming at the side of Faintary's mouth.

"I'm a stickler for the rules," the commander affirmed. "I know it makes me a pain in the arse. I suppose you even think I'm depriving you a bit of fun by denying your meager request to go frolicking about the sky."

"Sir, I—"

Faintary held up his hand. "I was like you once." He took a step back, nodding in a manner that told Sid to stand at ease. "It was late in the War, an operation off Borneo. My squadron was tasked with sinking troop transports, but we had more torpedoes than targets. On the way home, my flight leader decided to peel off and attack—in his own words—'targets of opportunity.' The squadron leader ordered him to return to the formation, where we had our Corsairs for top cover, but Hensley didn't listen. And I, thinking I'd have a little fun, followed, along with two other crews. After all, we thought we'd had the enemy licked. It'd be a walk in the park.

"And it was—for the Japanese. As soon as we were out of sight of the formation, a swarm of fighters swooped down out of the sun. Do you know what an Avenger's chances against a Ki-84 are? Less than a lamb's in a fox den. They had us in flames before our gunners could even home in on them. I was able to ditch and get out, me and my radioman. Bristow, my gunner, wasn't so lucky. Or maybe he was; he didn't have to spend the rest of the war in a Japanese prison camp. I don't know how long I was there; certainly not as long as some unfortunate souls, but more than long enough. Long enough to learn my lesson."

Sid bowed his head. "I'm sorry, sir."

Then, to Sid's shock, Faintary laid a hand on his shoulder—not a reproving hand, but a gentle embrace, almost fatherly. "Those rules and regulations exist for a reason," the commander said with uncharacteristic calmness, "and that reason is that, at the end of the day, we all come home. Do you understand, Lieutenant?"

"Yes, sir."

"Very good." A smile finally broke through Faintary's stony veneer. "You may take Willie Love," he said, referring to Whiskey Lima Eight-Niner-One. Sid couldn't help but be amused; despite his unflinching adherence to regulation and propriety, Faintary stubbornly refused to use the new NATO standard phonetic alphabet introduced earlier in the year, clinging to the old system as if it were a family heirloom. "She may not even make it back to the ship anyway, what with all the fuel I burned going after that bandit."

Sid risked a smile of his own, the kind that, no matter how much he tried to restrict, ended up overtaking his face. "Are you quite serious, sir?"

"You will not engage in the kind of unsafe maneuvering the woman spoke of," the commander made crystal clear. "You will make a standard pass over the area at a reasonable altitude, two passes if need be, but no more. Is that understood?"

"Yes, sir. Thank you, sir."

Faintary nodded, a cordial gesture, but never so much as to eschew his rigid formality. "Before you go, Lieutenant, please, get some rest. With all you've been through since this morning, you're in no condition to fly. Good luck, Lieutenant."

"Good night, sir." Sid turned for the ramp, his body and heart suddenly as electrified as whatever strange phenomenon gave light to the majestic world around him.

Lucretia leaned over the raised surface next to the projector, staring blankly at the empty wall panel, ever and anon glancing down at her fingers, blue in the glow of the translucent screens and hologram projector. The aviators had all left; the dashing Englishman Wellington and that prick Wickler to their beds, the commander outside to seek solitude, and Sidney Daventry to stew. Jeremiah had gone to bed, and the Racosku had gone to do whatever Racosku did in those hours that were, to Lucretia's eyes, no different than any other hours in this blissfully unchanging place.

Lucretia couldn't sleep, not now. Not even if she'd tried, which she hadn't. She could only wallow in self-pity for so long. Being in the lab at least allowed her to indulge the delusion that she could do something. As much as it reinforced the reality that she couldn't.

The lab felt so empty, not merely devoid of Racosku and humans, but devoid of hope, joy, and all the things that Lucretia had all but forgotten from the world she'd left behind, only to rediscover here. *And now, to have them snatched away.* What a cruel tease, to bring her here, show her all this beauty, only to slap her in the face with the revelation that it was about to be snuffed out and there wasn't a damned thing she could do. If there was a god out there, then he must have hated her.

A soft, thin limb coiling around her wrist startled her from her thoughts.

"Oh," she yelped, spinning around. "Hey there, Noodles. Haven't seen you in a while."

The creature held something in its forelegs, awkwardly, presenting it to Lucretia as if it were a gift. It was a tattered box, square in shape: a game of checkers.

"Ha! Where'd you get that?" She assumed it had come with the space capsule, buried under the bad movies. "Do you even know what that is?"

Noodles held the game higher, desperately balancing it on top of its legs. It was as if Noodles knew that Lucretia was sad, and that giving her the gift would make her feel better. She blinked a tear from her eye.

"Come on," she said, taking the box before Noodles could drop it. "Let's play."

She led Noodles to an open space of floor—there was nothing vaguely resembling chairs in the Racosku's abode—and placed the box before her, unfolding the game board and arranging the pieces, with the blacks on her side and the reds in front of Noodles. Then she sat down, cross-legged.

"I'll go first," she said and moved her piece a space to the right.

Noodles only stared back at her, flashing blue across its head. Lucretia gestured to the red tokens, pantomiming the motion of moving the piece.

Instead, the creature's proboscis flared out, the smaller branches pushing the token right off the board.

"No, Noodles, that's not how it goes." Lucretia shook her head like an admonishing schoolteacher. "We're gonna have to work on this." She placed the token back on the board. "Your move, Nood."

Noodles nudged the token to the space adjacent to Lucretia's.

"Yes!" She clapped her hands, then held out her fist for a bump.

Noodles drew back, as if it had interpreted the gesture as a threat. Lucretia withdrew, holding up her hands and smiling, then bumped her fists together. She held out her fist again, and, hesitantly, Noodles touched it with the end of its proboscis. Lucretia giggled like she was twelve again.

"Unfortunately," she said, "you opened yourself right up." She jumped Noodles' token and collected it.

Noodles, in mature adult fashion, reached its cranial tentacles out and began knocking Lucretia's pieces off the board.

Before Lucretia could scold her opponent for throwing a hissy fit, she heard footsteps racing up the ramp. She turned to the doorway.

And there was Sidney Daventry, panting, grinning ear to ear like he'd just been named Ace of Aces.

"We have a plane!" Sidney exclaimed. "Commander Faintary will let me run a reconnaissance flight."

Lucretia sprang to her feet, almost jumping for joy. It wasn't perfect, but it was a start.

She wanted nothing more than to run downstairs and give the disturbingly handsome commander a big, sloppy kiss on the lips.

CHAPTER VII

NEVER BEFORE HAD Sidney Daventry thought any aircraft, let alone a Westland Wyvern, could look so beautiful as WL891 did in that moment. It was more than the blues and reds and purples and yellows floating upon the plane's glossy grays like swarms of fishes in an aquarium. She was a sight for sore eyes, that was for sure.

But it was even more than that.

He ran his hands over the tailplane, over the joint between the fixed horizontal stabilizer and the slightly drooping elevator, as if it were his first time touching an aircraft. It was all part of his routine preflight check, but it hadn't lost its luster He was ready to fly, ready to save this world like the hero in the old stories.

And he was ready to go home, to Marie, to the girls. To the things he loved the most, even more than flying.

Walking around the Wyvern, Sid gazed up at its brilliantly brutish, splendidly utilitarian lines. In that moment, it *did* look as graceful as a Spitfire, if only in the image Sid's mind painted over what was actually there. He thought back on the stories his oldest brother, Edwin, had told of his time flying that most legendary of fighters, dueling in the heavens against Messerschmitts and Butcher Birds over the verdant fields of Europe. Sid had barely seen any combat in the War, contrary to what he'd told Hags in his moment of rage a few hours earlier, being among the last Canadians sent over to fight. He remembered being so green with envy listening to those tales of triumph. Now, after a week of raining Hell down upon the Egyptians for reasons known only to God and Anthony Eden, he'd had more than his fill of it. As much as he loved flying, the kind of flying a man could only do in a marvel of human ingenuity like the Wyvern, he wasn't sure he wanted to do it anymore. Not like that.

Until this very moment. It was as if his wish, and Marie's prayer, had been heard. How often she'd recite that passage from Isaiah, the one about beating swords into plowshares and spears into pruning hooks, as if to beatify her displeasure at the ugly reality of her husband's work. Here was his opportunity to use his passion for something good, something noble. Not taking life but saving it. Maybe even giving it.

He was about to place his boot on the footstep on the left main undercarriage leg when he heard his name being called. He spun around to find Tom Wickler traipsing toward him, head slightly bowed, as if he'd discarded the haughtiness and rage he'd worn so boldly like an old hat.

"A moment, mate?" Hags supplicated, the words falling from his lips like leaves from a gutter.

Sid placed his helmet on the wing, folding his arms behind his back. "Lieutenant."

"I was out of line last night," Tom confessed. "I'm sorry, mate."

"Water under the bridge," Sid said flatly, still skeptical.

"I've not been myself lately, I know." Tom's feet shifted like those of a man under interrogation. "It's just that…I've not told anyone this yet, but…well, before we embarked, when I was kissing my Susannah goodbye at the dock, she gave me the news… we're having a baby, mate."

Suddenly, any lingering anger vanished from Sid's heart. "Well, congratulations, Tom!" He grasped the suddenly exuberant pilot's hand, giving it a good hard shake while clasping the Scotsman's shoulder.

"Thank you!" Tom let out a deep breath, and in that moment, he was the boy he looked to be, joyful and naïve and proud and terrified.

"A word of advice, though, from someone with experience: there's no enemy on earth so terrifying as a little girl. So, if you end up with one of those, beware."

Tom's mien grew pensive. "I wish she hadn't told me," he confessed. "It's all I can think about now. When I bailed on you in the fight…I'm sorry, Daventry, really, I am. I wasn't thinking straight. It was like the voice in my head saying, 'Get back, get back home.' And ever since we got to this place…"

The words trailed off into nothingness. The silence that followed yielded to Marie's voice speaking those very words to Sid a week before he was shipped off to Europe. He remembered the unbridled joy in her eyes, how her soft cheeks turned red, how the dimples in them grew with her radiant smile. How he thought of her every day, trying to imagine little baby Emily, born while Sid was half a world away. All he could think about was getting home to them, holding them in his arms. He knew exactly how Tom Wickler felt.

Yet there was something that disturbed him, some hidden lie lurking behind the lad's apology. Wickler *had* been himself; ever since Sid had met him, he'd been brash, cocky, even reckless. He was grudging in his respect for authority, though he seemed to crave it plenty for himself, often harassing younger men like poor D.B. Barluck. He was like the schoolyard bully who beat up the little kids but tucked his tail and ran when a bigger guy showed up. Sid often wondered how he was still in the Navy.

But fatherhood changed a man, and maybe, just maybe, this was the beginning of Tom Wickler's long-overdue transformation into a grown man. *Maybe.*

Without a word, Sid patted Hags on the back, nodding as he collected his helmet and began the long ascent to Willie Love's cockpit.

"Will you do it?" Tom called out. "The water trick the lass showed us."

Sid chuckled. "Negative. I've got my orders." He climbed over the cockpit railing, pulling the harnesses over his waist and chest.

"You know you want to." Hags slapped the Wyvern's wing. "See what the old girl can do, *eh*?" He exaggerated the last word, as if to mock Sid with it. "Besides, you want to impress the little lady, don't you?"

There's the Hags I know, Sid feared, glowering back at the lad. "Clear the prop, Lieutenant."

He slammed the canopy hood shut before Hags could answer.

&

Ejection seat safety pin fitted in strap. Parachute verified.

The prestart checklist had become rote in Sid's mind, but just hours after nearly going down with his ship, after having several reasons to fear that his flight back through the swirling clouds would be his last ever, there wasn't a classic novel or penny dreadful he'd rather be reading.

Cockpit ventilation louver in position. Emergency oxygen pin removed. Main oxygen supply connected. Undercarriage selector down.

Undercarriage emergency release fully aft, locking wire in place—and pray to God I don't have to use that again, and if I do, it works this time.

He went through the long list of routine motions, checking the flight control movement, the circuit breakers, trim wheels, levers, propeller fine-pitch stops, fuel tank selectors, ordnance controls; all those pesky necessities to ensure that the skipper's favorite aircraft wouldn't end up next to VW888. Though every plane was manufactured to the same specifications, each one had its own quirks, its own unique character, as if it were a living thing. "Willie Love," as Commander Faintary so affectionately called the Wyvern entrusted to him, was newer than Triple-Eight; she was the youngest ship in the squadron, in fact, and Faintary had kept the cockpit looking as neat and spotless as the utilitarian confines of a warplane pilot's office could be, as if she'd just come off the production line.

Sid opened the high-pressure cock to check the operation of his compass and tank booster pump, the last checks before start-up. Then he tripped the ignition switch, and his ears filled with the mellifluous scream of the turboprop roaring to life. The propeller blades swirled like the arms of ballet dancers going this way and that, the forward prop spinning the way Sid was used to and the second slashing at the air counterclockwise. He remembered how the blades' churning had mesmerized him the first time he'd sat in a Wyvern's cockpit, almost to the point of hypnosis.

He revved the props up to six thousand RPM, checking the oil pressure: a perfect thirty pounds per square inch. Going through the rest of the checks, he felt like a conductor in a symphony, the kind Marie always dragged him to the theater to see. The droning growl was like a deep bass interlude, the darkest, most alluring part of the composition. He chuckled a little as he remembered her telling him that the Toronto Symphony Orchestra was performing Brahms the weekend before Christmas—a not-so-subtle hint that a pair of tickets would be the perfect gift. He was her favorite. *When I get back, baby, we're going to the big city.*

Sid nudged the throttle ahead, checking his wheel brakes and artificial horizon, glancing over the nose. Unlike the Avengers and Sea Furies he'd flown in Canada, the Wyvern offered such a good view from the cockpit that he didn't have to zigzag to see where he was going. The empty strip between the forest and the river was narrow, but long and straight enough. He noted that he'd need to make a swift left turn straight away to avoid the trees. *No problem.* He lined Willie Love up, locking the tailwheel in place and tightening his harness.

He muttered a perfunctory prayer, as he always did even amid his doubt that his supplication would be heard, before releasing the brakes and opening the throttle. Willie Love lunged ahead with a spryness that belied the aircraft's bulk, a spryness that Triple-Eight would have scoffed at. The Wyvern leaped into the air, quicker than Sid had expected. He raised the landing gear and flaps, massaging the throttle as he entered a shallow, banking climb leftward.

Once Sid was certain he was clear of the trees, he glanced down at the myriad dials and indicators in his cockpit, following his normal routine after takeoff. Willie Love had just over half her fuel load remaining. By Sid's estimations, that would give him one good run at the pond and back, and just enough fuel to reach the coastline when they went back through the storm. *Provided nothing unexpected happens.*

Yet something unexpected *was* happening. Sid found he was having trouble keeping the aircraft at the usual initial climb speed of 165 knots—Willie Love wanted to go faster. He extended the air brake, ready to compensate for the usual slight nose-down pitch that accompanied it, but the plane flew straight as an arrow. *Is it a tailwind?* If so, it wouldn't account for the smooth ride, particularly the absence of the moderate buffet that so often came with popping the brake.

To Hell with it, Sid thought, retracting the brake and letting Willie Love race along. The additional speed didn't seem to be having any negative effects. Even as he passed three hundred knots, the point at which the controls grew heavy in normal air, the plane flew as light as a feather. *The quicker, the better.*

He turned his attention to the map provided by the creatures Lucretia called "Racosku"—if it could indeed be called a "map." It was a moving image, almost like magic; a three-dimensional, transparent depiction of the ground below that moved with the aircraft. He didn't read the chart and plot a course through it; he simply followed the triangular blue shape through the richly detailed orange path. He'd placed the small box that generated the image in the notch on the port side panel behind the gyro angling unit, securing it atop the torpedo depth setting control wheel that had been rendered superfluous with the Wyvern's change in role. Yet the image it projected was right there before his eyes, in the center panel of his windscreen as if painted upon the glass. All Sid had to do was follow the line.

This was *so* much better than dead reckoning!

The mountains rose on either side of Sid, their summits seemingly level with his wingtips. His altitude indicator read five thousand feet. The glowing trees and ferny plants dressing their slopes were so bright that, even if Sid ignored the pointer in front of him, he'd have to be blindfolded not to see the mountainsides. It was like flying down Broadway.

Forty-three minutes after takeoff, the gulch veered right. The mountains suddenly fell away, and the land before Sid was nearly flat. And there was the pond, no more than five miles ahead, green, glowing like everything else in this strange world, as if there were neon beneath its surface. The "pond" was in fact a small lake, maybe a mile across its longest side and half as wide. Sid switched on the cine camera in the starboard wing, once used to verify the effectiveness of the Wyvern's weapons, now to find a way to save those wonderfully silly Racosku.

Sid put Willie Love into a shallow descent, extending the air brake. Once again, the Wyvern gave no protest. He would make the pass at one thousand feet off the deck—low enough to gather clear film but not so low as to put his aircraft, and himself, in peril.

And there was peril enough, for, as Sid approached the pond, he noted a number of birdlike creatures soaring over the still green water. He couldn't get a good look at them, but they appeared quite large, maybe the size of egrets, and rainbow colors flashed upon their wings in the way that such iridescence cascaded over the Racosku's bodies. *Best to stay above them*, he knew without much concern; the birds seemed to be content to fly just a few feet above the surface.

After passing over the pond, Sid disengaged the camera, pointing the nose up slightly and retracting the air brake. Willie Love lurched ahead even without Sid advancing the throttle. Sid glanced down at his fuel indicators, surprised to discover just how little fuel he'd burned. The indicator had moved only a few notches. *She'll have enough to make it back to the ship!*

Or to make another approach to the pond. This time lower. Much lower.

His left hand crept to the undercarriage selector.

⌇

Don't even think about it, the voice of reason bellowed, but Sid was only halfway listening. He banked gently to the right—*south,* by the geography of this world—extending his turn more than he needed to as he looked over his shoulder in the direction of the lucent pond, taking measure of the lay of the land. The banks were shallow; assuming that the soil was the same as the takeoff strip and could support the weight of a Wyvern, he could touch down there, holding the aircraft just above its stall speed so that the wheels were kissing the ground, then advance the throttle just before touching the water. The tires would be spinning; they'd only need to be in contact with the surface for a split second to get soaked.

It would be easy. Faintary wouldn't have to know. Lucretia wouldn't tell. She had said that the camera footage was only part of what she needed. She needed whatever was floating on the surface of the pond to work her magic. To save the Racosku. Sid had to get her that sample. As he leveled his wings, the pond directly in front of him two miles out, he lowered the landing gear.

You have your orders, he reminded himself. *You are a military officer; you don't have the luxury of choosing which orders you follow.* Fanny had the right of it, he knew; those orders existed to safeguard Her Majesty's instruments of war, sure, but, as the commander had emphasized, they also existed to safeguard human life—*his* life.

But this time, it's bigger than me. Here was a shining chance to give help to the helpless. *God's work*, Marie might have called it; the Lord knew she'd have pitied the poor creatures in their desperate plight. More than Sid did, anyway, and he had plenty of pity. *She would do everything she could to help them.*

What would she think of him if he passed up the chance? What would his daughters think—Emily, whose tears had convinced him to spare a mangy, rabid feral cat all those years ago, and little Rhiannon, that gentle little girl whose angelic soul had never seemed to harbor even the whiff of a malicious thought?

What would he think of himself? The churchmen had warned of the perils of sin, not merely sins committed but sins of omission. To do nothing when the chance to do right was there was every bit as offensive to God as an act done out of ill intent.

But this was not church, and those preachers had no authority here. God Himself might not have. Here, God's name was Lieutenant-Commander Eugene Faintary, and the wages of sin were permanent grounding and dishonorable discharge.

And, yes, quite possibly…death.

A storm raged inside Sidney Daventry. His mind knew that Faintary was right, that his orders were what they were, and that obeying them was the right thing to do. Yet his heart screamed that what was right was wrong, that there was no order to follow but that given by his conscience, and that the duties of a naval aviator paled in comparison to those of a good man. Would such a man turn a blind eye to the suffering of desperate creatures to satisfy the myopic commands of another, a man as flawed and fallible as himself?

As Sid descended, Willie Love began to exhibit more typical handling characteristics. The plane slowed as it should have, and Sid had to adjust the elevator trim to compensate for the effects of the air brake. He kept the plane just above one hundred twenty knots; below that, the ailerons had a tendency to float, and he needed precise roll control to line up. He fully extended his flaps and lowered the undercarriage. The pond spread out before him like a dream he was watching from outside, his waking eyes unable to observe or comprehend, calling out to him, beckoning him to come inside. Of all the beauty around him, none could match the allure of the vastness of bright green shining ahead. He descended lower, lower, until he was fifty feet off the ground, forty, thirty…

No! That blasted voice was shouting now, and against it, even the roar of the turbine was a mewling whisper. Sid slammed the throttle forward, much too violently. Willie Love jolted upward into the purple sky as two rainbow birds whooshed past the right side of the canopy, barely missing the tail. Sid quickly engaged the flight fine-pitch stop to keep his propellers from overspeeding, setting his flaps to the takeoff position and raising the landing gear as he turned toward the gulch. He couldn't press his luck again. He'd won a small victory from Faintary; maybe, having followed orders dutifully and brought WL891 back with more fuel than expected, he could win another one.

Maybe.

Damn it, he thought, pounding his fist on the canopy hood as he peered back at the green pool growing smaller and smaller behind him. *Goddamn it.*

Sid, you bloody coward.

CHAPTER VIII

THE FOOTAGE WAS all but useless, as Lucretia had feared. Between the low light, the poor image resolution, and the lens's paltry thirty-five-millimeter focal length, all she could make out was a series of grayscale blurs. *At least the pond itself is bright in the video.* Yet she didn't have the heart to tell Sidney that all he'd done was for naught.

"It's a good start," she lied instead. "I mean, now we know... that..."

We know that I've quickly run out of bullshit.

Sidney chuckled in that way someone did when they were trying to cope with failure. "It's useless, isn't it?"

So much for trying to be nice. "Yeah, unfortunately I can't see much." She blew into her hands, glancing around the empty laboratory, running her fingers over the bulky camera that, as far as she could tell, was a leftover from World War II. Yet the Racosku were still able to develop the film, digitalize it, and interface it with their projectors, somehow. "If only we could jury-rig Jay's camera in place of this one. The dimensions are around the same; it ought to fit."

"We might be able to," Sidney said, and his face brightened. "Skipper keeps a maintenance manual in his plane at all times. From what the gents tell me, he was over in Belgium on exercise and had to make an emergency landing. Well, no one at Beauvechain had the parts to fix a Wyvern, so they had to fly the stuff all the way from Ford, and Skipper wasn't too pleased about having to wait around listening to everyone speaking French. He swore that, if he ever found himself in such a predicament again, then, by God, he'd get himself out of it!"

Lucretia got a genuine laugh out of that. "Well, Jay might have something to say about us commandeering his camera. He protects that thing like it's his dick." She bit her lip; people in Sid's time didn't talk like that. "Sorry. Anyway, his camera's sensor is way better than this old film. The telephoto lens might be too long to fit, although we could probably just leave off the glass cover. Might increase your drag a bit."

"That shouldn't be a problem," Sidney said. "Even the air seems to work differently here. I hardly burned any fuel."

Lucretia jolted back, and suddenly her idea to smuggle away her brother's prized camera felt less like a thought born of frustration than a cruel yet necessary plot. "Even with a wider lens, we could blow up the image. Try to do that with this, and you'll just see a bunch of big white blurs."

"I'll ask Commander Faintary for permission to conduct another flight. Though, like I said before, I make no promises."

"Yeah, I know." Lucretia exhaled as she refocused on the footage, like a moving Jackson Pollock piece spattered across the wall panel, pretending to study the film as if to reassure the airman that his efforts weren't wasted, even though he knew very well that they were.

"So," Sidney said kindly, "whereabouts in America are you from?"

The question caught Lucretia off guard. "East Texas, about forty-five minutes from Shreveport, Louisiana. That's where I live now, anyway; I'm originally from Pittsburgh. Lived in California for a while, before my career went to shit anyway. Back when I was actually a respected scientist. Jay lives in Houston; that's where the lab we work for is based. I usually spend half the year down there, in the summer when the skeeters are bad in the bayou. I'm usually back at my cabin in November; it's still hurricane season on the Gulf Coast, so we don't do much flying. I do my work from home, and in the meantime, my neighbor and I make a little extra renting out canoes and swamp boats to the fishermen and photographers."

Sidney nodded, politely but with a face that suggested that she'd shared too much, enough that he pitied her, and she didn't want his pity. She caught herself from returning the question. *He'll tell me if he wants me to know.* He was already becoming too familiar.

She turned back to the screen, tucking her hair behind her ear. Sidney's chortle drew her attention.

"What?" she asked.

"Oh, nothing. Just…the way you play with your hair. It reminds me of Marie. She does the same thing. I never told her how much I loved watching her."

Lucretia's heart fluttered, even against the spear of pain that pierced it. In that moment, she wasn't hearing Sidney's voice but Mark's.

She forced a smile. "Well, I'm guessing she's slightly less Chinese than I am."

"I'm not so sure just how Chinese you are, with a name like Lucretia!"

Lucretia raised an eyebrow, and she had to remind herself that Sidney was from a different time. *Not that ignorance is okay, intentional or otherwise.* "My mother loved the opera," she said. "My father loved the Bible, hence Jeremiah. But, if it makes you feel better, you could call me Chao-Xing. That's my Chinese name."

Sidney lifted an eyebrow. "You've got two names?"

"There isn't just one thing that defines us, so why should we only have one name? My brother's is Jia. That's why I call him 'Jay;' it could be for either Jia or Jeremiah."

The pilot smiled, nodding as if to concede her point. "So, Chao-Xing Tang—"

"No, no, it's Tang Chao-Xing," she corrected him. "In the Chinese tradition, surname comes first. Family before self, I guess." She shrugged nonchalantly. "Or just a different way of doing things. I don't know. I've never been to China. America and China aren't the best of friends where I come from…I mean *when*."

"They weren't in '56 either."

Good point. "I've got mixed feelings on traditions, to be honest. Half of me laments that people don't seem to cherish them anymore; the other half can't stop bitching about how restrictive they are."

"Well, you did say that there isn't just one thing that defines us."

"Touché!" Lucretia's eyes lilted away from Sidney's, toward the projection she wasn't watching, off into the silence. "I think of Lucretia as the scientist," she said, and only now realized that she was about to pour her heart out, and she didn't care. The door had been opened, opened by her own hand. "Sure, she's a goofball sometimes, but she's grounded. She has goals and limits, she works hard, plays harder; she aspires to be something better than what she is. Chao-Xing is the dreamer, the one chasing meteors, the one with elf ears and fairy wings, the one who lives in a place like this, flying through the trees, dancing in the moonlit water-falls, talking to her auspicious dragon. The one with the hair the shade of hot pink that Lucretia is afraid to dye hers because she's still afraid she'll get in trouble at work.

"I think Chao-Xing is who Lucretia wants to be, who she sometimes forgets that, in her heart, she is. They need each other, I think. Lucretia needs Chao-Xing to tell her to remember that she's never too old to dream, and Chao-Xing needs Lucretia to wake her up. The problem with dreamers is that, sometimes, they get so swept up in their dreams that they forget there's a real world out there, a big wide world that needs them."

"A world like this one," Sidney said with a smile that wasn't mere politeness. It was as if her words had stirred in his soul.

"Yeah," she said, backing away. "So, Lieutenant Daventry, your turn. Why'd you want to become a pilot?"

"Oh, I just was always fascinated by aircraft." His tone and expression were suddenly sheepish.

"Hey now, no generic answers! Come on, tell me."

He looked up at her; his smile seemed to strain against his thoughts. "My oldest brother, Edwin, was in the Air Force."

"Ah, wanted to show him up, did you? The Navy was where the excitement was, right? You wanted to be top gun?" She bit her lip. "I guess you wouldn't understand that reference."

Sidney bowed his head. "There was a story he told me once when he was home, reassigned to a training unit, right before I joined up." His tone was grave, and melancholy rippled aloft his suddenly deep voice. "You ever heard of the Channel Dash?"

Lucretia shook her head.

"It was early in '42," Sidney explained. "The Germans decided to sail two of their battleships, a heavy cruiser, and a bunch of destroyers right up the English Channel."

"That couldn't have gone well."

"It should have been a suicide mission, but, between the winter weather, some communications snafus, and just plain bad luck, the Brits were caught totally off guard. By the time anyone knew what was going on, the ships were already halfway up the channel.

"There was a group of Royal Navy pilots, 825 Naval Air Squadron, led by an Irishman named Eugene Esmonde. Eddie was sure to include that part; Marie is Irish too. Protestant Irish," he added quickly and emphatically, as if that were a vital piece of information. "If you heard her talk, you'd think she was straight off the boat from Belfast.

"Anyway, back to my story, Esmonde and his men took off from Manston in horrible weather. They were flying old Fairey Swordfish; pilots called them 'Stringbags.' They were biplanes, old and rickety, with a top speed not far off that of a constipated pelican."

A chortle tore through Lucretia's nose at that.

"They were supposed to have RAF escorts," Sidney continued. "The escorts had to alternate, because the Spitfires couldn't fly slowly enough to keep up with the Swordfish. Eddie's Canadian squadron was one of them. Most of the escorts never made the rendezvous in the bad weather. But Esmonde and his men went in anyway." He drew a deep breath. "He'd been one of the pilots who led the first air attacks on the *Bismarck*; the guns on that ship were so modern that they weren't calibrated to shoot down planes as slow as a Stringbag, so they got through unscathed. Well, *Scharnhorst* and *Gneisenau* didn't have that problem."

"What happened?" Lucretia dared to ask.

Sidney closed his eyes. "Every damned one of those planes got blown out of the sky. Out of eighteen men, only six survived." His eyes opened, moist and wistful. "You know, I think they knew they were flying into certain death. But they did it anyway. They knew that, if those ships reached Norway, there was nothing to stop them from obliterating the convoys that were keeping the Allies in the war. The Nazis would have won. They say that Esmonde was the one who made the choice to go out, not his superiors on the ground. He was willing to give his life for something greater than himself. That's the kind of man I want to be." He stared at the moving pictures on the wall, exhaling. "I just…hope I have the courage."

They stood in silence for a long while. *You have the courage*, Lucretia wanted to say; she'd spent all her life hearing those stories of war, stories of men charging headlong into certain death, and she wondered if they truly believed what they were dying and killing for or just doing what they were told. But there was no lie in Sidney's eyes, no falsity in his voice. He wanted to be a hero, as he saw it, if such a thing as a "hero" indeed existed. He wanted his choices to matter, to be for good. Because, unlike so many in Lucretia's world, he believed in good.

Such naïve idealism, she thought. Sidney's was the kind of bravery straight out of folklore, it seemed; the kind adored by cultures the world over, the kind all too often molded by kings and commanders, presidents and prime ministers for barbarous ends.

Yet there was something innocent in it, something noble, something strong, strong enough to endure even through the attempts at corruption by the warmongers. Something Lucretia couldn't help but admire…and love.

She took the airman's hand, now trembling a little, and rested her head on his shoulder.

⋦

The moment had passed as soon as it began, like a dandelion seed blown across an open field in a brisk wind. *It didn't mean anything*, Lucretia assured herself. *He needed emotional support, nothing more. There's nothing. There was no "moment."*

Of course there was nothing. There couldn't be anything. Anything would be wrong.

Sidney had gone to bed, he and his mates, alone in their bunks, the others no doubt giving Sidney a ribbing, as was the wont of such men. Especially the younger men, both still in their twenties—boys, really, at least to Lucretia's eyes, even though the handsome one was second-in-command.

What was he thinking about? Some noble quest, where he gave his life to save others? Was that what he truly wanted, or was that simply the archetype he aspired to, all the while praying that he'd never be called upon to become it? Was that how he rationalized the nature of his work?

Was he up there thinking about dying?

Or was he dreaming of something else, imagining himself living forever in a world like the one that now ensconced them? Was he thinking of Chao-Xing, with her pink hair and pointy ears, and her wings, and her dreams? Did Sidney have a dream-self, a Prince Charming, a King Arthur, a Paul Bunyan, that he morphed into in the sanctuary of sleep?

Or had he stopped dreaming long ago? Had he, by the travails of war or merely the advance of years, become an adult, inside and out?

Why the hell do I care what some man I'll never see again after a few days is thinking about? For heaven's sake, Lucretia, what is the water here doing to your head?

Jeremiah entered the laboratory, jarring Lucretia from her thoughts. He had his earbuds in and was muttering rap lyrics under his breath, complete with certain words that someone of his ethnicity probably shouldn't have been repeating. *His phone should be dead by now*, Lucretia knew, for he'd been fiddling with it for hours. *There must indeed be a way to recharge here.*

"Can't sleep?" she called out to him.

He pocketed his phone, ripping the speakers out of his ears—a rare look for Jeremiah Tang. "Not tired. I haven't really been tired since we got here; I lie down mostly because I'm bored, and I drift right off to sleep, then I wake up and I'm raring to go."

"This place has that effect, although I'm not sure how you're managing to get bored." Though, if Lucretia was honest with herself, the only thing keeping her from falling into the same ennui, majestic as her new surroundings were, was her worry for the Racosku. Her work had always been her refuge.

"Still watching that?" Jeremiah asked, gesturing to the gun camera footage playing on repeat on the wall panel.

"Nope. Why? Did you want to put *Sharknado* on?" Lucretia rolled her eyes.

"Well, I never did see the sixth one." Jeremiah's chuckle had momentarily infected Lucretia. "Actually, I have some movies on my phone. I figure Brain could come down here and hook me up again. Maybe our buggy friends will want to watch with us."

"*Racosku*, Jay. They're called Racosku."

"According to you," he reminded her. He turned back to the screen, as if to inspect the picture quality for whatever cinematic experience he was planning on embarking upon. "Wait...freeze that frame."

Lucretia complied, cocking her head to the side. "What's up?"

He gestured to a black blotch at the edge of the white blur that was supposed to be the pond. "Did you see that?"

"Jay, all I see are blobs. Why, are you seeing something?"

"I don't know. Keep playing."

She touched the screen to restart the footage.

"Pause again," he said after one second. "It's moving."

Lucretia peered closely at the screen. The black blob had indeed ventured further from the white space and was spreading into the gray area beyond. "Wow, you're right. But...what am I looking at?"

"Well, if I had to venture a guess, I'd say it's the critters that make the goo coming out of the water."

She scratched her bottom lip. "Have you ever seen anything like that before?"

Jeremiah turned an admonishing sneer at her. "Uh, Lu? Alien planets aren't exactly the kinds of environments I study. I've never seen anything like *anything* around here."

"I meant sea anemones coming out of the water like that."

"Lu, based on the schematics your pal Brain showed us, they *look* like sea anemones. But there's no evidence that they're anything like marine invertebrates on Earth."

"What about the DNA readouts? Do you see any similarities?"

"Genetics is your baby, Lu."

"Yes, but you know enough about it. You've banged enough geneticists. Have you even looked at them yet?"

Jeremiah bit his lip. "I was waiting for you to do your thing."

Lucretia uttered an exaggerated harrumph. "You were dicking off." She refocused on the panel, resuming the playback loop. "Okay, I need to know what's going on out there. If that really is the spiny goo-pooping thingies coming out of the water, it changes our whole approach."

"You know, Lu-Tang," Jeremiah said with a grin, "Carl Linnaeus would stand in awe of your system of animal nomenclature."

Lucretia snorted out a chortle.

"I agree with you," Jeremiah continued. "We don't know what other organisms are in that water. If you're going to shower it with CRISPR plasmids, we want to minimize the adverse effects it might have."

Lucretia nodded. "Plus, it'll be easier to saturate the population if they're on dry land. Wouldn't have to worry about the compounds getting swept away or not sinking deeply enough. Anyway, I need better footage than this to determine if that's really what's going on. Gotta convince Sidney to go over again— or rather, convince that stick-in-the-mud commander to let him." She drew a deep breath. *Now for the unpleasant part.* "I'm gonna need to borrow your camera. Is it still in the plane?"

Jeremiah raised an eyebrow. "Uh, yeah…but…you're going to have the guy take pictures while he's supposed to be flying his plane?"

"No, Jay, we're going to mount it inside the wing in place of this." She slapped the bulky camera unit.

"Like hell you are!" Jeremiah snapped.

"Jay, please! I need better pictures—"

"You're not using my camera, Lu! That thing was expensive, and you couldn't rig it to the plane even if I were stupid enough to let you play with it." He sighed aloud. "I don't get it. The Racosku showed us those videos before; why can't they just go over and take more?"

"I don't know," Lucretia admitted. "It's fairly obvious that they want to avoid that area at all costs, and we shouldn't ask them to go. They asked for our help. Jay, I could really use your camera. If it breaks, I'll buy you a new one, I promise."

"Or, you know, you could just use the marvel of modern technology you've got in your pants pocket."

Lucretia screwed up her face. "My phone?"

"It's got a camera, doesn't it? A very high-resolution camera."

"You want me to rig my camera to the plane's wing?"

"No, Lucretia, I want you to hand it to the pilot to take with him. You think that uptight commander is going to let you go around making modifications to his aircraft? Besides, what ever happened to the path of least resistance?"

"My phone is secured using facial recognition, Jay."

Jeremiah heaved a sigh, clawing at his face in despair. "Then disable it, for fuck's sake! God, Lu, why are you being so god-damned obstinate?"

"You know, just a minute ago, you were chiding me for wanting him to fly and take pictures at the same time."

"My God, woman." Jeremiah slapped his forehead. "Then mount the damned thing above the control panel. I'm sure there are ways to fasten it. Don't planes have those heads-up displays nowadays? Use it like one of those."

"Those are transparent, though."

Jeremiah turned and stomped away.

"Fine!" Lucretia yelled, throwing up her hands. "You win. I'll use my phone. I'm sure it'll be just fine."

"Quit pouting," Jeremiah snapped, spinning around, jerking his finger in her face. "You do this all the time, and I'm tired of it."

Lucretia jerked backwards. "What is your problem?"

"All the time we've been working together, you've treated me like the sidekick, there to be used as you need me. You have this attitude like what's mine is yours. I've put up with it because I know what you went through, and because you're my sister, my family. But I've had enough of it. That camera belongs to me. I sank a lot of money into that gear, money I worked my ass off to earn. It's not about it getting broken, or you owing me a replacement. It's about you acting like it's yours to use at your convenience, you telling me that you *need* it."

He spun around, the flash of his hair a knife across Lucretia's soul.

"Jay!" she called out. "I'm sorry! I mean it. Please."

And she was. She'd never even stopped to think; she'd always just assumed that they were of a like mind when it came to work.

You know what they say about people who assume. Except the only ass this time is me. The regret swallowed her up like a straitjacket.

Jeremiah turned around, exhaling his frustrations. He approached her, laying a hand on her shoulder. "You know I love you, Lu."

"And I love you," she said, choking back her guilt. "I owe you so much. I never meant to—"

Jeremiah held up a hand. "I know. No need to get all emotional on me."

She threw her arms around him. "I'm sorry, Jay. You know I never meant to be disrespectful."

He backed away, smiling. "It's all good. I'll go and tell your boyfriend that we need another flight, and show him how to use your phone camera. I'm sure he can figure it out."

"He's not my boyfriend!" Lucretia bellowed with all the fury of a fifteen-year-old.

"Sure," Jeremiah said with a wink. "And after that, I'm afraid you'll need to atone for your transgressions against me. And it turns out I've got just the punishment you deserve."

Slowly, dramatically, he stepped closer and closer to the box full of bad movies. *No*, Lucretia prayed. *Not that!*

Her brother's face was overtaken by a diabolical smile as he pulled the sleeve containing the sixth *Sharknado* movie from that accursed package. *I'm doomed!*

The man Jeremiah had delivered Lucretia's request to Sid. He had come, he said in his typical jovial fashion, to keep the two of them separated. The hours of courtship were over for the evening.

Sid had to chuckle. He'd quite come to like Jeremiah, despite his rather puerile demeanor—though, Sid figured, that might've just been how people behaved seventy years into his future. The current attitudes about decorum, dress code, proper speech, and reverence for the sacred had clearly gone out the window. He wasn't sure if that was a harmless development or a surefire sign that human civilization was in a downward spiral, but the Tangs seemed like decent enough people, so he assumed the former. And, considering he didn't think it likely he'd live long enough to find out firsthand, he was perfectly content with that assumption.

Though he did find the insinuation about courtship to be rather crude.

He doesn't understand, Sid lamented. But why not? How could the brother who had lived with Lucretia all his life be so blind to what had been apparent to Sid within an hour? The woman had lost everything: her husband, her career, her reputation. She was lonely, looking to fill the void inside her, the one she may have stubbornly refused to admit was there. She had loved this Mr. Leibovitz; Sid could tell by the lightness in her voice, the nostalgic glimmer in her eyes. What could have come between two people who were truly in love, that love itself could not heal?

She hadn't said, and Sid knew better than to ask. And he sure as hell wasn't about to ask the brother. It was no matter; Jeremiah had already retreated to the laboratory with Jim Wellington and Tom Wickler eagerly in tow to watch the film about the tornadoes and sharks.

Sid would almost have rather joined them, silly as the flick sounded, than have to petition Gene Faintary for another crack at the pond.

The commander hadn't said a word. A man of lesser wisdom might have assumed that Faintary's silence spoke for him, but Sid knew the skipper better than that. The gears in his head were turning like the wheels of a runaway freight train, mulling over every possibility, every eventuality, every cost and benefit.

"Sir," Sid prodded, "based on the significant reduction in fuel burn, I am confident that the aircraft will have sufficient fuel to reach a friendly aerodrome."

Faintary gave a slow, dramatic nod. "Have you considered that you may have simply had a favorable tailwind? That may not be the case if you were to conduct a second mission."

Sid shook his head. "Sir, the performance was the same in both directions. The air here, it seems thinner, much thinner. I experienced none of the adverse effects of air brake extension, and the controls were light and fluid throughout the air-speed envelope."

"And if your analysis proves incorrect? If you empty the tanks, not leaving sufficient fuel even to reach Port Said?"

"Then I'll ditch in the Mediterranean, sir. If we exit the storm in the same location where we entered, then I could put down in the sea and wait for the helicopter that's coming for Barluck."

Faintary's glare was sharp enough to cut diamonds. "You make too many assumptions, Lieutenant. For instance, that you will be piloting Willie Love back through the storm, when in fact she is assigned to me."

Sid lowered his eyes. *Damn it. Of course, you fool.*

"Furthermore," Faintary said firmly, "you've already made a submarine out of one of our aircraft. Just how many more do you intend to put on the sea floor?"

Sid pinched his face to hold in his urge to chuckle. "None, sir."

"You find that funny, Lieutenant?" Faintary's tone was deadly serious. "You find humor in wrecking Her Majesty's naval aircraft?"

"No, sir. Not at all."

"Very good." Faintary folded his hands behind his back, pacing this way and that with a look of surety on his face. "The answer is no, Lieutenant."

Sid exhaled his deflation. He wasn't about to press his luck again. "Yes, sir."

He pivoted around, about to retreat to the ramp leading into the tree city, when Faintary's powerful hand clasped his shoulder.

"I know how much this means to you," the commander said, his voice gentle and compassionate yet unmistakably firm. "However, every minute you spend in the air, you expose your aircraft—and yourself—to risks."

Sid thought of the birds he'd nearly struck on his climb-out from the pond. What would happen if he'd hit them? How heavy were they? Even a sparrow could bring down a Wyvern if it struck the wrong component. And those were definitely bigger than sparrows.

"We have no support infrastructure here," Faintary went on. "No maintenance depot, no spare parts. Have you stopped to think that even minor damage to these aircraft could see us stranded here permanently?"

Sid nodded. "You're right, sir."

"Every second that engine runs, the risk of failure increases. You and I both know that the Wyvern has demons that she's never fully exorcised. She's a good aeroplane, better than some of those coffin dodgers in the Admiralty seem to think, but she needs her guardian angels to keep the demons at bay. And those angels are all in *Eagle's* hangar deck or back in West Sussex."

"Understood, sir."

Sid backed away, watching out of the corner of his eye as Faintary stared off into the luminous wilderness. The commander's face betrayed nothing, but his left hand busied around his right, and Sid knew that their movements mirrored those in his mind.

After what seemed an hour, Faintary turned, his stark eyes locking onto Sid's. "I will authorize one more sortie, Lieutenant."

Sid jolted back; he genuinely hadn't expected the skipper to give in. "Sir, I'm most grateful. Thank you, sir." Sid saluted and turned for the ramp.

"This is your last one, Lieutenant," Faintary called out, and Sid knew he meant what he said. "And even this is against my better judgment." The commander approached Sid, and the severity of his authority was made manifest in the stony glower on his face, in the emphatic hardness of his words: "Do not make me regret this."

Lucretia lay in the surprisingly soft and perfectly warm lucent hammock, staring up at the lights on the ceiling, thinking about the past—the distant past, if seventy years, a mere double her lifetime, could indeed be called "distant," then the not-so-distant one, the one where she was a respected scientist and an inspiration to little girls. The one that seemed like ancient history, like a fairy tale written upon the parchment of her dreams.

She hadn't gotten much rest since she'd woken up in this strange new world. Part of it was that she just wasn't tired, as if the magic of this world affected the human body's physiological processes. But mostly, it was the work and the worry. She'd felt guilty about taking so much as a break. Hell, she reasoned, she was only in her quarters now because the laboratory was occupied and she'd had enough of *Sharknado* within the first three minutes. Plus, the Scotsman was down there, and he made her uneasy.

You've really mucked things up, Lucretia. She'd pissed off Jeremiah, possibly engaged in improper behavior with a married man, and was no closer to helping the Racosku. *Par for the course.* Failure and disappointment had been her constant companions for the past three years; of course they would follow her even to the edge of the cosmos. She supposed that this was her punishment. All those years of thinking she'd had it made; it was only a matter of time before she flew too close to the sun.

She found herself thinking about the day Mark had told her he wanted the divorce. At the time, she'd been heartbroken, angry, depressed; she'd just had her reputation torn to shreds by the Daniken piece, lost her job, been shunned by her colleagues—even the ones doing the same kind of work. It was as if she were toxic waste that everyone was tripping over themselves to get away from. To make everything worse, the mother she'd loved so dearly had just passed, and her father was in the early stages of dementia. How she'd wanted nothing more than to run away, *fly* away, to some faraway place, away from the cynicism and ruthlessness of her world. A place like the one she found herself in now.

Yet there was little respite. She couldn't escape the past's shadow. For a long time, she'd been telling herself that Mark was only doing what was best for him, and it hurt him as much as it hurt her. But why? Why was she rationalizing that betrayal? Why the hell hadn't he stuck by her side, been the rock that she needed to lean on? What ever happened to that "love conquers all" nonsense? "Through thick and thin?" Why was Jeremiah the only one to stand beside her?

She thought of her conversations with Mark after the divorce, how courteous and even apologetic he was, how she just wanted to punch him right in the mouth just as much as she wanted to kiss him. But even those trailed off in time. Mark was in another woman's pants within a couple months. And Lucretia was all alone, with no one. No one but her brother, who deserved a life of his own.

Her thoughts shifted to Sidney Daventry. Why was she so drawn to him? It wasn't love; it couldn't have been. Not the kind of love she'd had for Mark, anyway. He was a friend, nothing more. She cared for him, enjoyed his company, even pitied him in a way, though she couldn't quite put her finger on why. Was it the shadow of Mark that she saw in his soft complexion, though the two of them looked nothing alike? Or was he merely a character in the grand fantasy playing out before her, like the operas her mother used to drag her to the theater to watch?

He isn't Mark, she told herself. *He isn't going to fill the hole inside you.*

Because there is no hole in you, except the one you imagine. A wise man had once told her: "It's up to you to make yourself whole. Another person won't do that for you. They may enrich your life, but the powers that be in the universe didn't create an 'other half' to complete the puzzle of your life." A wise man indeed—a man named Mark Leibovitz. *You are whole, Lucretia. Wake up and remember that.*

She hefted herself out of the hammock. It was time to get her ass back to work.

CHAPTER IX

COMMANDER FAINTARY'S CONCERNS about the second flight not going as smoothly as the first were entirely unfounded. If anything, Sidney Daventry noted, the second flight was even more pleasant. Even with Lucretia Tang's "phone" blocking part of his view.

The device was affixed horizontally above the instrument panel. Sid found it more distracting than obstructive. The small, thin rectangular wonder was a telephone, and a television, and a stereo, and a camera, and a writing pad, and an encyclopedia, and a thousand other things that Sid could only imagine. *What else will they come up with in the future?* He thought about the aircraft that Lucretia and Jeremiah had arrived in, powered by electricity. Its lines were so sleek, so smooth; no paneling, no rivets, almost as if the plane had been molded out of blown glass.

He refocused on his instruments. Once again, Willie Love was speeding along smoothly and swiftly, her controls light to the touch even above three hundred knots, the fuel level indicators hardly budging. The hum of the turbine and the propellers' buzzing played in his head like a song, yet he couldn't shake the urge to change the tune. He grasped his right glove between his teeth and wriggled his hand out of it, pressing his thumb to the small round part on the bottom of the phone—now on his right side—which, Lucretia had said, was a fingerprint reader. Since it didn't recognize Sid's print, he had to type in the code on the numerical pad that appeared on the screen that she'd given him to unlock the device. He was about to click on the icon with the musical notes, which would open what Lucretia called an "app," when at the last second he pulled back. Though the plane was flying straight and level, he knew better than to take his focus off the flight. *How the hell do people in the future keep from getting distracted all the time?*

He pressed the gray button with the black rectangle that was supposed to represent a camera. The image that appeared on the screen matched the scenery before him, moving as Willie Love moved. *Remarkable!* The image was so *clear!* It even seemed to be compensating a little for the low light.

As the pond came into view, Sid pressed the video camera icon, then hit the red button to start recording. He slid his glove back into place with much more effort than it took to finagle the device, then put Willie Love into a shallow descent, slowing to one hundred thirty knots and overflying the sea of verdant splendor at five hundred feet. This time, there were no birds flocking about. Good luck was on his side.

Or, as Marie would say, the luck of the Irish. He chuckled to himself. *My love.*

He slowly moved the throttle quadrant to takeoff setting, climbing to a thousand feet before putting the Wyvern into a gentle bank to make a second pass. He didn't know how much film the phone had left—if it even used film, which he had a sneaking suspicion it didn't, for where would it go?—but it hadn't stopped recording, and Lucretia could surely use as much footage as could be taken.

He repositioned Willie Love two hundred seventy degrees, then banked left to align with the pond in the direction from whence he'd approached. Throttling back and extending the flaps, he began his descent. His fingers inched for the undercarriage buttons—only to increase the amount of drag, so that he could fly slower, down to one hundred twenty knots, maybe even below. The slower speed should yield better footage that Lucretia could study more closely.

That was all he was going to do. He wasn't about to press his luck, or do anything stupid. He would obey his orders.

This is your last chance, the voice chanted.

I need genetic samples.

A gene bomb.

Sid took a deep breath. *There are no birds, no obstructions. The way is clear. This is my last chance to help Lucretia—to save this world. To do the right thing.*

Could his conscience let that chance pass by?

Halfway bristling with resolve and halfway hating himself for thumbing his nose at a direct order, Sid gritted his teeth. He descended lower, lower, lower.

And this time, he didn't pull up.

Commander Faintary was standing on the riverbank, past the two parked Wyverns, staring out in the direction Sidney had flown. *He seems to do a lot of standing around and staring into the distance*, Lucretia noted. Maybe he was meditating, maybe imagining himself in the air barking commands over the radio, or maybe he was worrying about his man and his plane. Or maybe he was just embracing the silence, the serenity.

Whatever he was doing, she figured it probably wasn't in her best interests to interrupt him.

Eugene Faintary wasn't at all what she'd expected a military commander to look like. He wasn't tall; she wouldn't quite call him *short*, but he stood only two or three inches above Lucretia. That modest stature was deceiving, she knew, for he was clearly built on a sturdy frame, his biceps forming bulges in the sleeves of the uniform a Royal Navy pilot wore under his flight suit, the one Faintary stubbornly refused to take off, even as his subordinates had long since stripped to their undershirts. His pilots towered over him, even the young Scotsman, yet he was still by far the most imposing among them. Maybe it was the aura of his authority, maybe the stony glower that his otherwise comely face seemed perpetually molded into, maybe the sheer force of the gaze of his starkly blue eyes.

So, when the time came for Lucretia to approach him, she did so as gently as humanly possible. And she'd never been especially good at handling things delicately.

"Uh…sir," she stammered. "Good evening, sir. Or afternoon…whatever it is."

Faintary offered a blank nod. "And to you, ma'am."

Lucretia stood there gaping like a speared fish. She cringed as she imagined just how ridiculous she looked, which only made her more nervous. "So, uh, sir—"

The commander held up his hand. "I've told you, Dr. Tang, you needn't address me as 'sir.' You're not a member of the forces; you aren't bound to our rules."

"Right, of course. So, uh, Mr. Faintary…is that what I'm supposed to call you?"

"How about Gene?" he said, and for the first time, he smiled. "Or Eugene, if you'd prefer; it seems to me that 'gene' means something quite different in your occupation."

Lucretia risked a snorting laugh.

"At ease, Doctor," Eugene said, clearly sensing her nerves. "I don't bite—no matter what my men tell you."

Lucretia exhaled, and at last, she was indeed at ease.

"In fact," Eugene continued, "I'm glad we've got a moment to speak. I believe I owe you an apology for my curtness."

"Oh, it's okay—"

"No, it is not. I am an officer of the Royal Navy, the commanding officer of this squadron and, as such, a representative of the United Kingdom. It is my duty to embody my country's values, to represent it with dignity, and I've failed to do that. So, please, accept my apology."

Lucretia nodded. "I, uh…accept your apology. Actually, sir…sorry, *Eugene*…I just came by to thank you for your help. I get why you were reluctant to risk one of your planes. So, I just want you to know that I'm grateful."

"You made a compelling case," Eugene confessed. "And I know that Lieutenant Daventry is keen to assist you. I wonder if I've made the right choice." He turned to her, and his glower had morphed into a look of grave concern. "In truth, ma'am, it was not the aeroplane that I was reluctant to risk. Machines can be replaced, albeit at great cost, and with much consequence to those who imperiled them. I learned long ago that men cannot."

Lucretia bowed her head. "I'm sorry, sir."

"Don't be. However, what I've told Lieutenant Daventry remains. I cannot authorize any more sorties after this one."

"Even if Lieutenant Daventry—"

"Sidney."

"Right, right. Even if Sidney can give me what I need, and we're sure beyond a reasonable doubt that we can help the Racosku?"

"You've got an aeroplane of your own," Eugene said, kindly

but adamantly. "I've pressed my luck as far as I'm willing to press it. I need to get those aircraft and their pilots back to our ship."

Lucretia cleared her throat. "That brings me to the other thing I wanted to discuss with you, actually." Suddenly, her nerves were raging again. "Earlier, you, uh, you said you were going to…how did you say it? Oh, yeah…*commandeer* my plane. Look, I know you're only thinking about your men, but how am I supposed—"

Eugene's callused hand on her shoulder cut her off. "I spoke in haste, ma'am. It seemed the only way to get my men back home." He raised an eyebrow, smirking. "I didn't actually use the word 'commandeer,' did I?"

Lucretia risked a chortle. "You definitely did."

"Ah, I suppose you could say it's a bit of the old privateer in me. You know, it's said that my forebears sailed with none less than Sir Henry Morgan."

"You mean…you come from a family of pirates? That's so cool!"

Eugene shook his head, chuckling like he was a boy again. "Hardly one of the prouder moments of my lineage, I deem." He clasped her shoulders. "Rest assured, ma'am, I've no intention of leaving you stranded here. If I have to carry Lieutenant Daventry back on my lap, then so be it."

"Can you even do that?"

"There's a first time for everything," he said with a wink.

Lucretia jerked her head at the Velis. "I'm not even sure you could fly that thing," she japed. *Of course he could fly it; a half-drunk one-armed monkey could fly it.*

"Oh, don't underestimate me, Doctor," the commander said with grave surety. "I was one of the few souls unfortunate enough to have flown the Blackburn Firebrand, an aeroplane designed by the Devil himself. At the risk of sounding arrogant,

I'm quite confident that there isn't an aircraft on God's earth I couldn't handle!"

They stood in silence for a while, Eugene staring stoically into the far purple empyrean, hands behind his back. He stood still as stone, not flinching but a finger, as if he'd morphed into a statue of puissance. His face betrayed nothing, no worry or regret. He was like a father calmly and confidently anticipating his cub's return.

"So, Eugene," Lucretia risked, "do you have a family back in England?"

"Negative," the commander said in a tone devoid of emotion. "The wife walked out on me eight years ago; I've been married to the Navy ever since."

Lucretia jolted back. "Wow. I mean...I'm sorry to hear that. I just...I didn't think that happened in the fifties."

Eugene raised an eyebrow. "Didn't think what happened in the fifties?"

"People getting divorced. I mean, I'm divorced too, but... well, it's kinda par for the course in my time. Not that it doesn't suck, but...I just thought things were...you know, better...back then. In your time, I mean."

Eugene shook his head. "I can only guess that you're basing your conception of 'my time' on the lies you've been fed by Hollywood."

Lucretia bit her lip. "Yeah, kinda."

Eugene drew a deep breath. "I come from a long line of naval officers. My father sailed under Admiral Jellicoe at Jutland. I grew up reading stories of Nelson at Trafalgar, the Holy Coalition at Lepanto, the Greeks at Salamis; looking at the paintings of those proud and mighty heroes, standing tall like gods among men. The past had seemed a better place, a nobler one. Everyone knew what they were fighting for, what they were living for. People were just *better*.

"And then I came to realize that the Romans shit just like we do." He patted Lucretia's shoulder. "If you're looking for perfection in the past, you're looking in the wrong place. We idealize the past to make sense of our discontentment with the present. It seems to me that you've got it made in your time, Doctor. Maybe not so much the bit about the sharks coming out of whirlwinds, but the things you can do, the things you've shown me, I still cannot comprehend them. And yet, it seems, the future is as imperfect as the past. After all, how can creatures as flawed as us ever achieve perfection, that which is the province of God alone?"

Lucretia's gaze lilted to the soil, glowing with a heavenly luster around her feet—perfection, such that, as Eugene had been so achingly right about, would never exist in the world she'd left behind.

Easy does it. Sidney Daventry couldn't remember making such a gentle descent since...well, *ever.* Landing on an aircraft carrier was famously compared to a controlled crash; hitting the soft mud and glowing water here in that manner would surely result in an *actual* crash. He had to kiss the surface, a gentleman's buss upon a maiden's wrist, not thrust down upon it, in typical naval aviator's fashion, as if he'd meant to impregnate it.

At least he had an unobstructed path to the pond. The mountains loomed ahead but had tapered off into a wide, flat expanse. No trees grew here, only some of those strange plants with their rubbery tubular fronds, little more than tall, thick grasses.

Sid extended Willie Love's flaps all the way and increased the power. The Python turbine didn't spool up in a hurry, so, if the need should arise to accelerate quickly, better to simply raise the flaps and decrease drag, while already having the power he needed. He kept his left hand on the flap lever. For good measure, he decided to extend the tailhook used to grab the arrestor cables laid across the carrier's flight deck to snap the Wyvern to a halt. Surely, some of the surface material that Lucretia needed would cling to it, maybe even better than it clung to the wheels. He didn't know how much she needed, but, he figured, the more, the better.

He eased the throttle back a little as Willie Love sank lower, then nudged it ahead to slow his descent. *Kiss the surface,* he reminded himself, chuckling. There was a first time for everything.

The tailhook's thud as it struck the surface was slightly more noticeable than it usually was. *Soft surface,* Sid knew; the shaft was designed for the hard deck of an aircraft carrier and had probably caught some of the mud. Unfazed, Sid nudged the stick back a little, advancing the throttle. The pond was about five hundred feet ahead and closing quickly. *Almost there.*

The Wyvern jumped a little when the wheels struck the surface, surprising Sid; his descent had been shallow enough and the soil soft enough that there was no bounce. He nudged the nose forward slightly, just as the vastness of shimmering green passed beneath the cowling. Sid advanced the throttle. The Wyvern glided across the surface as if she were indeed waterskiing.

Sid exhaled, relaxing, only now realizing just how tightly he'd been clenching his cheeks.

But the relief was ephemeral.

Another jolt rippled through the cockpit, more pronounced this time. Without a thought, he raised the flaps.

Too late.

With a loud thud and a shudder that nearly ripped Sid out of his harness, Willie Love veered sharply to the left. Sid shoved the throttle forward even as the nose fell forward, green waves splashing across the windshield. He pulled back on the stick, and the Wyvern leaped out of the pond like a wounded fish desperately fleeing a charging shark. The whole aircraft juddered. He was about to stall.

This low, he was a goner for sure.

He shoved the control column forward, his view filled with those surreal swaying, glowing plants racing to meet him. The Wyvern rolled sharply to the left, and when Sid slammed the stick right, the aircraft was dreadfully slow to respond.

I'm dead.

With one last defiant heft, he pulled the stick into his chest, bracing against forces of gravity that were sure to overstress the airframe, but it was his only hope. Sid's head felt light. The plants' glow was a neon spiral in his waning view. His hands felt like boulders, his body a planet.

Willie Love pulled level just inches off the ground. Sid eased off the control column, attempting to put the aircraft into a shallow climb toward the mountain pass. But the Wyvern was still shaking like it was trying to rip itself apart, all the while rolling and veering leftward.

As the green liquid streaked off his canopy, Sid suddenly realized why: Willie Love's left wingtip had been sheared away, and the aileron was hanging by its cables, useless as nipples on a boar. The violent shaking, he feared, meant that the propeller blades had been damaged.

Willie Love was wounded, but she was still flyable, though Sid needed all the strength he had to keep her flying relatively straight and level. If he could get her down, then maybe something in that maintenance manual Faintary kept with his charts and clipboards could help them get her at least to a state where she could make it back through the squall. *I just have to get her back on the ground. I can do that.*

Such naïve hope. When he attempted to raise the landing

gear, there was a loud banging from under the left wing. Now he understood what had happened: the left main strut had struck something, and now it was bent. It would almost certainly collapse upon landing.

Willie Love wasn't going home.

And, Sid feared, neither was he.

CHAPTER X

THE RETURN FLIGHT had felt like a lifetime. Sid's hands hurt from working the control column, pushing hard to keep Willie Love flying as straight and level as he could, but never so hard as to roll the aircraft too far to the right, risking an unrecoverable downward spiral. Every turn was a herculean task, tap-dancing on the rudder pedals while making minuscule adjustments to the amount of pressure he placed on the stick.

All that with an aircraft that was shaking like a motorcar being driven over sharp rocks. Sweat poured down Sid's face, so much that his helmet felt like it was floating.

His arms were jelly, his hands catatonic as if made of lead. The adrenaline surging through his veins was the only thing keeping him conscious and alert. Still, he managed to hold Willie Love on course until the tree city came into view, and beyond it, the landing strip. He didn't bother with the landing checklist; with all the buffeting, he wouldn't have been able to read it anyway. At that moment, the only literature he wanted in his grasp was

Marie's prayer book. Because holy wrath was about to fall down on him, whether that of God or Gene Faintary.

He couldn't land on the strip. With such limited control, he might hit the other Wyverns or Lucretia's plane. At the very least, he'd crash in the middle of the makeshift runway, blocking it for the other aircraft and trapping everyone at the edge of the galaxy. There was only one thing to do: put down in the glowing grass beside the forest, and pray he didn't hit any trees.

He pulled his harness so tight that it was squeezing his chest and waist in preparation for what was certain to be the worst landing he'd ever make.

Reality had a tendency to whack Lucretia right in the heart, and every time, the blow came from a place most unexpected. She almost wanted to thank Eugene Faintary for the reminder as much as she cursed him for it. The world she had left behind, the one to which she'd soon have to reluctantly return, wasn't perfect, and probably never would be. And it didn't want to be.

She was lost in her thoughts for what seemed an eternity, and yet was jarred from them all too quickly by the distinct sound of tandem propellers chopping at the tranquility.

Eugene leaned forward, as if tuning his ear to the distant sound. His eyes squinted slightly to catch the first glimpse of the incoming Wyvern. His countenance betrayed little, though it seemed to Lucretia that he was concerned. Jim Wellington, who had been lounging against the wheel strut of the Wyvern marked 335, sprang to his feet. Something was wrong.

Lucretia heard it too. The timbre of the sound was different, ever so slightly—rougher than usual, rattling, like a household fan that had gotten tilted slightly off its shaft, causing the blades to buffet and slap the casing.

Something was wrong, indeed. As the Wyvern came into view, Lucretia could see that the left wing had been shortened, and that a piece—the aileron—was dangling from it, threatening to break away entirely. The left wheel assembly was tilted inward and backward at a sharp angle, and, as the aircraft drew closer, it was clear that the strut was bent, the tire shredded. *He skimmed the pond*, she knew.

And hated herself. *Sidney almost got killed because of me.*

"Goddamn it!" Eugene growled, and he shoved Lucretia out of his way as he stomped in the direction the Wyvern was going. Wellington followed at a brisk pace, wiping sweat from a face wrought with worry.

Sidney just missed the narrow open strip and was hurtling toward the forest. Lucretia covered her mouth, holding her breath as the Wyvern impacted the ground, the left wing slicing through the flora, leaving swirls of neon light in its wake like an Expressionist painter's brush slashing through perfectly arranged dots of dye. The propellers stopped as soon as the plane hit, the lower blades curling backward into the cowling. The plane was hurtling for the trees…

Lucretia exhaled as the Wyvern halted just before striking two of the behemoths. The canopy was already open, and, as she sped toward the wreck, she could see that Sidney was alive and conscious, though he was making no attempt to extricate himself from the cockpit. *Hurry up, Sidney!* She feared that the plane would explode at any moment.

But there was no blast, not even a puff of smoke. Not even the rockets, five of which had been ripped from the left wing and were now strewn across the wrecked ground, had detonated.

Jim Wellington was the first to reach the twisted ruin of an aircraft, having outrun Eugene. The young executive officer deftly unfastened Sidney's harness while he and the commander yanked the trembling pilot from the cockpit. Even with one arm over each of his colleagues' shoulders, Sidney nearly collapsed when they hefted him away from the plane, and would have had Lucretia not caught his chest. Together, they lowered Sidney, panting and drenched in sweat, to the ground.

Sidney's head seemed to protest turning to face his commander. "I'm sorry, sir—"

"Enough," Eugene said firmly. "Are you all right, Lieutenant?"

"Yes, sir. I think so, sir."

"Yes or no?"

Sidney stumbled to his feet, at last standing erect and sturdy, exhaling. "Yes, sir. Thank you, sir."

"Return to your quarters immediately," Eugene commanded.

"Yes, sir." Sidney saluted his commander, then beat a maladroitly brisk retreat to the tree mansion.

Wellington stepped forward. "Sir—"

One glower from Eugene cut him off.

"I'll see to Lieutenant Daventry, sir," Wellington said and scurried off after Sidney, catching up just as the Canadian was about to topple over.

Lucretia looked over the Wyvern, a thousand emotions surging through her body. Gratitude, both to Sidney for sticking his neck out to help her and to whatever god or good fortune had gotten him home. Shame, for asking others to do what she should have done herself. Relief, for there was indeed a wealth of material clinging to various parts of the aircraft from which she could take DNA samples, and even the spattered remains of a few of the anemone-like creatures glued to the right tire. Despair at the charred and twisted wreck, and guilt that it was her plea and her idea that had trashed the plane.

And, as the gelid gaze of Eugene Faintary fell upon her, fear.

"It would seem you've got what you sought, Doctor," the commander hissed. "I hope you're happy."

Lucretia turned contrite eyes on him. "Please, Eugene—"

"I've heard quite enough from you." He pivoted about with military precision and stormed off, leaving Lucretia alone with the reminder of her brash folly.

She sank to her knees, leaning her forehead on the side of the plane, exhaling. *This had damned well better not be for nothing*, she told herself as she stared at the gunk coating the Wyvern's wheels, wingtip, and extended tailhook, afraid to touch it for fear that it would be as toxic to her as it was to the Racosku's pollinators.

She hefted herself to her feet. There was nothing to gain from moping and cowering. *What's done is done.* She had what she needed; the uptight commander had no authority over what she did in the lab, or how she used her airplane. The situation wasn't ideal, but when was the last time she'd found herself in the perfect scenario? *It won't be for nothing. Come Hell or high water, I'm making this work. I'm making this right.*

CHAPTER XI

Sid had expected Commander Faintary to chew him to pieces, spit those pieces on the floor of their suite, and stomp them into formless mush. He was as ready for the reaming as he could be.

But there was no yelling, no finger-wagging. No tendons bulged from the commander's neck; no color marred his pale face. He paced back and forth before the door, hands behind his back, standing tall and stoic as ever. His gaze never left Sid, as if he knew exactly how many paces he could walk without tripping over a hammock or a folded flight suit. Those cold blue eyes were devoid of the wrath Sid had expected.

It was then that Sid realized that he hadn't just thumbed his nose at his orders. He had let his commander down, betrayed his trust. Indeed, it was not anger that festered behind Fanny's stolid façade but disappointment.

"Sir," Sid said, the words barely squeezing through his tightening throat, "it wasn't Lucretia's fault—"

"Of course it wasn't." Faintary spoke as plainly as if he were ordering lunch. He didn't raise his voice, and his tone betrayed nary a hit of emotion. "Dr. Tang was not the pilot in command of the aircraft that now lies damaged beyond repair in the forest, significantly depleting our chances of making it back to the ship alive. Nor was she holding a knife to the throat of the pilot who chose to violate a direct order, to operate his aircraft outside its approved flying envelope, to act recklessly and in a manner wholly unbecoming of an officer of Her Majesty's Royal Navy, exchange program or otherwise."

Sid shuffled his feet. "Yes, sir."

"I suppose you presumed you could wing-walk back to *Eagle*, like the old barnstormers of the Roaring Twenties. I can think of no other reason, particularly in the wake of your mishap upon our arrival, that would embolden you to operate your aircraft in so rash a manner."

Sid caught himself from chuckling at the image flashing through his mind, of him in a bowler hat and a silly mustache standing on a Wyvern's wing.

But there was no humor in Faintary's glower. "Do you have something you'd like to say, Lieutenant?" he demanded.

"No, sir." Sid squeezed his eyes shut. "I simply did what I judged to be right—"

"It isn't your duty to decide what's right!" Faintary bellowed. "Nor is it your choice—especially when your judgment is quite clearly compromised! The Fleet Air Arm is not the Lyceum, Lieutenant. You don't get paid to debate what's right and what's wrong. What's 'right' is what I say it is, and the 'right thing to do' for you is to carry out my orders without question. Do you understand?"

"Yes, sir."

Faintary exhaled, approaching Sid with ponderous steps. "Have you ever lost someone you love in combat, Lieutenant?" He spoke with such unguarded openness, almost vulnerability, of which Sid had hitherto seldom heard or sensed but a flicker.

Sid drew a deep breath, thinking back to five years before. His youngest brother, Henry, hadn't been in the Army more than a few months when his outfit was sent to fight in Korea. Henry had been gravely wounded at Kapyong; he'd pulled through, but the battle had changed him, broken him. Gone was the jovial boy who used to speed up and down the street on that rusty old Super Chief tricycle, the one with the red frame and yellow wheels, shouting and singing. Now, he was always looking over his shoulder, wincing at a pain that never left him. At twenty-nine, he was already an old man.

But Henry had survived, and every now and then, a little bit of the old Henry would break through that tormented, paranoid façade.

"No, sir," Sid admitted.

Faintary nodded. "Then there isn't a warning, lecture, or parable I can give you that'll make you understand. You're confined to quarters, Lieutenant. You will not leave except by my express permission or in the event of an emergency. You will have no further contact with Dr. Lucretia Tang. Is that understood?"

"But, sir—"

"Is that understood, Lieutenant?"

Sid exhaled, plunging into his hammock. *You did this to yourself, Sid.* He nodded to the commander. "Understood, sir."

Something about Tom Wickler had unnerved Lucretia from the moment she'd first laid eyes upon him. It wasn't anything overt; not the cockiness, not his liberal usage of racial epithets, not even the fact that her first encounter with the Scotsman had seen him aiming a six-shot revolver at her face. Those things could be explained away: he was a naval aviator, and arrogance came with the territory; he was a product of his time; he was afraid.

No, there was something in his eyes, something in his manner, that betrayed something sinister, some darkness festering deep within him. Even his squadron mates seemed to notice it; Eugene and Sidney in particular seemed wary, and even the carefree Jim Wellington seemed to be keeping his distance of late. The other men had been cool and collected, focused on their tasks; even Sidney had seemed to compartmentalize his first accident, carrying himself with the composure of an officer. Only Wickler was acting strangely; the only time he'd seemed remotely calm was when he was watching the movie. And Lucretia had left minutes into the screening; who knew how long that tranquility had endured?

Now, he was back to his fitful pacing beneath the trees, muttering under his breath, spitting on the ground, cursing Sidney for wrecking another plane, and Lucretia for—in the young lieutenant's words—"seducing" the Canadian. He made sure she could hear him from where she was standing on the ramp by the laboratory doorway, though he pretended to be talking to himself. He'd glance up at her, his piercing blue gaze gelid as the void of space, eyeing her the way a tiger would a wounded deer that had no chance of escape. The man was dynamite in disguise, and Lucretia feared lighting the fuse—or rather, that the fuse had already been lit, and it was just a matter of time before the spark reached the bomb.

Lucretia ducked into the sanctuary of the laboratory, suddenly shivering.

෯

"You weren't wrong when you compared these guys to sea anemones," Jeremiah said, transfixed by the readout on the projector wall. Brain had linked the microscope Lucretia had produced from her flight bag to the holoscreen and brought up the transliterated DNA sequence from the spattered remains Lucretia had scraped off the wrecked Wyvern's good tire, placing it next to the one it'd shown the humans earlier.

For her part, Lucretia was still astounded not only by the level of technological advancement the Racosku had achieved but by how well they understood, or at least were quickly able to make sense of, human tech. These weren't static documents and schematics she was looking at; these were functional data—the kind she could work with. The kind that could save the Racosku.

"The genome is remarkably similar," Jeremiah continued. Then, with a puerile chuckle, he added: "Of course, you know, sea anemones don't walk or come out of the water." He played back the video Sidney had captured on Lucretia's phone that confirmed that the blob she'd seen on the gun camera footage was indeed the creatures coming out of the water. "But the similarities are astounding—like, way more similar than humans are to chimpanzees."

Lucretia shot him a wink. "Are you able to see what might be causing the problem?"

As she spoke, she felt soft sensations pressing against her body. The Racosku—Noodles, Violet, Pinky, Ramen, and now three more—were huddled around her, peering over her shoulder in the way only faceless insectoid creatures could peer, clambering over one another to the point that poor Brain was getting boxed out, much the way a group of friends might huddle over too small a television set to watch the game on a Sunday night. *Of course they're invested,* she knew. The stakes for them were so much higher than a couple hundred bucks bet on fantasy football. Their species' very survival hung in the balance.

Jeremiah nodded, gesturing to a line of minuscule letters that Lucretia couldn't read over the noodly appendages slipping into her view. "Here's the only discrepancy I can find between the sample on file and the one taken from the plane."

"Are you sure that's from the anemone thingies? I mean, could it be foreign DNA that got into the sample, like, from a bug or something?"

"Not likely. This is similar to a mutation I've observed in marine invertebrates back on Earth. I'm guessing it's responsible for the increase in production of the toxin."

Lucretia thrust her hands into her hips. "Guessing?"

"Hypothesizing." Jeremiah pinched her cheek, winking as if to say *you know what I meant.* "The genetic expression is in line with what I'd expect to find. Although, I have to add the caveat: we're dealing with an alien species—alien to us, of course—and I'm biased toward the species back on Earth that I have studied." He swiped the screen, pulling up the readout from the sheen that had clung to the Wyvern's tattered wingtip, adjacent to the one the Racosku kept on file. "Look, there's the spike in the cytolytic protein—holy crap, it's through the roof. No wonder the bees are dying."

"I wonder what's causing it."

"Well, it's probably a defensive adaptation that just sort of went too far, and now the excess proteins are ending up in the goo, where they serve no purpose but to poison the bees. It's almost like when your stomach makes too much acid, you end up with heartburn. But in this case, they end up with toxic poop."

Lucretia peered at the small lettering, trying to resist the urge to bat Noodles' noodles out of her way. The defective nuclease sequence was small—a minor mutation, an easy fix. "So, I could easily knock it out with an RNP."

"What's that?" Jim Wellington asked from the corner, where Lucretia hadn't noticed him lingering. He had his service weapon holstered at his waist, which made her uneasy. "You keep talking in acronyms; I can't keep up with them all."

"Oh, a ribonucleoprotein; basically the Cas9 knockout

protein plus the guide RNA, which I should be able to engineer with what I've got, and in sufficient quantities. It's pretty much the simplest way to do it and minimizes the risk of off-target effects." Fairly certain she hadn't clarified the matter for the pilot one bit, she turned to her brother. "How certain are you that deleting this sequence will stop the excess protein production?"

Jeremiah scratched his beard, sending a flurry of dandruff flakes to the floor. "If these were sea anemones back on Earth, I'd say better than ninety percent. Ninety-nine, really, leaving a one-percent margin for human fallibility. Since we're dealing with an unfamiliar species, I'll be conservative and knock it down to eighty-five percent. But I'm confident this is it, Lu."

That's good enough for me. "Okay. But, if I do run this interference, what's that going to do in the big picture? I mean, that mutation had to have happened in response to some kind of predation, right?"

"I don't know, Lu," Jeremiah admitted. "You're the one who's always saying that nature doesn't have a conscious mind, and that mistake is part of the evolutionary process. Maybe this is just a mistake. Or, at the very least, nature massively overcompensating. The thing is, Lu, ecosystems are complex things; you mess with one variable, and it tends to have a ripple effect. Now, obviously, this mutation is causing a massive problem for the Racosku. But what happens if you knock out the mutation, the anemones stop producing the toxins, and whatever had been preying upon them comes back and hunts them to extinction because you've stripped them of their natural defenses, and there's no more goop for the pollinators to feed on, and the Racosku go extinct anyway?"

Lucretia bit her lip. She opened her mouth to speak, but no words came out.

Jeremiah continued: "The point I'm trying to make is that we've been here, what, a couple days? There are ecosystems back on Earth that we've been studying for centuries and don't fully understand. Listen, I'm not saying you shouldn't do it. I want to help as much as you do. What I'm saying is that there's way too much I don't know. Even with the data we do have, I don't have the means of modeling out all the possible outcomes."

God, how she hated when her brother was right. She glanced around the room: at the Racosku, their sublimely expressive featureless heads pointed at her as if expecting some concrete answer; at Jeremiah, sympathetic yet adamantly refusing to give her false hope; at Jim Wellington, standing there spellbound the way a man who'd been whisked away through space and time ought to be.

Lucretia exhaled. "Jay, I know this is as unscientific as it gets, but…give me your gut feeling."

Jeremiah pinched his face. "It would help if I knew what the predators they're defending against are."

"Could it be the birds?" Jim asked.

"Birds?"

"Aye, Moose said that, when he flew over, he saw some birds flying over the lake. Or something like birds, anyway."

Jeremiah shrugged. "Certainly could be. We have no documented evidence of birds feeding on sea anemones back on Earth—although I have heard of sea anemones eating seabird chicks that fell from their nests into the shallows—but, once again, we're not on Earth, and we're dealing with an entirely different species here, even if the genetic analysis doesn't show it. Did he say how many birds he saw?"

"Only a few."

"So, if the birds are the anemones' predators, then it stands to reason that the toxins are driving them away; otherwise, there'd be way more than 'a few.' It's not like any animal to pass up a banquet like there is when those guys come ashore."

There was a long silence. Jeremiah leaned against the raised black plateau next to the holoscreen, still as a sculpture, as if frozen in time, rendered catatonic by indecision. But Lucretia knew her brother. Behind that expressionless façade, the wheels of his brilliant mind were racing toward a solution.

At last, Jeremiah stood up straight, drawing a deep breath. "The mutation is causing an *excess* in toxin production," he said to no one in particular, his eyes floating around the ceiling, "not the production of the toxin itself." He locked eyes with Lucretia, and there was surety in his gaze. "So, if you were to knock out that sequence, it should still leave the anemones with a layer of defense, if my assumptions are correct. And, if the birds are the main source of the depredation, then the small numbers lingering over the lake would suggest that the majority have found an alternative food source. I'm not an ornithologist, but I wouldn't think they'd all suddenly come flocking back. I mean, it's not like there's a bird hotline that says 'Come and get it' or anything." He gave a sharp nod. "You should do it, Lu. I know there are a lot of 'ifs' and 'maybes' in there, but I'm confident that the benefits outweigh the risks."

Lucretia wanted to hug him, but, in that moment, it seemed…inappropriate. She *was* at work, after all. She sighed aloud. "All right, time to get this show on the road."

"Well," Jim said, "I'm right knackered. I'll leave you two to your work."

Good, Lucretia thought. *Take that blasted gun with you.*

"I reckon you must be knackered too, doll," Jim said to Lucretia. "Might do you some good to take a breather, get your head in order. Five minutes ain't gonna hurt you."

"He's right," Jeremiah added.

Lucretia and her brother gazed at each other for a moment, as if each were waiting for the other to blink. *I've never been good at staring contests.* "All right," she said, blinking. "Five minutes."

She followed her brother and the young airman down the ramp, the Racosku filing in behind them, thinking on how, if Eugene hadn't beaten her delusions about life in the old days out of her thick skull, then being called "doll" had done the trick.

⸙

Jim Wellington was sitting on a raised root, still fiddling with his revolver. Was he cleaning the pistol, or just showing it off? Lucretia had no idea; she hated firearms with every fiber of her being. They had no place in a civilized society. She wanted nothing more than to rip that hideous contraption from the young airman's hand and chuck it into oblivion.

She tried to ignore the executive officer but couldn't help glancing out the corner of her eye as he placed a bullet into the open cylinder, then turned the chamber to add another, then another and another. All the while, Tom Wickler was pacing back and forth by the ramp, glancing furtively at the weapon.

The Racosku seemed to know to give the revolver a wide berth—all but Noodles, who drew closer, probing at the barrel with its proboscis, spinning it around until it was pointed at Jim.

"Whoa, mate!" Jim yelped, holding up his hands as if he were the banker and Noodles the robber holding him up.

"Noodles!" Lucretia hissed, having none of the joviality. "You get away from that thing!"

Noodles turned to her, seemingly ashamed, and, at Violet's prodding, ambled away.

Put it away, you idiot, she wanted to yell at Jim Wellington. But would the young officer listen? He must have known that there was no use for the revolver here. There were no threats. What was he afraid of? The Racosku? The most docile creatures in any part of the universe? Had the kid watched too many American movies and fancied himself some kind of cowboy? Or was that just what military men did, having a wank with their trigger-equipped phallic symbols, even at the most inappropriate times?

As for the even younger man, Tom Wickler? The look in his eyes when they'd fallen upon the revolver was that of a virgin boy in a strip club. As far as Lucretia knew, Commander Faintary still had Wickler's service weapon in his possession. *Thank heavens.* Every time she looked at the Scotsman, she grew more disconcerted. Behind his arrogant façade lurked something more, something sinister; maybe it was the fear that he'd never get home, or maybe it was the darkness that resided within every person, the darkness that the conscious mind tried so hard to lock behind fortress walls. Whatever it was, its tentacles were slithering through the cracks in its prison, slithering free, morphing into a parasite latching onto the young man's mind, slowly consuming him, strangling all semblance of rationality.

Lucretia forced herself to ignore the airmen. She watched the Racosku for a while, wondering just how old they were, how long they lived on average, how they learned so much, if there were more Racosku out there in other parts of this surreal planet. They behaved like children sometimes, playful, innocent, yet behind those faceless façades lurked brilliance and wisdom. How much of that had they gleaned from random boxes passing through wormholes, or even perhaps through contact with humans in their past, and how much had they learned on their own? *So rich in knowledge*, she thought, *yet uncorrupted by it. Why can't humans be like that?*

She wondered what the Racosku were thinking about, how they perceived the strange and crude bipeds trespassing in their world. What were they feeling? Were the conversations she'd been having with Brain an accurate reflection of what the creature was thinking, or was it simply using its knowledge of human thought and human emotion to manipulate her? Were they afraid? Did they even have concepts of fear, hope, love? Or were they merely animals driven by the most primordial instincts—survival and procreation—who had evolved to find ingenious means to ensure their species' continuity?

Eugene Faintary's heavy footsteps plodding down the ramp jarred Lucretia from her thoughts. She turned to the commander, forcing a nervous smile.

"Lieutenant Daventry will not be joining us," Eugene said firmly. His declaration was directed at everyone, but his eyes were on Lucretia.

"I guess I got him in trouble," Lucretia mumbled, sitting down on another raised root that was quite soft to her backside.

"You did no such thing, ma'am," the commander affirmed. "You may have influenced him to disobey his orders, whether willingly or nay, but the decision was his and his alone. He understands that."

Lucretia nodded her head. "Well, uh, I got the stuff! What he did worked. So it wasn't all for nothing…"

Idiot! That's the last thing he wanted to hear. Eugene's curt nod affirmed her overdue suspicion.

"Don't know how much good it'll do you," Jim chimed in. "You wanted a bomb; I'm afraid we jettisoned ours over the Med."

"In violation of my orders," Eugene grumbled.

"You dropped yours too, Skipper."

"As the circumstances dictated, as I recall."

Jim turned back to Lucretia. "As I was saying, ma'am, all we've got left are rockets."

"Those could work." Lucretia was thinking aloud and, for a moment, forgot that Eugene Faintary was standing there. Only after the words left her mouth did she feel his gaze boring into her flesh. *Oh, what the hell,* she thought. *I'm already on his naughty list; might as well let it all out. Maybe he'll have a change of heart.* "If there were a way to remove the warheads, rewire them so that they'd explode over the lake—or, better yet, over the anemones when they're on shore. I have a reagent in my kit that I could coat the compounds with that would help the guide RNA penetrate the cell and find the locus."

"We won't be making alterations to our aircraft or their armaments," Eugene said. "I'm sorry, Dr. Tang, but our work here is done. Those remaining aircraft won't be flying until it's time for us to leave this place."

"I understand, sir. But I was thinking, maybe you could make a detour that way on your way back, fire off the rockets, and then head straight for the wormhole."

"I'm afraid that's not an option, Doctor. We need to conserve what fuel we have left, which leaves no latitude for deviating from our courses. We don't know how long those 'wormholes,' as you say, will remain open, though from our prior experience I estimate that it will not be long. We cannot idle airborne, either, as that will only burn more fuel, fuel we need to reach safety."

"Sir, if I may?" Jim ventured.

Eugene spun around. "Lieutenant."

Jim cleared his throat. "Sir, we've heard Lieutenant Daventry's testimony about the lessened fuel burn on the way to the target area."

"Yes, we have."

"Right. And I was also thinking: if we are indeed planning on flying back with two men to an aircraft, we're going to increase our aircraft's weight. By that logic, we may not even have enough fuel to reach the ship even if we do fly straight for the storm. Wouldn't it then be prudent to make for Port Said after exiting the cloud? After all, if Moose—correction, Lieutenant Daventry—is going to be sitting on my groin, it's going to be hell trying to land on the ship. And what are the chances that Daventry would survive the rigors of a carrier landing sitting that way? He's liable to go right through the windshield and into the props. My point is, sir, that if we are forced to divert to dry land, we will have more fuel than anticipated. It wouldn't hurt us to make a slight detour."

"The unconventional nature of our return is exactly why we won't be venturing off course, Mr. Wellington. We'd be performing intense maneuvers at low altitude, which would be strenuous enough with just one man in the cockpit. No, Lieutenant, we must make for the storm as directly as possible, then for our landing site—Port Said, as it must be—as directly as possible. And even this way, there is no guaranteeing anyone's safety; I'm making the best of a bad situation." Eugene turned to Lucretia. "Again, Doctor, I am sorry. But you've seen what can happen if we make rash decisions with our aircraft."

Lucretia nodded. "I get it, Commander, I really do." She drew a deep breath, glancing at the Racosku, playing some game by twisting the lower limbs of their proboscises together. "It just sucks, frankly. I'm so damned close! It just seems like these guys brought us here for a reason. They need our help—"

"Wait," Tom Wickler barked, his face twisted in terrified fury. "What did you just say? Did you say they *brought* us here?"

"No!" Lucretia gasped. "I mean, yeah, I said that, but I didn't mean it literally—"

"Shut up!" the young Scotsman shrieked. "I've had enough of your fancy talk!" He covered his face with his hands. "God! Good God! We're stuck here, and it ain't no bloody accident!"

Jim stood up, approaching the lad, leaving his revolver on the root. "Now, settle down, mate—"

"They did this to us, Wimpy!" the lad wailed, and Lucretia could see that he was nothing more than a terrified boy, that terror breeding a mindless anger. "They took us away! Now we'll never get home! I'll never kiss my Susannah ever again, never see my wee babe!"

Lucretia's heart went out to him, even as she trembled in fear of what might become of that anguish.

"It's all right, Hags," Jim said calmly, clasping Wickler's shoulders. "We're gonna get home, mate. In a couple hours, you'll be back on the ship, and we'll be headed back to Blighty, and you'll be kissing your pretty little missus in no time at all."

But Wickler was having none of it. "Don't you see, mate? We're doomed!" He thrust an inimical finger at the nearest Racosku, which happened to be Noodles. "*They* doomed us! Those Hell-spawned abominations! I'll kill them all!"

"We're not doomed, mate. Just calm down. You heard the commander. We're going home. It'll be all right."

"Bollocks!" Wickler turned manic eyes upon Eugene. "He lies! There's no way we're all fitting in those cockpits! Not after that stupid Canuck wrecked half our planes." He pointed frantically at the commander. "His stupidity got us here—"

"That's enough, Lieutenant!" Jim barked, straightening, and Lucretia marveled and trembled at the executive officer's sudden change in demeanor. "Commander Faintary is your superior officer. You *will* afford him the respect he deserves. Is that understood?"

"We're all gonna die," Wickler muttered.

"No, we're not. Now sit down."

But without a word, Wickler shoved Jim out of his way, lunging for the gun. Lucretia gasped.

"Whoa, mate! What the hell are you doing?" Jim tried to catch the frantic airman, but Wickler was too strong. The two of them scrambled for the weapon, wrestling on the ground, Jim gaining the upper hand, pinning Wickler down by his wrists.

But Wickler's eyes were those of a man possessed. He roared, an infernal sound as if belched out of the very pits of Hell, and head-butted Jim, knocking the executive officer off-balance. Then he landed a left hook straight to Jim's temple. Jim crumpled to the ground.

"Lieutenant!" Eugene bellowed, charging at Wickler. "Stand down right this moment—that's an order!"

But before Eugene could restrain him, Wickler was on his feet with the revolver raised before him. Lucretia screamed as the gun went off, a single shot impacting Eugene's chest right inside the shoulder. An inch lower, and it would have found his heart. The commander stumbled backwards, clutching his wound, gritting his teeth as he fell.

Then, Lucretia watched in horror as Tom Wickler turned the gun on the Racosku.

❧

Sid was pacing back and forth before the narrow passage in his quarters that led outside when he heard raised voices. That startled him; before now no sound from below had reached the chamber, which, in Sid's estimation, was the height of the tenth floor of the typical building back on Earth, as if all sounds from the floor were swept away by the songs of the trees.

But the voices were distinct, even if the words were not. He recognized the frantic nasal shouting of Tom Wickler.

Stay out of it, Sid. Whatever was going on down there, Fanny would handle it. Sid wasn't to leave; the commander had made that crystal clear. If he were to disobey yet *another* order...

Still, something wasn't right. Sid could feel it. He wasn't to leave his quarters, except by Fanny's leave—or in case of an emergency. Well, Tom Wickler losing his bloody marbles seemed to count as an emergency. Faintary would need all the help he could get to restrain the lad from doing something stupid.

Sid made for the passage but quickly halted, his eyes falling upon his service revolver, which sat atop his folded flight suit and uniform jacket. He'd nearly forgotten about the Webley, and to brandish the handgun among civilians would be a massive breach of protocol, but the hairs standing on his neck were pleading with him to take it.

And he did. *No harm taking precautions.*

He'd beg for forgiveness later.

His decision was swiftly vindicated, for he'd sped down only one spiral of the ramp when he heard the gunshot, followed by a man's cursing grunt, then another three in quick succession, these accompanied by the most heartrending inhuman shrieks he'd ever heard—and with them, a woman's screams.

When Sid reached the bottom of the ramp, Wickler was in a fury. Gene Faintary was wincing in pain, clutching his shoulder, stumbling over as he tried to clamber to his feet, his uniform stained a deep scarlet. Jim Wellington lay writhing on the ground, his nose and mouth bloodied badly.

And one of the kindly creatures that had welcomed them, the one Lucretia had named Noodles, lay motionless, the colors quickly waning from its graying body, yellow embers spilling from the wounds in its abdomen. A second, Violet, was shuddering and screeching, stumbling over its own lithe limbs as it tried to get up. The rest seemed bewildered, running this way and that, too naïve or stupid to run away. Wickler was pointing his gun at the reddish one, Brain, but the weapon only clicked. He was out of bullets.

Undeterred, Wickler charged at Brain, raising his weapon and bringing the butt down on the Racosku's head. The creature rubbed the hairs on its forelegs together, making a blood-curdling sound as it stumbled backwards. Wickler raised his hand for another blow, but Jeremiah caught him around the chest, dragging him away, attempting to kick his feet out from under him. Wickler beat himself free, striking Jeremiah's collar with a vicious blow, sending him crumpling to the ground. At that moment, Lucretia lunged at him, chopping at his wrist with the flat of her hand, sending the revolver spiraling across the ground. With eyes devoid of anything resembling humanity, Wickler growled, seizing Lucretia's throat with both hands, tackling her, bearing down on her with all his weight and strength. She clawed at his wrists, writhing, her face swelling and reddening, but he was too strong, too diabolically strong.

"Wickler!" Sid shouted, raising his weapon. "Let her go!"

"She's a demon!" he hissed. "She's in league with these devils! They brought us here! I heard it from her own wretched mouth!"

Sid caught a glimpse of Tom Wickler's eyes—no, not Tom Wickler's. That was not cocky young Hags crushing Lucretia's trachea. Brash and reckless as he could be, Tom Wickler would not murder innocent creatures or unarmed women. He would never have assaulted his fellow officer or attempted to kill his own commander. The madness had consumed him wholly.

"I'm not saying it again, Hags!" Sid bellowed, cocking the revolver, his finger kissing the trigger. *Don't make me do this.*

The creature that had once been Tom Wickler turned infernal eyes on Sid, baring his teeth. There was no recognition in those blue eyes, only anger and profound fear.

He released Lucretia and lunged at Sid, clawing at the weapon. They wrestled for a while. Wickler was stronger than Sid, but his strikes were too erratic to get a good hold on the gun. Sid managed to get him off-balance, punching him in the temple. Maybe the blow would jar him back to his senses.

But Wickler was beyond all sense. Even as Sid turned the

revolver on him, he clawed at it, at Sid's wrists, at his fingers, prying at his grip. Sid tried to yank the gun away.

And then, it went off.

He hadn't meant to fire it. He wasn't even sure if he'd been the one to squeeze the trigger. The shot's crack stabbed his ears like an ice pick.

Wickler's hands fell flaccid. Blood bubbled from his mouth as he slumped to the side, motionless. A red lake poured from his chest.

Sid stumbled to his feet, dropping the Webley at his feet. Dazed, trembling, he glanced around. Jim was fretting over Faintary. Jeremiah was back on his feet, his hand on Lucretia's shoulder as she wailed over Noodles' body.

None of it made sense in that moment. Not the confused stillness of the Racosku, not the sorrow and worry all around him, not even the blood on his hands. Why? What had happened?

He stared down at Tom Wickler's frozen face, into his mate's hollow eyes. There was no madness left in them, no rage or hate. Only fear, the fear of a young man trapped in a faraway place, torn away from everything he loved—the fear that he would never return to the place he called home.

And now, he wouldn't.

CHAPTER XII

METAMORPHOSIS. A CHANGE, a transfiguration, a new beginning.

In the eyes of the Racosku, there was no such thing as "death." Only the next stage, shedding the old skin that encased the spirit, breaking free from the precious ephemerality of time.

Lucretia watched with humid eyes as Brain, Pinky, Ramen, and a fourth Racosku carried the shell that had once contained Noodles' lifeforce to the edge of the forest. The yellow flecks that poured from the body flickered like fireflies amid the trees' somber requiem, settling onto the ground like a luminous snowfall. Then the little lights sank into the soil, and veins of gold spread out from the muddy bier, and the forest shone with renascent vigor.

And then did Lucretia come to understand that it was the energy that gave life to the Racosku that, when they shed their mortal forms, found its way back into the world, giving the flora its glimmer. It was the Racosku's gift to the world that nourished them. Noodles wasn't gone from that world, not really. On the contrary; Noodles was now part of that world. Just as Lucretia knew that, in time, she too would wither and die, and her corpse would decay and turn into nutrients that spread into the ground where she lay, nourishing new life, to live and to die and to live anew.

Did Noodles have a soul? Were the last moments of its life spent in anguish and fear? Was it still suffering, even separated from its body? Did the Racosku have gods they prayed to, or the promise of Paradise, through which they came to accept the finiteness of life and the finality of death? Did any of it matter?

Our bodies are made from the stuff of stars, someone very wise had once said to her, *stars not unlike our sun that died millions of years ago, driven by a deathless force birthed at the very dawn of the cosmos. Who is to say that we are not the suns that gave life to worlds now long extinguished?* Jeremiah's words had comforted her then, in her time of confusion and spiritual stasis, filling her with awe that she hadn't known since she was a child staring up at the heavens, and they brought that same warmth back to her soul now. Indeed, those kind, charmingly innocent creatures who had sheltered Lucretia were children of stardust as much as she and her brother, born of the phenomena that spread light and warmth throughout their galaxy. And now, Noodles was giving it all back, giving the gift of new life to the world that had nourished it. New births, new beginnings, all from a singular tragic, unjust end.

The circle of life. It was beautiful, if one viewed it from the right angle.

Yet, no matter how she looked at it, Lucretia couldn't see that beauty. Only the injustice, the unfairness of it all. She thought back to the first time she'd seen Noodles, how she'd been so needlessly afraid, for such was that most unfortunate of human wonts, to regard the unknown with fear and suspicion. She remembered Noodles' proboscis softly probing her, almost as if in wonder of its new discovery, and the single limb coiling around her neck, for it must have thought that was the proper way to embrace a human being.

Lucretia was watching from the ramp as more Racosku assembled around their fallen friend when a hand on her shoulder startled her.

"You all right?" Jeremiah asked.

Lucretia drew a deep, strained breath, only now taking notice of the pain lingering in her throat. She'd thought about rubbing some soil on it to heal the ache Tom Wickler's thumbs had left, but how could she, now that she knew that it was the stuff inside Noodles—its blood, essentially—that gave that soil its healing qualities? Could she soothe her pain on the death of the creature that had been so kind to her, so playful and silly—the creature she had come to love?

"I'm fine," she said instead. She blinked a tear from her eye. "How about you?"

"Tip-top. Head hurts a little, and my shoulder, but I'll live."

Lucretia smiled back at him. "This place seems a little darker now, doesn't it?"

"Nah, Lu, that's just your sorrow talking." Jeremiah's strong fingers sank into her shoulders and nape. His hands had a way of extracting all the negativity out of her body. "I don't think Noodles would've wanted to see you like this."

"I know," she whispered, exhaling. She turned around, forcing a smile. "You should get some rest, Jay. I'll be in the lab if you need me."

Back to work, she told herself. Back to science, her refuge. Even though the endeavor was more hopeless now than ever. Commander Faintary had been unyielding before being wounded; when had a close call with death ever softened a man's heart, especially a man like that?

She rubbed her throat, wincing at the tenderness. There were bruises, she knew. She'd gotten off easy. As she gazed out at the Racosku, watching them gather in mourning or in duty or in confusion or whatever went on behind their enigmatic façades, she knew that, very soon, they would all become like Noodles, pouring their life force into the soil, giving life and light to their world.

Light and life that would soon be extinguished forever.

⌁

The blood had seeped deep into Sidney Daventry's hands, as if it had marked him permanently. He sat in his hammock, staring down at the patterns of red, like deep stains, like amorphous tattoos, like curses put there by demons. His hands were still trembling. His teeth chattered. Tremors surged through his heart. Even amid the warm breeze wafting through the comfortable suite, he felt cold, a chill like the third of the three fell winters ere Ragnarök. He thanked God that there was no mirror, lest he see in it the face of ignominy—the face of a killer.

A firm hand on his back startled him, a jolt as if his soul had meant to flee the cage of corrupted flesh that imprisoned it.

"Whoa!" Jim Wellington yelped. "It's only me, mate."

Sid exhaled. "Sir." His voice was weak, stumbling over the anger and regret and loathing and fear churning in his gut.

"I just came to ask if there's anything I could get you."

Sid shook his head. After what must've been hours, he at last raised his eyes, glancing around the room. No sign of Gene Faintary. "The skipper?"

"He's up and about," Jim affirmed. "Looks like the same can't be said for you." The executive officer sat down, wrapping his lithe but powerful arm around Sid's shoulder. "I know you're hurting, mate. It's a terrible thing you had to do, but there was no other way. Hags lost his bloody mind, mate. There was nothing else for it."

Sid squeezed his eyes shut. "Somewhere in Scotland, there's a young woman eagerly awaiting her husband's return. She doesn't yet know that she's a widow. And in her belly, there's a little boy or a little girl who will never know their father."

He thought about the exuberance in Tom Wickler's eyes when he told the news—how, in that moment, all the arrogance and the rashness that had defined the young airman had disappeared, and there was hope in his eyes. There was only a man, terrified of the mandate that had been laid upon him.

Jim took Sid's hand, clasping it tightly between the two of his. "And, if you hadn't done what you did, there'd be a beautiful woman back in Canada who'd never see her loving husband again, and two wonderful girls forced to mourn their father. You're right, mate, it ain't right at all. It's not fair." Jim stood up. "Hags never told me Susannah was with child. Rachel and I will do what we can for her."

"Thank you, sir." Sid's eyes lilted to his profaned hands.

"Sid, you've got to pull yourself together," Jim ordered, clasping Sid's shoulders. "We've got to focus on getting home, mate. We've got lives to live, families to provide for."

"I hate killing the enemy," Sid confessed. "It's part of my duty, I know, but I take no pleasure in it. *Thou shalt not kill*, you know. But to kill my own mate?"

Jim placed a hand on Sid's shoulder, sympathetic yet firm. "You've got to stop crucifying yourself for sins that aren't yours, Daventry. If you're to blame for Hags' death, then I am too for being careless with my weapon, and the American for not minding her tongue, and the skipper for leading us into that storm, and God for bringing us to this place, filling the poor lad with the fear that he'd never get home. It's no use worrying about whose fault it is. Wickler is gone, and may God have mercy on his soul. But you're not gone, Sid. Not yet."

Sid looked into Jim's eyes, and it was as if he were hearing his father's voice from the lips of a man a year younger than his youngest brother. He smiled at the irony.

"Now get your arse out of that hammock," Wimpy commanded. "We're not licked yet."

Lucretia hadn't gone back to the lab, as she'd told Jeremiah she would. For one thing, she didn't feel welcome there anymore—not because of any actions of the Racosku, but out of her own guilt.

Instead, she followed the slow, somber procession, keeping far enough behind as not to announce her presence but close enough that she could see the remnant of Noodles lain upon a bier of lucent leaves. The two Racosku at the head of the march—Brain and Pinky—and those immediately behind them gripped the bier with their abdominal tentacles, while Ramen and another held the rear of it with their inside forelegs. Dozens of their companions, creatures that Lucretia had not yet seen, followed closely behind in perfect regiments, each one radiating rainbow colors that danced in the perpetual purple twilight.

But no color played upon Noodles' body, not anymore. All that was left of Lucretia's friend was a pallid husk, grayed, rubbery, stiff as stone.

At the riverbank, the Racosku set the bier on the ground, turning it to the side so that Noodles' body rolled off to the left. At first, the crassness that Lucretia perceived in the act made her wroth. But, as she watched the Racosku busying at the leaves, she began to understand. They were folding the bier into a funeral boat.

Reverently, they nudged the vessel into the water, and veins of silver shone from the leaves' warm red like rivers of heavenly light, their reflection dancing upon the gentle waves lapping against the sleek hull. Then, as two Racosku held the boat fast against the shore, the others took hold of Noodles' body, lifting it in their forearms with the care and respect of a steward handling the Crown Jewels. They gently placed the darkened exoskeleton in the center of the boat, and Lucretia climbed onto a raised root to observe the final preparations. Each of Noodles' abdominal limbs was stretched out, then neatly folded into an impeccable spiral with its end facing the center of the body. *The heart.* The forelegs were pulled out over the boat's gunwales, rising at a slight diagonal over the water like little wings.

With a slight extension of its forelegs, Brain nudged the boat into the river. As it sailed off whither the current would take it, the Racosku dropped to their abdomens, raising their bodies on their forelegs the way Lucretia had seen them do in the pollination footage. They rubbed the bristles together, all at once, and the calm purple sky filled with *racosku racosku racosku racosku racosku*, so many voices that it should have been a maddening cacophony, but somehow, each voice was unique, singing in perfect harmony with the others, and the sound romanced Lucretia's ears as if it were a concerto played expertly by a string quartet.

She watched the boat slowly moving away, thinking of the autumnal fog settling over the cypress bayous back in Texas. How she would paddle into the mist, losing herself in it, in the silence, losing sight of all but the flared trunks rising out of the water, the leaves of orange and russet hanging low and reflecting faintly in the still water, the Spanish moss hanging low over the lake like an arboreal gown. The one thing she missed about the world she'd left behind, the only comfort that would welcome her home. How she wished those moments would last a lifetime, and yet how all too quickly they faded, the mist yielding to the garish sun. They were as fleeting as life itself.

As the glowing boat grew small in the argent flow, the music ceased. The Racosku extended their proboscises, the upper tendrils glowing green, and from those lights little specks of green took flight, like Chinese lanterns gliding over the river, their glow reflected in the water, a spectacle more beautiful than anything Lucretia's eyes had ever beheld. She blinked and blinked again, but her eyes were glazed with grief. She thought of the first time she'd heard Noodles vocalize. She remembered it offering her the game of checkers, and knocking her pieces asunder. And her heart ached, and there was no magic in this sublime place that could take that pain away.

As the boat bearing the last physical vestiges of Noodles disappeared in a shower of shining green lanterns, Lucretia Tang fell to the ground, weeping.

CHAPTER XIII

LUCRETIA MUST HAVE been lost in anguish and reverie longer than she'd realized, for when she arrived at the laboratory, Brain was already there. Its movements were slower than before, as if every motion were weighed down by grief. But did the Racosku really grieve, or was Lucretia merely projecting her own experiences and biases onto them?

Maybe she had been projecting all this time. She felt like she'd been able to sense what the creatures were feeling, even when those thoughts and emotions did not take the form of holographic words. But now, she felt only confusion.

That must be what they're feeling. Confusion. The Racosku had seemed at peace with the finality of physical death; they didn't yearn for it any more than humans did, but neither did it seem that they clung to life. But the death of the body was not a tragedy, merely a transformation of matter and energy. Perhaps it was even a choice for them—if not in its inevitability or lack thereof, then in its time and manner. They had probably never conceived that death could be so violent. That must've been why they hadn't run away when Tom Wickler had begun firing the revolver. They didn't understand.

That was the real crime that the humans had brought to this place of prelapsarian perfection, more than the murder of sweet Noodles. Through the maddened fury of one man, perhaps aided by the follies and failures of others, Lucretia among them, this world had lost its innocence.

"Hey, Brain," she said softly. She couldn't bring herself to look at the creature amid the shame pulling on her heart like an anchor. "I just came to get my things."

By Lucretia's estimations, there were twelve hours left until the wormhole reappeared. Twelve hours in which she could only sit idly. Twelve hours until she had to abandon the Racosku's paradise for a world that had long since abandoned her.

"Bet you can't wait to get rid of us," she muttered without thinking.

Brain noodled the projector screen, and the words appeared on the far wall: YOU MUST NOT LEAVE.

Lucretia raised an eyebrow. "You're…keeping me here? Am I a prisoner?"

Hurriedly, Brain scrawled another message: THAT IS INCORRECT. FORGIVE ME, I MADE AN ERROR. YOU ARE NOT REQUIRED TO LEAVE. YOU ARE WELCOME TO STAY AS OUR GUEST. YOU ARE VERY AWESOME. THIS IS FACTUAL.

Lucretia couldn't help but chuckle, even amid that stubborn grief that weighed on her spirit. "No, Brain." The words formed upon her lips with reluctance. "We need to go home. We've brought enough of the ugliness of our world here."

Brain's limb encircled her wrist, as if to console her. YOU ARE MADE UNHAPPY BY THE ABSENCE OF THE SPECIMEN WHO HAS PREMATURELY METAMORPHOSED, the Racosku correctly deduced. YOU ARE NOT AT FAULT FOR THAT ABSENCE. WE WOULD LIKE YOU

TO BE HAPPY AGAIN, AS YOU WERE WHEN YOU ARRIVED HERE. YOU ARE MORE AWESOME WHEN YOU ARE HAPPY.

Even now, after all that's happened, they hold on to their innocence, their kindness. Lucretia sniffled. *Why can't humans be this understanding, this compassionate, this forgiving?*

Another text block materialized on the wall: THE SONOROUS AIRBORNE HUMAN BEINGS ARE ALSO WELCOME TO STAY AS OUR GUESTS, FOR THEY ARE ALSO VERY AWESOME. THIS IS ALSO FACTUAL.

Lucretia turned to the door, where Eugene Faintary was standing, a length of muddied leaf over his injured shoulder, which he seemed to be favoring. Her heart took wing when she saw him.

She drew Eugene's eyes to the writing on the wall. "That means you and your men, Commander."

Eugene offered a chivalrous bow to Brain, then implored Lucretia: "Please, relay to our most gracious host my sincerest thanks."

YOU ARE WELCOME, GREAT LEADER OF THE WINGED HUMANS.

Lucretia patted Brain's foreleg. "May the 'great leader' and I have a moment alone, please?"

Brain scurried away, and the words disappeared.

"How are you?" Lucretia asked.

"I've been worse," Eugene said, shrugging off her concern. "I believe I owe our hosts an apology—and you as well."

"It wasn't your fault. You didn't pull the trigger."

"No, but I was Lieutenant Wickler's commanding officer. I was responsible for his actions."

Lucretia shook her head. "You were his commander, Eugene. Not his father, not his puppet master, not his god. There was only so much you could do. I learned a long time ago that people are people, and no matter how hard you try to change them or control them, they're going to do what they're going to do. You can't hold yourself responsible for other people's mistakes, even if your rules say you are." She drew a deep breath. "Besides, it was what I said that set him off. Stupid!"

Eugene smiled. "Ma'am, I'm going to tell you exactly what you just told me." His eyes lilted to the floor, gazing blankly at nothing in particular, as if deep in thought. "What you said may have been the spark, but the fuel for the fire was already there. Lieutenant Wickler was…troubled. A good lad, but…fragile, perhaps. I wonder if I was too severe with him."

"Well, you aren't exactly delicate," Lucretia said with a smirk. "Although, in your profession, you probably shouldn't be. Besides, Jim and Sidney turned out okay, didn't they? I think you just have to do what you think is right. How other people respond to it is up to them."

"I wonder if that was truly Tom that shot me, that shot our hosts, or if he had indeed broken." Eugene stiffened, as if only now realizing that he was opening himself up more than was proper for a military commander. "And how is our injured host—I believe Violet was the name? That wound should be healing well, if mine is any indication."

Lucretia shook her head, her heart suddenly heavy again. "The others are with Violet now. I think it'll survive, but that wound won't ever heal." That was a guess, but Lucretia had seen that the Racosku wasn't healing. Violet would carry those scars until the end…until metamorphosis.

Eugene cocked his head a little. "But…the soil. It seems to have some sort of medicinal quality to it."

"It's because of the Racosku," Lucretia said. "All the light in the trees and plants, all the healing power in the earth, it comes from inside them. It's their gift to their world, a gift they don't receive for themselves." She squeezed her eyes shut, drawing a deep breath, exhaling slowly. "That's what I've just come to realize, sir. Without the Racosku, this whole ecosystem will darken, will wither away. And, sure, maybe something better will evolve to take its place; nature always finds a way, right? Even if that way is awful. But I can't imagine a world as brilliant as this one coming to pass after them. God, I'm afraid it'll become like ours."

Lucretia glanced furtively at the commander. Reading his face was like trying to read a book in the dark, without a flashlight, with only the slightest ambient light to illuminate the text. It was as if the rules and regulations he'd so rigorously adhered to had always existed in perfect harmony with his conscience, until this very moment, that moment when the voice in his head was screaming that following the rules wasn't right, even though ignoring those rules was, by its very nature, wrong. His eyes were those of a man who had hitherto seen the world in black and white discovering gray for the first time.

Eugene pursed his lips, then blew into his hands. "Tell me what you need," he said with gentle authority. His eyes met Lucretia's, and though she could read the fierce conflict behind them as clearly as if it were etched in stone, there was no vacillation in his gaze. "I'll give the order. I'm in no condition to fly yet myself, but I'll see to it that the chaps make it happen."

Mouth agape, Lucretia needed all the conscious thought she could muster to express her thoughts—her gratitude. "You… you mean that, sir?"

"Affirmative, Doctor. And the name is Eugene."

With joy she hadn't known since she was a child surging through her veins, she threw her arms around Eugene Faintary— drawing back as he winced when she pressed a little too tightly to his wound—and broke into tears.

She took a moment to compose herself, blinking her eyes dry. "I'm going to need those rockets."

Eugene nodded, then turned to the door. "Lieutenants!" he yelled.

In a flash, Sidney Daventry and Jim Wellington were in the lab, as if they'd been waiting outside, hoping against hope that their names would be called. Both men came to attention, standing straight and stoic and handsome.

"Lieutenant Wellington," Eugene began, "you've spent some time in the bowels of the ship shadowing the ordnance technicians."

"Yes, sir," Jim said.

"Then you are familiar with the procedure for unloading armament, removing and reinstalling the warheads, and replacing it on an aircraft's hardpoints?"

"Yes, sir."

"Very good. I want all munitions removed from Three-Three-Five and Eight-Zero-Three and brought to this facility within the hour."

"You can borrow Jeremiah," Lucretia said, girlish excitement and unblemished hope dancing upon her voice. "I'm older than him; I'm invoking my big-sister privilege to boss him around."

Sidney and Jim looked at each other, eyebrows raised, making bewildered faces. The poor dears, Lucretia thought; they must've thought the water was messing with their heads and they weren't hearing things right anymore.

"Gentlemen," Eugene said firmly. "You were given an order. Do you intend to carry it out, or shall I have you brought up on charges of insubordination?"

With a wide smile overtaking his comely face, blue light glimmering off his perfect teeth, Jim Wellington nodded, saluting even though they were inside. "As you command, sir!" Giggling like schoolboys at recess, the pilots slapped their hands together and ran out the door, making swiftly for the two remaining Wyverns.

Lucretia approached Eugene with tepid steps, daring to reach out and take his wrist. "I don't know how to thank you, Eugene. I know we owe it to these creatures—"

Eugene shook his head, and there was no doubt, no conflict in his beautiful blue eyes. Only stony resolution. "It's the right thing to do."

❧

Jim Wellington had certainly studied the ordnance boys well. Sid watched the executive officer removing the RP-3 rocket projectiles from WP335 with a mixture of awe and guilt, the latter for effectively standing around and doing nothing. He'd offered to assist, as had Jeremiah Tang and even Commander Faintary, but Jim had kindly informed them that he wasn't in need of their services, instead instructing Sid and Jeremiah to cradle the rockets as he removed them, lowering them gently so that they could be carried back to the lab. For his part, Fanny seemed equally miffed by his subordinates telling him that he was in no condition to be handling the weapons as he was by the realization that they were right. Sid couldn't help but pity the old man, who was still clawing at his wound, as if enraged by its stubborn refusal to obey his direct order to heal immediately.

The Wyverns each carried sixteen rockets, mounted in pairs—one atop the other, the lower protruding slightly ahead of the upper—on simple launcher racks attached to each of the eight small underwing stations, two to either side of the joints where the wings folded and the main hardpoints where there'd been bombs when they took off. Kneeling in the soft, soothing soil next to Jim, hands outstretched to collect the projectile, Sid ran through the math in his head. Short of some kind of miracle, there was no way they were getting all the rockets to the laboratory within the hour Fanny had allotted them. The walk from the lab to the beach took a good ten minutes either way, and that was at a quick pace. And a man could only carry one rocket at a time. Crews referred to the rockets as "sixty-pounders," but that was just the warhead; the whole assembly was just shy of a hundred pounds. Sid could carry the weight but knew that his arms would be on fire after the first three or four, and he'd have to walk slowly if he didn't want to risk dropping the projectile, potentially breaking his foot—or worse, somehow triggering the explosive. He didn't think the warheads would be *that* sensitive, but he wasn't in a hurry to find out. Jim could remove the warheads here on the beach; Lucretia Tang was going to have to take them off anyway to install whatever she was making in the lab. A forty-pound body would be easier and probably less cumbersome to carry, and Sid could walk at a normal pace. But the time it took to remove the warheads would negate the time saved in transit. Would there even be enough time to get them all to Lucretia? The hours were waning, and they had to make it through that vortex when it reappeared. They *had* to.

The realization set upon him that they might very well have been too late.

As Sid took the rocket in his arms and hefted himself up, he felt the futility writhing over his body like a fungus encasing a tree. The weight was distributed over a projectile longer than he was tall, difficult to balance. He had no cart, not even a wheelbarrow. And he had to carry it uphill over a dauntingly long distance, then up a steep ramp, careful not to catch the tip on any trees or knock anything over inside the lab. And he'd have to repeat the procedure thirty-one more times. Even if Jeremiah shouldered half the load, their muscles would turn to jelly long before the last projectile reached the lab.

And, if by God's good grace, they were able to haul every rocket the distance without keeling over, even with the two of them working together, the whole thing would take nearly seven hours. Just to get the rockets to the lab. Without a moment to rest. There'd be only five hours left, at most, to retrofit the warheads, carry them back to the planes, reload them, conduct the mission, and prepare for the journey home. The numbers simply didn't add up.

If only Fanny hadn't taken so damned long to come around. Sid understood why, of course. There was no point crying over spilled milk, he knew. At the same time, he knew just how Lucretia felt: the promise of success dangling before her eyes, tantalizingly close, yet just beyond her reach.

Every step was a labor. Sid's arms and back already ached. His legs groaned as if they were trying to raise up a mountain. He wasn't used to exerting himself this way. At this rate, he'd be lucky to get the first rocket to the laboratory without throwing out his back.

He hadn't taken five steps when a soft sensation on his arm—*around* his arm—drew his attention. He turned his head, and there was a Racosku, the one that wasn't pink but whom Lucretia had named Pinky nonetheless, standing with forelegs outstretched. The hairs on the creature's limbs rubbed together, and Sid smiled; the noise really did sound like *racosku*.

Sid stared at the creature for a short moment, marveling at its immense size and gentle grace. He couldn't comprehend the sounds it was making, of course, but it seemed to be saying, *Lay your burdens on me, for I can carry them.*

Either that, or it was having a laugh at Sid for being weak.

"Here you go, lad," Sid said, placing the rocket atop Pinky's forelegs. Pinky didn't budge or shrug at the weight. "Much obliged!" Sid said with a bow of his head.

"Cor, mate!" Jim exclaimed. "Why didn't we think of that before?"

"Yeah," Jeremiah said, "they're more than welcome to carry my load."

Sid smirked back at the man. Jeremiah clearly wasn't in any shape at all, much less the kind of shape a man needed to be in to transport a heavy, volatile object over a long distance, and Sid feared the poor fellow's heart would give out long before he reached the tree mansion. And that would be catastrophic in more ways than one.

As for the Racosku, of course they'd be willing to help in the labors that would lead to their salvation.

Pinky accepted another three rockets from Sid and probably could have taken four more but seemed to be having some trouble balancing the spindly, front-weighted projectiles without hands to grip them. No matter; the creature just extended its proboscis, the lower limbs coiling around the weapons, keeping them relatively steady, enough that they wouldn't fall to the wayside. Pinky sped away, shockingly quickly and smoothly on its tentacles. Another Racosku, whom Lucretia had given the name Ramen, quickly ambled forward, eager to collect the remaining rockets from WP335's right wing.

And there were plenty more of the creatures lining up behind it.

Lucretia, too, was thinking about time—or rather, the lack thereof—but right now, it wasn't her primary concern. What consumed her thoughts the most was how she was going to replace warheads designed to go boom and cause lots of carnage with something that could spread CRISPR compounds over a wide swathe of wetland in a manner that minimized any collateral damage, preferably avoiding said damage altogether. It was a bit like using a hairdryer as a paintbrush, but with the proper application of human ingenuity, she deemed it could be done.

Fortunately, she knew enough about air-to-ground rockets to know that they were wonderfully simple devices, consisting of little more than the warhead, a solid-fuel flight motor, and a long tube three inches in diameter with some fixed fins at the tail to keep it flying straight. No high-tech guidance systems, no fancy electronics or even gyros; in the profound and elegant parlance of the military man, a "dumb" weapon. It stood to reason, then, that taking it apart and putting it back together would be a straightforward affair. So easy a caveman could do it. She hoped.

After all, she really just needed to take the front end off. But what to put in its place? Could she remove the explosives from the warhead and fill the fattened casing with her gene bombs? She'd spent so much idle time going over the gene modification sequence that she'd barely given any thought to the delivery mechanism. Such things were hardly her area of expertise.

She was jarred from her thoughts by a rustling at her side. Violet was on the other side of the lab, prodding at the checkers game that Lucretia had played with Noodles, still on a shelf carved into the wall just out of the reach of its proboscis. The creature still couldn't move as well as it had but didn't appear to be suffering. For that, at least, Lucretia was thankful. She'd forgive it for being too damned lazy to get up and get the game down for itself.

"Maybe later, Vi," Lucretia said with a smile. "Kinda busy at the moment."

Just then, another Racosku—Pinky—appeared in the doorway, clumsily clutching four of the rockets with its proboscis, supporting them on its forelegs. Lucretia gasped, tendons flaring from her neck as her teeth gritted. The projectiles looked like they'd slide right off Pinky's legs at any moment—and she didn't want to think about what that would mean.

But the Racosku managed to finagle the projectiles deftly enough to dump them on the raised table. Not five minutes after Pinky dropped its load, Ramen sashayed in with four more rockets. Lucretia screwed up her face; never in her thirty-five years had she imagined herself in a highly advanced laboratory on an alien planet, surrounded by sapient noodly mantises, staring at a mountain of high-explosive aircraft armaments. With a box full of *Sharknado* movies somewhere behind her. Life was, indeed, full of surprises.

The raised platform was quickly filling with rockets, piled like sticks for a campfire, as more Racosku brought more projectiles. Grateful as she was, Lucretia was running out of workspace. She moved to pick up one of the rockets, nearly ripping her arms out of their sockets and throwing her back out. It was heavier than it looked, and she'd never been particularly strong. She grumbled out her frustration under her breath.

Sidney Daventry and Jim Wellington followed the last Racosku into the lab, each of them hefting a rocket over their left shoulder. The two pilots were huffing as if they'd just run three consecutive marathons, their faces glistening with sweat, and yet they were trying so damned hard to look tough, like their labors were a minor inconvenience. Lucretia chuckled to herself. A good thing it was that they'd had the Racosku to help out, or else they wouldn't have made it three trips.

"Aw," Lucretia said in as saccharine a tone as she could muster, "look at you big strong boys!" She was certain that the men had carried the rockets all that way, rather than handing them off to the last Racosku, just to impress her. She saw no harm in indulging their delusions. "Hercules would be green with envy."

Jim wheezed as he laid down his rocket. "It was supposed to

be your brother carrying this one. I did my part taking them off the planes."

I'll bet he didn't make it twenty steps. "That's my Jay. Hey, would you mind doing me one little favor? Just help me put these into a line so they're not piled up like a bunch of deadwood. It'll make it so much easier to work with them."

Jim gave the most debonair bow he could in his winded state. "We'd be delighted, ma'am."

She smiled at the young executive officer. "So, uh...*Wimpy*? What's up with that?"

"Ah, just a bit of fun; nothing meant by it. Anyway, seeing as you know so much about aeroplanes, I'm right gobsmacked you don't get the reference."

"Right, because your last name is Wellington, and there was a bomber called the Vickers Wellington that was also nicknamed the 'Wimpy.' That's a pretty insulting nickname, if you ask me."

"Aye, can't say I know the tale behind it." Jim smiled, flexing his biceps before lifting the first rocket from the stash, he and Sidney, placing it neatly next to the ones they'd just delivered. "But don't be fooled, doll. There ain't nothing wimpy about a Wellington."

She shot him a puerile smirk. "We are still talking about the plane, right?"

Jim winked back at her, peacocking about like a high school jock...or like the stereotypical flyboy from the movies. Lucretia rolled her eyes. *Kids.*

Sidney, for his part, seemed to share her sentiments. But there was something else in the way he looked at his colleague, and at Lucretia, that irritated her. Behind his carefree laugh, his face was reddening. Was he envious that she was talking to Jim, and not him? No, that couldn't have been it. He was much too old, much too mature for pubescent jealousy. If anything, he was probably just embarrassed at his mate making a fool of himself.

And…why was that the first thought that entered Lucretia's mind? *For heaven's sake, woman, stop being a damned child.*

She shifted her attention to the rockets, which the two lieutenants were now well into the process of arranging before her, the warheads facing her direction. That probably should've made her afraid—having enough firepower to take out a column of vehicles or a battalion of troops aimed at her body—or at least given her pause, but that thought hadn't registered. She was becoming far too acclimated to being in the vicinity of destructive objects.

"Is it hard to get the warheads off?" she asked, not directing the question at either of the pilots in particular.

"Nay, doll, it's a piece of cake," Jim said. "The tips are interchangeable. The same body can house either these sixty-pound heads or twenty-fives."

Lucretia nodded. "James, a favor, please? Don't call me 'doll.' That's not cool where I come from…*when* I come from."

Jim's face flushed red even as his mien suggested that he couldn't comprehend why a woman wouldn't appreciate being likened to a child's toy, an inanimate object. "Sorry, ma'am."

"What will you do with the warheads?" Sidney asked quickly, seemingly more to give his mate an escape than out of genuine interest.

Lucretia scratched her lip. "I'm not sure yet. These things detonate on impact, right?"

Sidney nodded. "These have nondelayed base fuses. They're not designed for deep penetration."

Lucretia pinched her face, needing every ounce of adult restraint she could muster to keep from making a juvenile dick joke. "You wouldn't know a way to modify them so that they exploded in the air, would you?"

"I could try, if I had the tools," Jim offered. "I know a mite about rigging explosives; used to blast wells on the farm with my dad when I was a lad. Although I've got to say, this would be a first for me, and I can't make any promises." He jerked his head at the Racosku, now gathering around Violet. "Don't think the lads would appreciate me blowing up their home if I mucked something up."

"Yeah," Lucretia said, "and I would strongly prefer if you didn't blow *me* up."

She pondered a moment while Sidney and Jim began the simple yet strenuous process of unscrewing the warheads. Even if Jim could rig the refitted tips to detonate over the beach, the explosion would shower the anemones with as much hot metal shrapnel as modified DNA. And how much of the compounds would burn up in the blast? No, the rockets were weapons of war, and trying to use them as they were intended wasn't going to work. She'd end up killing more of the goo-poopers than she saved.

Sometimes, a thought struck her as if a little fairy were flying around inside her head, giving her a swift kick to the brain. This was one of those moments, or so she hoped. She thought back to Noodles' funeral, and how the Racosku had folded the leaves into a boat. Those leaves must've been quite strong, and were perfectly pliable. Strong and pliable enough to fashion into an aerodynamic casing—one whose fragments wouldn't slice the poor anemone thingies into smithereens when it rained down upon them.

But what about the superfluous warheads? They couldn't just leave them there for a curious Racosku to potentially blow itself up. Nor did she like the idea of burying them, or throwing them in the river, or simply discarding them at the periphery of the forest. Who knew what kind of environmental damage the explosives could cause if they leaked out, or the casings rusted, or they somehow got triggered and detonated?

Worry about that later, she told herself. She'd have time to think about that once the Wyverns were airborne with the modified rockets. Right now, she had to figure out how to get her hands on some of those leaves, and find a way to get the heads to fragment in the right place. There was still the matter of the rocket bodies, which would end up littering the area around the lake, but those would be harmless once the cordite propellant was burned through, and she figured the Racosku were resourceful creatures, and could worry about those once their species' continuity was secured. She hated leaving her mess in their laps, but time was of the essence.

"Thing is, d…ah, *ma'am*," Jim stammered, "I *don't* have the tools. Unless the locust chaps have some electrical wiring and a capacitor lying around, I'm afraid I can't make you a detonator."

Locust chaps? Really? "I actually wouldn't need it to explode," Lucretia said, speaking almost in parallel with the thoughts coming to her. "In fact, I'd rather it didn't. I just need to puncture the skin I'm going to make, enough that the compounds will just sort of spill out over the beach."

"Could you use the fuses from these heads?" Sidney asked, slapping one of the disembodied warheads, causing Lucretia to squeeze her eyes shut like a character in a movie in that split second where he foresaw the impending blast that would kill him. She was sure the weapons weren't so sensitive that they'd go off at the slightest touch, but she really wished that these intrepid naval aviators wouldn't display such a cavalier attitude when dealing with volatile objects.

"Maybe," Jim said. He turned to Lucretia. "What kind of material are you using to make the new heads?"

"I'm not a hundred percent sure," Lucretia admitted. "But it's not metal; it's some kind of organic material. My guess is that it's about the thickness and texture of the stuff they make mail crates out of."

Of course, the postal services of Planet Earth probably used something entirely different in 1956, but Jim seemed to get the gist. He nodded. "The action of the firing pin ought to be able to punch through that. Only problem is, like Moose told you, these things are designed to blow on impact. Sounds to me like you don't quite fancy us shooting our rockets directly into the mass of tentacled critters."

Lucretia exhaled. "No, I really don't. I'm trying to save the little fellows, not crush them. Besides, I want to disperse the compounds as much as I can, and they'll spread farther from above."

"There's got to be a way to wire it to fire before impact," Sidney mused, though nothing in his tone suggested that he believed that, or that he was doing anything besides trying to placate Lucretia.

"Sure," Jim said, "if I had some electrical wiring."

"What about the rockets from Eight-Niner-One? You could use the firing wires."

Jim's eyes flashed as if a lightbulb had just illuminated in his brain. "The ones under the left wing will be a bugger to get at. Besides, you think the skipper would let us mess with those?"

"Why wouldn't he?" Sidney flashed a rebellious grin. "Jim, Willie Love isn't going anywhere. Unless we're planning a second mission, we can't use those rockets, and who knows if they're even functional after the crash?"

Jim nodded. "I don't have the means to rig a delayed fuse. The firing pin would activate as soon as the flight motor ignited."

"So, we launch them over the target area," Sidney said. "Use glide-bombing tactics, compensating for the different trajectory of the…compounds, is it? That way, we're firing the rockets away from the animals."

And pray they don't end up hitting some other wildlife we haven't seen yet. "That would be perfect," Lucretia said. "Are you sure you can do it—safely, I mean? It's no good if you end up, you know, dead, or missing limbs."

Jim shot her a haughty wink. "I assure you, Dr. Tang, I've got this." He gestured to the warheads. "I should probably take these outside, though."

"Just the heads. I need the bodies." Lucretia chuckled under her breath, barely able to contain her excitement. *I need the bodies? Good God, I really do sound like a mad scientist!*

That excitement soon dampened once Brain slid into the room, as she could read in the creature's faceless mien that something was wrong.

CHAPTER XIV

THE SKIPPER'S SHIP was in worse shape than Sid had remembered. She still resembled a Westland Wyvern, to be sure…from the right side, anyway. From the left, she looked like a Westland Wyvern that had been roasted and mauled by an actual wyvern. The spinner had been sheared off its bolts and was leaning slightly to the right, the forward set of propeller blades twisted around the second four. The dangling aileron had been ripped away and was now a full three hundred feet behind the wing, bent as if by a lathe.

Also lying on the ground behind WL891 were five of the eight rockets that'd been under the port wing; the only ones remaining were the two mounted on the inmost rack and the one on the top rack next to them. The rest had been ripped away in the crash, and Sid was still gobsmacked that not one of them had detonated. *Something in the soil around here…*

The three rockets still mounted to the left wing were nearly buried, their firing wires blocked by the Youngman flaps, preventing Wimpy from getting to them. But Sid figured thirteen should've been plenty. Jim's insouciant demeanor seemed to confirm that.

Once again, Sid felt perfectly useless, standing by and watching Jim working the wires loose with his pocketknife. Jim had courteously declined his offer to help. He had to content himself with holding the detached wires while Wimpy cut the rest free. The short wires didn't seem like they'd be nearly long enough to reach the front of the projectile to activate the firing pin, and they'd be three wires short. The thought of diving after Triple-Eight and snatching the rockets from its wings had crossed Sid's mind, vanishing like a motorbike that'd blown through an intersection at top speed. Even if he could remember where he'd ditched, there was no way he was going back in that water, or letting anyone else.

No matter. Jim knew what he was doing. He'd always been a resourceful bloke, that Jim Wellington. That had been made abundantly clear when Sid had visited his home, and the first thing Jim had shown him—aside from Rachel and little Oliver, of course—was the workshop he'd made from an old woodshed, full of all sorts of electrical contrivances.

"So," Jim said as he wrenched the fifth wire free, "what'd you think of her?"

Startled and blindsided by the question, Sid only muttered a few wordless sounds. *Why is he asking that? What does he think is going on between us?*

"She's…charming, I suppose," Sid said at last. "In her own way, I mean. Very strange. The way she talks, I mean; the way she behaves. It's very charming, of course, just…very unusual. I'm certainly fond of Lucretia. She fascinates me. She's…not like any woman I've ever met. Though I suppose they're all like that in her time, eh?"

Jim turned to him, screwing up his face. "I meant the

aeroplane, mate." He gazed longingly at the twisted remnant of WL891. "I'd always wanted to get my hands on her, all new and shiny, like. Before you went and ruined her, that is."

Sid turned away to hide the blushing he felt burning in his cheeks. "She's no different than any Wyvern, Jim. Cockpit's a little cleaner, maybe, and she flew quite splendidly, though I reckon that was to do with this place and not the machine."

With a carefree chuckle, Jim turned his focus back to his work. He snipped the sixth wire, then the seventh, then the eighth.

"She fancies you, you know," Jim said amid cutting the ninth.

Sid raised an eyebrow. "Willie Love?"

"No, *she* hates you, and I don't blame her after what you've gone and done to the poor girl." Jim stood up, looking hard into Sid's eyes. "I'm right, mate, and you know it. You're blind as a bloody bat if you've not seen it in the way she looks at you."

Could he be right? Sid had suspected something at first, an infatuation, though he'd convinced himself that was just his vanity run amok. And maybe she had, for a moment, though by now the varnish had worn off.

No, he knew exactly what it was. It was the same thing he felt.

"I don't think it was ever *me* she fancied," Sid said. "It was a hero, an archetype, a figment of her imagination. After all, she's a dreamer."

He smiled as he reminisced on Lucretia talking about Chao-Xing, the little pink-haired sprite she'd dreamed of becoming, and how, in that moment, as she stared off into the purple majesty of the everlasting twilight, she had almost morphed into Chao-Xing. She had nearly become one with her dreams, only pulling herself back at the last second. *Alas.*

"You want to know what I think of her?" Sid mused. "I think I'm being shown a glimpse of a future I won't live to see. And I don't know what to think about that. That future seems so incredible: those 'phones,' the aircraft—superb! I'm not so sure about the music, all that hollering and cussing; maybe the tunes Lucretia likes are more pleasant, though I wouldn't bet on it."

"Ah," Jim said nonchalantly, "look on the bright side. At least you won't live to see the sharks coming out of tornadoes."

Sid had to laugh. "Thank God!"

Jim laid a hand on Sid's shoulder, and his tone was suddenly serious. "I wouldn't fret too much about not living to see that future, Moose. Look at the lady and her brother. All that fancy stuff they have, all the mind-bending things they can do, and do they seem happy? I should say not, mate. Their smiles are like garments, worn on special occasions to keep up appearances, then tossed in the wash bin with everything else. You said she fancied the hero she saw in you; I reckon that's because they don't have heroes anymore where she's from. Bloody shame, that."

Sid nodded somberly. "When we go back to Earth, I'll be separated from her—not by distance but by time." He drew a deep breath, blinking the moisture from his eyes. "By the time she's born, I'll be an old man. I'll have hung up my wings long before she ever learns to fly. When she's Rhiannon's age, I'll be sitting there decrepit, whether on my porch or in a hospital bed, staring at the setting sun, waiting for its last rays to illuminate my name etched in granite. When she reaches Emily's age, I'll be frail and forgetful, yearning for that sun to set at last. And when she grows into the woman she is today, I'll be nothing more than a memory. Will she remember me? Or will all this pass like a moment in time—a moment that never truly existed?" His voice creaked as he wiped his eyes. "That...I don't know why, Jim, but that hurts."

Jim clasped Sid's shoulders. Nary a word passed between the men, but the silence was its own comfort, its own counsel. Would he remember Lucretia and Jeremiah when he returned home, longing for the fleeting friendship they'd had, that they could never have again? Or would the magic of this world wash away that memory?

Either way, he knew, he couldn't dwell on it, lest it distract him from his duties. He had a family that needed him, that he needed to get back to.

And right now, he had a job to do. Jim handed him the last of the wires, then knelt beside WL891's left rear fuselage, just behind the wing's trailing edge, and opened a small door, barely big enough for a man to stick his head through. The tailwheel had propped the empennage up just enough for Jim to open the door all the way, giving him clear access.

"What are you doing?" Sid asked.

Jim shot him a cocksure wink. "Getting more wiring, mate. You think this little bit is gonna do the trick?"

Sid chuckled. There was the Jim Wellington he knew. *He loves the old girl so much he's willing to cannibalize her for parts. I'm glad he doesn't love me that way.*

They didn't have twelve hours to spare, or even eleven hours. According to Brain's calculations, they had eight hours left until the alien bees returned to their breeding grounds. Which, for all intents and purposes, meant Lucretia had four hours to engineer the compounds and retrofit the rockets. The nucleases had to be released well before the pollinators settled over the lake, to give them time to take effect. The flight to the breeding ground took a little under an hour, and, with so much having already gone wrong, Lucretia wanted to make damned sure they'd left a margin for error.

Suddenly, she was under the gun. *But fortunately, not literally this time.* She shuddered at the thought.

She opened her travel pack, the one so big and bulky that it barely fit in the Velis's tiny cabin, and placed her portable clean bench on the raised surface beside the holographic projectors. The device, the size of a household microwave oven, was essentially a CRISPR lab that fit in her backpack, and she'd rigged it up so that the electron microscope was already installed. Beneath the polypropylene hood was a small opening, shielded by flexible static-dissipative PVC laminae, about four inches high and three-quarters the width of the workstation; Lucretia would have preferred a little more freedom of movement, but she'd gotten quite adept at manipulating her instruments through the limited space.

She donned a white lab coat and a set of latex gloves, prepared an N95 mask fitted to a respirator and safety goggles, tucking her smooth black hair under a hairnet, then opened the armored case containing the *E. coli* samples from which she'd extract the Cas proteins. She chortled to herself; most people would run like hell from such a thing. *Scientists really are a different breed, aren't we?*

Jeremiah was across the room, playing checkers with Violet, every now and then glancing at Lucretia, winking slyly as if to say, "Better you than me." *At least he's enjoying his vacation.* Although, in fairness, there wasn't much Jeremiah could do at this stage.

"You're losing, you know," Lucretia japed.

"Yeah," Jeremiah said with a shrug. "I'm trying to give Violet a confidence boost. Poor fellow could use it, after all."

Lucretia snickered. "You're such a gentleman, Jay."

"Shut up and get back to work."

With a roll of her eyes and a middle finger to her brother, Lucretia turned to Brain, watching her from beside the doorway. She had everything she needed except the leaves to make the casings.

"Hey, Brain," she called out, "come over here. I need your help."

The Racosku approached more tepidly than usual, and Lucretia wondered if it sensed that the bacteria samples were dangerous.

"It's all right," she said. "This stuff won't hurt you. The filter will prevent it from getting out."

Still, Brain was slow to approach. It extended its proboscis, the lower limbs reaching not for the workstation but for Lucretia's hairnet, prodding at it, carefully at first but then more forcefully, as if to save her from whatever strange growth was consuming her head.

Lucretia burst into laughter. "No, Brain, it's okay, really! It's just a hat." She took it off. "See? My hair's all still there." She placed the cap back on, cursing herself for having so much hair to have to finagle. "I can't let any stray hairs get into the samples. Plus, it gets in my face when I'm working and annoys me."

Brain's proboscis retracted, though the creature still appeared quite flummoxed.

"I need those leaves you made the funeral boat out of," Lucretia said. "Could you bring me some of those?"

The creature just stared at her, in the way that only a creature without anything a human could descry as facial features could stare.

Lucretia squeezed her eyes shut, realizing how insensitive she'd been. After all, that wasn't just a boat they'd sent downriver. She embraced Brain's foreleg. "When you sent Noodles—the specimen who metamorphosed—down the river, you fashioned some leaves into the vessel that carried the body away. I was thinking that I could use those to carry my compounds, if that's all right with you."

Brain fumbled at the screen, and there was a distinct melancholy in the way its limbs roved over the screen.

THESE MATERIALS CANNOT BE PROFFERED TO YOU, the translation read. THEY ARE SACRED GIFTS GIVEN TO US TO HONOR THE REMNANTS OF THE METAMORPHOSED. THEY MUST NOT BE USED FOR ANY OTHER PURPOSE.

Lucretia grumbled under her breath. *Now they decide to get religious on me?* "Brain, I need those leaves! I need something that I can shape that'll be strong enough to endure the forces of flight; anything I've got in my bag is either too flimsy or too rigid."

YOU MUST FIND ANOTHER WAY. THESE GIFTS CANNOT BE GIVEN AWAY. THIS IS FACTUAL.

"Brain, I'm trying to save you! Is it more important that you cling to your stupid superstitions than *survive?*"

The next words to appear wrought Lucretia's heart: OUR LIVES ARE FEW AMONG MANY. WHY SHOULD OURS BE MORE VALUABLE THAN OTHERS'? IF WE ABANDON THE TRADITIONS OF OUR FOREBEARS AND USE THE GIFTS OF OTHER LIVES FOR OUR OWN BENEFIT, THEN WE WILL HAVE ABUSED THOSE GIFTS.

Lucretia exhaled. "Brain, don't you understand? Without you, there is no life in this world. Without you, the beings that grow those leaves die. Are you willing to sacrifice them and all the life in this world just for your outdated traditions? This isn't just about you!"

WHY ARE YOU BEING UNKIND?

"Because you're being obstinate! If you aren't going to let me help you, then why did you bring me here?" Suddenly, Lucretia's veins were electric with rage, her face wrought into a glower. "You *did* bring us here, didn't you? It was no accident that we got sucked through that wormhole."

Brain backed away. YOUR ARRIVAL HERE WAS AT RANDOM. THIS IS FACTUAL.

"Oh, yes, the two people with the knowledge and skills to help you. I suppose that it's just a coincidence that you knew who we were, had our credentials in your files. After all, the internet access here is just stellar!"

THAT INFORMATION WAS FOUND IN THE DEVICE ON YOUR PERSON. IT WAS LINKED TO OUR DATABASE UPON YOUR ENTRY TO THIS LABORATORY.

"Oh, sure it was—"

"Lu!" Jeremiah shouted. "Listen to yourself, damn it. You're losing your grip. Remember what happened to Tom when he lost his shit?"

Lucretia gasped. She opened her mouth, but no words came out.

Jeremiah approached softly. "Let me handle this, okay?"

She nodded contritely.

Jeremiah turned to Brain. "I understand how you feel. Back on Earth, we have things that we revere, too. Sometimes, I think we revere them a little too much. But, whether because the stories about their power or their sanctity have been passed down to us for generations, or simply because we want to believe in them, they take on lives of their own. And we want them to, because they represent something that's bigger than us, something we want to believe in.

"Thing is, there *is* something bigger than us, bigger than us all. It's called 'love.' That's why Lu and I want to help you guys, Brain. Look, I know all about tradition. We grew up in a very traditional family. And, yeah, Lu and I, being scientists, we want to push ahead, make new discoveries, fix what's broken… change the world. Tradition tends to feel like an anchor. Thing is, though, anchors exist for a reason. I believe that wisdom is in knowing when to drop anchor and when to weigh it. I think this is one of those moments when you raise the anchor and let the winds take you forward."

Lucretia blinked the moisture from her eyes. God, how

she loved when Jay talked like that…how proud she was to be his sister.

Brain stared at Jeremiah for a moment, then turned to Lucretia.

"I'd only need one or two leaves," she promised.

The reddish Racosku glanced around the room, to Violet, to Pinky and the others. They rubbed the hairs on their forelegs, first one creature at a time, then in harmony. In agreement. Slowly, Brain's proboscis prodded at the screen.

YOU SHALL HAVE WHAT YOU REQUIRE. WE ARE GRATEFUL FOR YOUR EXPLANATION AND YOUR HELP. AND YOUR LOVE.

Brain and the others save Violet disappeared to collect the gifts, leaving Lucretia alone with Jeremiah.

"Thank you, Jay," she said with the deepest sincerity. "I couldn't do it without you. Any of it. You know I mean that. You're the best, Jay."

Jeremiah gave a warm laugh, nudging her shoulder. "Hey, every superhero needs a sidekick, right?"

"You know, you're only the sidekick because I'm older," she said with a wink.

"Well, I am taller than you, and way heavier, so, I mean, in terms of balance and general aesthetic, you'd look way better as the sidekick."

Lucretia shook her head. "Get back to your game, you dork!"

Jeremiah began backing away, chuckling, but halted. "I just thought of something." He tiptoed to one of the rockets, running his thumb over the open end where the warhead had been removed. "Once you've made your casings, how are you going to attach them to the rockets?"

"Oh, I'm way ahead of you there, Jay. As it turns out, I'm in possession of the most versatile creation the human mind has ever conjured up. Behold the cure for all faults, the solution to every problem that ever needed fixing." She reached into her bag, quickly finding that most advanced and prestigious of scientific tools and raising it up into the electric glow, bathing it in the spotlight it deserved. The cool blues and yellows danced upon the silver roll, in utter awe of its profundity. "Duct tape!"

❧

The process was as close to perfect as Lucretia could have hoped for. While she engineered the CRISPR compounds and cloning vectors, Pinky and Ramen hauled the rocket bodies outside so that Jim could splice the new firing wires to lengths of control cable he'd pulled from the crashed Wyvern and connect it to the firing pin. All the while, Sidney brought the firing pins to the laboratory, placing them next to the conical tips that Brain was molding the leaves into—much more elegant, Lucretia couldn't help but note, than the bloated warheads that had been removed from the projectiles. Gene Faintary, still in some pain from his wound as much as he tried to hide it, placed the firing pins in the tips after Lucretia had inserted the proteins and the guide RNA she'd made from the anemone remains, deftly fitting the heads to the modified rockets that the courier Racosku brought back using that most miraculous of human inventions. Everything was running smoothly.

Everything but the clock.

Time. The one thing of which there was never enough. The one thing that was Lucretia's constant adversary. Time. They needed more time.

And there was no more to be had.

CHAPTER XV

THE FINAL ROCKET was ready with only a little over two hours to spare before the pollinators were due to return to the lake. Plenty of time to get there and back, Sid knew, but Lucretia had wanted a lot more time. She had suggested launching the mission with only half the rockets modified but then caught herself, deciding that it'd be better to wait as long as possible, get as many rockets refitted, and be able to spread her strange life-rewriting substance as much as possible. For his part, Commander Faintary had left the timeline to her—a rarity indeed, Fanny letting someone else make the decisions!

When it came time for the mission briefing, there was no mistaking who was in charge. Faintary stood before the strange white panel on the wall where the words would appear, Lucretia to his left, the creature called Brain on his right. While Brain drew the eye most simply due to its size, and Lucretia was certainly most pleasing to the eye, looking sublime in her shiny white coat and braided hair, both Sid and Jim knew damned well that they'd better keep their focus on the man of modest stature between them.

"Pay attention, gentlemen," Fanny began. "The mission profile is quite straightforward. You will approach the target area at five thousand feet above ground level, descending to five hundred feet to release your munitions. Lieutenant Daventry, based upon your prior experiences over the area, would you confirm that this is a safe altitude?"

"Yes, sir," Sid said with certainty. *Just watch for birds.*

"Very well. You will overfly the targets at no more than one hundred fifty knots. Lieutenant Wellington, you will lead the flight."

"Yes, sir," Jim said. "But, sir, with all due respect, I thought that, due to Lieutenant Daventry's familiarity with the mission area, he would be better suited to lead in this instance."

"Duly noted." Fanny turned hard eyes on Sid. "However, considering the results of Lieutenant 'Moose' Daventry's last foray, I'd rather a literal moose lead the flight. He may consider this his penance."

Sid couldn't help but notice the grin penetrating the commander's stony veneer. He nodded, risking a chuckle of his own. "As you say, sir."

Fanny turned back to Jim. "On your first pass, you will fire a salvo of two rockets. You will note the pattern with which the material falls and adjust your subsequent runs accordingly."

"I injected the compounds with markers," Lucretia said. "It's blue ink; it's biodegradable, so it won't hurt the anemones or anything else. But it'll show you where the compounds are falling."

Fanny continued: "Once you've ascertained the trajectory of the spread, you will continue in kind, altering your approaches to spread the material over as wide an area as possible. Remember, gentlemen, these are not the rockets you're used to. If you fire them directly at the targets, you'll only spread the material on the ground, where it'll be of no use to anyone, and you'll have wasted all our efforts. But don't expect it to fall like a bomb, either."

"Hence the initial shots," Jim said.

"Precisely." Fanny turned to Lucretia. "Is there anything else, Doctor?"

Lucretia bit her lip, slinking backwards a step.

"Spit it out, Doctor," Fanny prodded. "We're running out of time. If you need something else, tell me now."

"Well," Lucretia said, her face straining, "I was hoping... after the compounds are released, I'd like to get another sample. I need to see if the knockout is working. This isn't exactly something that's ever been done before."

"You wish for one of my pilots to repeat Lieutenant Daventry's maneuver that resulted in the loss of our aircraft?"

Lucretia pinched her eyes shut. "Yeah."

"Very well," Fanny said to the shock of everyone in the room. "Lieutenant Daventry, do you think you could replicate the maneuver *without* destroying your aeroplane?"

Sid wasn't sure whether to laugh or to kowtow. "Yes, sir," he said meekly.

"Sure you don't want me to do it?" Wimpy asked, grinning. "I mean, it's like the skipper said, mate: your last attempt didn't go too well."

"I can do it, sir," Sid assured both officers. "Now that I know where *not* to set my wheels down, I'm fully confident I can get Dr. Tang what she needs."

"One more thing," Lucretia said timidly. "It'd have to be a while after the compounds are delivered, so they have time to take effect."

"What's 'a while'?" Fanny asked.

"Maybe a half hour."

The commander nodded. "That can be done. Lieutenant Wellington, you will vacate the target area once you've released your munitions and return here immediately, as to preserve your fuel supply. Lieutenant Daventry, you'll orbit the area at flight idle for exactly thirty minutes after your last salvo has been fired, then perform the maneuver in the safest manner possible. Is that understood?"

"Yes, sir," Sid said.

"With all due respect, sir," Jim said, "I'd like to remain with Lieutenant Daventry throughout the mission." He winked at Sid. "If naught else, I'd feel better keeping a set of eyes on him so his silly Canadian arse doesn't go and get into trouble again."

Fanny held back a chortle. "That's very generous of you, Mr. Wellington, but if we're to try to put two to a cockpit to return, we'll need to preserve as much fuel as possible to compensate for the extra weight."

"I understand, sir. But I'd feel terrible leaving my wingman behind. Please, sir. Safety in numbers."

The commander pursed his lips, his hands folded behind his back. He pondered for a moment, a moment in which he seemed frozen in time. But Gene Faintary wasn't one for indecisiveness. He nodded. "Very well. You will observe Lieutenant Daventry's approach to the lake, and render any possible assistance if necessary. But go easy on the throttle."

"Yes, sir."

"Well, then." Faintary approached Jim, shaking his hand, then did the same for Sid. "I wish you the best of luck, gentlemen—and I only wish I could be up there with you."

The Racosku had been so kind as to carry the rockets to the beach during the briefing. All the humans had to do was mount them.

Everyone had pitched in: Sid and Jim, of course, and Fanny as much as he could with his bad shoulder, and the Americans, who had already worked their magic and could only wait for the valiant fliers of the Fleet Air Arm to perform their tricks.

As he slid into VZ803's cockpit, the first thing Sid noticed was a small sepia photograph tucked into the windscreen railing on the left side. There was a young woman, certainly not one whom any lingerie company would hire to model their catalog, what with her pronounced front teeth not unlike a beaver's, her mouth canting to the side, her right ear bigger than the left. Yet there was true beauty there, in her smile, in the radiance of young love. Radiance that would, alas, soon be dimmed. *Susannah Wickler.* Reverently, he plucked the picture from the glass and placed it in his flight suit's pocket. How could he tell that vibrant young mother-to-be that he was the one who had widowed her?

He shoved the thought aside, glancing to the right as he ran through his prestart checklist. The Wyvern's cowling still bore the scars of its collision with Triple-Eight in the storm, but the damage was superficial, a mere dent that an unwary eye might've missed, and certainly nothing that would affect the engine's performance or the aircraft's handling. Commander Faintary was standing tall as he observed his pilots' departure, and Sid could see the yearning behind the skipper's stony mask. Lucretia and Jeremiah were waving, and Sid was tempted to blow a kiss back at Lucretia but thought better of it, for women of the future didn't seem to appreciate chivalry. As for the gaggle of Racosku, he had no idea what the hell they were thinking.

Sid watched as Jim took off, then nudged Eight-Zero-Three forward and into the air. The older Wyvern had seemed a little more sluggish than Willie Love had been, as if her heart were heavy with mourning for her fallen former handler, but once there was wind beneath her wings, she was light as a feather, dancing through the purple sky, reaching for the strange astral patterns glinting from above.

He maneuvered into a loose right echelon formation. Flying was so much more satisfying when sharing the joy of it with his friend. Tight as the valley was, Sid never felt that he was in danger of impacting the mountains, for so precise was the navigation mechanism given to them by their hosts. Only now did Sid take notice of how smooth the flight was. Back on Earth, flying through mountains was often fraught with turbulence, but here, it was like ice skating. *For my daughters, anyway*, Sid thought with a chortle; Emily in particular was as graceful as a ballerina on skates, while Sid moved with all the panache of a three-legged black bear.

The mountains fell away, and the glowing green lake spread out before them, glimmering like the dance of the aurora. "Well, there's a sight for sure!" Jim said, his voice rich with awe.

"Sure is," Sid replied.

And yet, apprehension gnawed at Sid's thoughts. *One chance*, he knew. *One chance to get it right. And not a moment to waste.*

The air brakes at the back of WP335's wings opened, and the large flaps inched downward. "I'm taking her down," Jim said, and WP335 slid beneath and behind Sid's ship. "Keep a high orbit, Moose. Tell me what you see."

"Yes, sir." Sid nudged his throttle forward, turning right away from the lake, then putting VZ803 into a shallow left bank so that the wing wasn't obscuring his view. He watched as Jim pulled level over the lake, and the flames shooting from behind his outboard right wing, and the orange flash as the two rockets zoomed off into the swaying forest and disappeared.

"Got anything?"

Sid peered down, descrying a little of the blue ink. "Hold on, let me get down for a better look." He pushed the control column forward, putting the Wyvern into a shallow dive. He could see the mass of dots, a darker and less lustrous green than the water, which he figured were the strange spiny creatures coming out of the lake. The blue ink seemed to have landed on some of them but was mostly in front of the blob. "Adjust your release a second earlier on the next pass, Spoke Two."

"Roger that, mate. And, seeing as I'm in command of this mission, shouldn't I be Spoke *One*?"

Sid chuckled. "My apologies, sir."

He observed as Jim made another pass over the lake, banking slightly as he fired the remaining six rockets from the right wing in a fan pattern. The blue cloud spread over the mass of creatures, some seeping into the lake where it swilled with the green.

"Perfect!" Sid shouted into his radio.

"Comes with the territory," Jim said smugly. He pulled up hard, putting WP335 into a Derry turn—a two-hundred-seventy-degree aileron roll into a turn in the opposite vector of the roll—and dove in to release the rockets on his left wing. *Show-off.*

As Wimpy made his final pass, Sid noticed him pulling up abruptly after the last rockets left the wing.

"Saw some of those birds you were on about," Jim said. "Beauties, they are."

"Can you tell what they're doing?" Sid asked, suddenly worried that the birds, or whatever they were, would attack the defenseless creatures, undermining everything the pilots were doing.

"Looks like they're just loafing. They're not on the side of the lake where the critters are. Caught a couple flying over the mass, but just kept going; I don't think they're interested in them. They're keeping low, so you'll be all right to launch your salvos. But be careful on your skim. There's more than 'a few' down there."

Relieved, Sid snorted a chortle. "*Skim*? Is that the official Royal Navy name for the maneuver?"

"It is now, mate!"

Jim entered a steep, spiraling climb, leveling off at Sid's altitude. It was Sid's turn to fire his rockets. He'd follow the same procedure: an initial salvo of two rockets to dial in his targeting, then spreading the rest over whatever area Jim hadn't saturated.

Sid leveled off, firing off his salvo as the blob of creatures passed under his spinner. "How'd I do?" he asked.

A long second later came the reply: "Got the opposite problem I had, mate. You're a little short."

"Copy that." Sid pulled up sharply…but instead of leveling out to turn around, he decided to have a little fun. After all, if Jim was going to do aerobatics with Her Majesty's aeroplane, then Sid would be damned if he wasn't joining the party. He kept pulling back on the stick until the aircraft was inverted, then pulled back some more until he was diving toward the lake at forty-five degrees, only then rolling wings-level and pulling level above the lake. It was what the stunt pilots called one-half of a Cuban Eight.

"Hey, now, hotshot!" Jim's voice crackled over the radio. "Go easy on the old girl."

"Ah, she's tougher than you think. Besides, I saved myself thirty seconds."

"Thirty more seconds of that, and you'd be in that lake!"

"Quit being such a wimp, Wimpy."

Jim keyed his radio for Sid to hear his harrumph. "Damned Canucks!"

Sid couldn't temper his mirth as he fired his next salvo in a shallow right bank along the edge of the lake.

"I've got a good spray," Jim affirmed. "Just do me a favor, mate. No more loop-the-loops this time, all right?"

"That wasn't a loop, sir; only three-quarters of one." *Almost.* "Besides, I've got something totally different in mind."

Sid yanked the control column into his belly, squeezing his muscles as the seat pulled his body into it, not letting go until VZ803 was going straight up. The airspeed fell like a thermometer amid a Canadian winter. As the dial spun dangerously close to the Wyvern's stall speed, Sid kicked hard left on the rudder pedal, twisting the controls to compensate. The Wyvern lurched sideways, making a fishhook shape in the sky until the nose was pointed straight down, the shining lake rushing up to meet Sid as he gathered airspeed. A stall turn, or, as the Americans called it, a hammerhead.

He hadn't even thought a Wyvern could do it. *You never know until you try.*

Jim grumbled through his radio. "You'd just better thank God that Fanny's not here to see you showboating like that. Your arse would be court-martialed in a second."

He's not wrong, Sid knew. And, in that moment, he didn't care.

⌘

"Think it'll work?" Jeremiah asked.

Lucretia looked at her brother, noting how weary he looked. Not worried, not conflicted, just tired. In truth, she felt it too, for the first time since passing through the wormhole. Maybe it was the adrenaline rush wearing off, or the concern weighing on her, or the feeling of impotence now that everything was truly out of her hands.

"I don't know," she admitted. "I hope so. Hope is the last refuge of the wretched, right?"

Jeremiah chortled under his breath. "You're playing with fire, you know."

"Damned right I am. Fuck you, Dick Daniken!"

"And if it doesn't work?"

Lucretia exhaled. "At least we tried. At least we did something." She patted Jeremiah's shoulder. "Get some sleep, Jay. You look like you need it. Don't worry, I'll wake you up when it's time to go home."

"Promise?"

"Pinky promise."

Jeremiah took her gesture and mussed her hair. "What about you? We need you to fly us home."

"You got us down here, remember?"

"I got lucky."

Lucretia smiled. "I'll be fine, Jay. I've worked on less sleep. I still have to run the samples when the boys get back. You worry about me too much, you know."

"You're my sister, Lu. You're my family."

"I know, and I'm grateful." She squeezed her brother's hand. "But it's time to stop. It's time you were your own man, and not anchored to me all the time."

Jeremiah lifted an eyebrow. "What's that supposed to mean?"

Lucretia shook her head. "Nothing. I'm sorry. Just…get some sleep, Jay. Please. You deserve it. You've done your part."

Jeremiah stared at her for a while, frowning as if she'd wounded him. But before she could say more, he shrugged and walked away.

What have I done? she pondered. *What am I doing, and what am I about to do? I should be with him. We should spend this time together. Cherish it, cherish each other.*

She shoved the thought aside. There would be time to tell him. At the very last. It could wait. It'd be less painful that way, for both of them.

She turned her attention to Pinky and Ramen, pulling on a

length of flora as if playing tug-of-war with it. Eugene Faintary was watching them, smiling. Lucretia's heart too was light again.

"They truly are magnificent creatures, aren't they?" Eugene mused.

"Yeah, they really are."

"I always loved birds," Eugene said, still transfixed by the playful creatures. "How sweet their songs were, and the freedom to shed the bonds of earth. I think that's why I chose to fly." He smiled at Lucretia. "When I was a boy growing up in Somerset, my father would take me to Westhay Moor to watch the king-fishers. Beautiful birds, they are, with their bright blue tufts and feathers, beaks like spears, bellies like orange flame. These crea-tures—Racosku, is it?—they remind me of kingfishers, in their own way. Maybe it's their colors, or maybe it's how they frolic.

"The more I think on it, I realize it's that they remind me of a better time—or rather, a time when I was naïve enough to believe in such a thing as 'better times.' Ah, to have back the innocence of youth! When we spoke before, I told you that there's no perfection to be found in the past, and I think you'd tell me that there's none to be found in the future. How cruel it is that we should find the perfect world, only to have to leave it, to go back to the chaos from whence we came."

What if we didn't? What if this could be our world, our perfect home? Lucretia opened her mouth, but no words came forth. She made to approach Eugene, desultorily, when he turned to her, smiling, patting her shoulder.

"Take some rest, Doctor," the commander said as if to give her a direct order. "You've earned it."

Precisely thirty minutes after Sid had fired his last salvo, he began his descent. He'd do it exactly the same as last time—except this time, hopefully, without breaking his aircraft.

The two Wyverns had been orbiting the target area in level flight, five thousand feet above indicated ground level, in a shallow left bank. No more stunts, no more excitement, no more blatant disregard for proper and safe aircraft operating procedure; they had to save what fuel they had left, even though the fuel burn was indeed noticeably lower here than back on Earth, certainly well below the typical 235 gallons per hour a clean Wyvern's turbine usually sucked down. With all the fuel they were saving, maybe they wouldn't have to divert to Port Said. They could make it all the way back to *Eagle*.

Sid preferred it that way. He was in no mood to be shot at again.

But until such time as they were underway for home, his focus was on the glowing lake. He went through his checklist as if this would be any typical landing. *Brakes off, good pressure. Air brakes closed. Undercarriage down and locked, indicator lights green. Tail wheel locked. Flight fine-pitch stop set to normal. Flaps at takeoff setting. Harness tight. Hood locked.*

Descending lower, he extended the flaps fully and dropped the tailhook. He'd gather as much of the stuff as he could. Lucretia would like that.

As he flew over the beach, he saw no sign of the creatures. He assumed that they'd all gone back underwater, and, while he had no idea how aquatic animals functioned, he took that as a good sign. *The luck of the Irish be with you,* he heard Marie's mellifluous voice cooing in his ear. Whatever substance they were emitting, the one causing all the problems, would hopefully be fixed and replacing the errant stuff. *I think that's how it works.*

Sid massaged the throttle lever as VZ803's tires and tailhook kissed the surface. He skimmed the surface as long as he could keep the Wyvern steady, a full seven seconds. By then, he figured, the stuff would be all over the wheels, catching in the tires' treads and the tailhook's notch, and probably spattered all over the flaps and rear fuselage. *Mission accomplished*, he thought with a self-satisfied smirk.

Too soon. Always too soon.

As he raised the flaps and began his shallow climb, two birds whooshed past his canopy—far closer than before. "Shit!" he yelped. *Too close. Too damned close.*

Then, as he faced forward, time seemed to stand still. He locked eyes with the bird headed straight for his windscreen's center panel. It was a beautiful creature indeed. And terrifying.

Then, a violent thump, and an earsplitting crack as the canopy shattered. Pain like a thousand knives sliced through the right side of Sid's face. He squeezed his eyes shut, screaming.

"Spoke Two, report!" Jim Wellington yelled over the radio. "Is everything all right?"

Sid opened his eyes...but only the left opened, glazed and blurred. Searing pain pierced his right, and he knew what happened before he could touch the wound. A piece of canopy was stuck in his eye.

"Moose!" Wimpy bellowed. "What's happening down there?"

"I...hit one." Sid's voice was weak and quavering. He glanced ahead; the mountains were racing toward him, and he was much too low. But, with one working eyeball, he could hardly read his instruments, spattered as they were with blood and feathers and bird guts. The navigation tool had been knocked out. He was as good as dead. "I...can't see. I'm not...I'm not going to make it."

"Don't you talk like that, Lieutenant!" Jim ordered. "Now pull up!"

Almost instinctively, Sid pulled back on the stick, nudging

VZ803 in the direction of the valley. But how could he make it through when he could barely see, couldn't navigate, couldn't read his dials and gauges, all in such agony that threatened to leech him of consciousness at any moment?

"Can you see at all?" Jim asked. "Do you see my aeroplane?"

Sid looked up, faintly descrying the blurred outline of WP335 growing bigger in his view. Jim was descending, he knew, putting himself and his aircraft at risk. "Yes, sir. I see you...you should leave me...don't do...anything stupid."

"It ain't stupid to get my mate back home." Jim's voice creaked as he tried to suppress his emotions. "Just follow my lead, Sid. Keep my aeroplane in your sight. I'll lead you back. I'll get you home."

"I can't make it—"

"Goddamn it, Sidney, you can, and you will! If not for yourself, then for Marie, for Emily and Rhiannon. Don't think about anything else. Look at my aeroplane, and see their faces in it. Let them bring you home."

And he did. The Wyvern's shape morphed into those of faces, the faces he loved the most, and he felt a new strength surging through his body, stronger than pain, stronger than fear. He *would* see them again. He would hold them in his arms, kiss them—he would *see* them again.

Come Hell or high water.

✍

"All right, mate." Jim's calm voice floated through Sid's helmet. "Let's get you ready to land."

Sid glanced around his cockpit the best he could. Nothing had been damaged save the gyro gunsight unit, knocked off its mounting but still intact and lying on the chart board, and the center panel of the windshield. But whatever instruments weren't covered in blood and mush were too small to read with one blurry eye. Had he been in a Sea Fury, he could have almost manipulated the dials and levers from muscle memory, but he hadn't had enough time to acclimate to the Wyvern.

Fortunately, he mostly remembered approximately where everything was.

"I'm gonna slow to one-fifty," Jim announced. "You'll be able to open your canopy hood at that speed. Let's have that open just in case, all right?"

"We're still a ways from the strip," Sid said weakly.

"I know. But you're best getting as much ready now as you can. Lessen your workload when it's time to put her down."

"We'll burn too much fuel."

"Don't you worry about that, Moose. Worry about getting down in one piece. Besides, you'd only burn an extra, what, thirty gallons? And not even that, the way this place works! Listen, Moose, I know you're in a hurry to get back, get some of that magic mud on you, but let's take our time, get back safely. All right?"

Even though every second was its own agony, even as the glowing trees passed dangerously close to Sid's wing almost in slow motion, he knew Jim was right. *Let me do as much as possible while I still can, while I've still got my wits about me.* "Yes, sir. Opening the hood, sir." He felt for the winding unit at his right side, grasping the knob's handle, his hand straining against the airflow rushing through the crack in the windscreen. He knew he was flying just ten knots below the highest speed the hood could be easily opened. With a groan, he turned the knob, and the glass bubble slid backwards. The extra rush of wind only exacerbated the pain in his face. His finger trembled as he pushed the radio button on the throttle lever. "Hood's open."

"Very good." Jim's voice was muffled amid the tempest of wind swirling through Sid's cockpit. "How are your trims?"

Sid let go of the stick; VZ803 continued straight as an arrow. "She's trimmed out perfectly, sir."

"Good. That's one less thing to worry about, yeah? All right, let's lower the flaps. At least get them down a notch. It's the big horizontal lever by your left knee."

Even amid the pain, and the vertigo from being slapped in the face with hurricane-force winds, Sid had to chuckle. "I think I've got that one, Jim."

"Of course, mate; that's the easy one! Now, lower your landing gear. Can you see the buttons?"

Sid glanced at the left side of the cockpit's front panel. The wind was blowing his eye dry, obscuring his view of the small, horizontally arranged controls.

"Last set of buttons on the front left. Press the bottom one. Take your time; we've got another twenty minutes to go."

Sid felt around, letting his thumb roam over the three altitude limit warning lamps arranged diagonally at the top of the panel, sliding down to the raised panel with two buttons. *Top is up, bottom is down.* He prodded at the two buttons, making sure he had the right one, then pressed the bottom. The Wyvern jolted as the wheels came down.

"Good," Jim said. "Now, I want you to keep your left hand on the throttle, your right on the control column, and don't let go of either one until it's time to dump the flaps."

"Yes, sir."

Those twenty minutes passed like twenty years, years that seemed to run to the end of time itself, and sometimes Sid felt himself slipping away, drifting into reverie. He thought of his first taste of flight, in the front seat of an old Tiger Moth at the local airfield; he thought of the day he'd met Marie by the lake, him with that ratty old fishing pole and her lying by a tree, pretty as an angel, lost in her book. He remembered coming home from the War to Emily's precious six-month-old smile, and Marie's bliss as she rocked Rhiannon in her arms, and his own when she placed her in his arms, the way he'd never gotten to hold baby Emily. He thought of Jim Wellington and Rachel and sharp young Ollie in their charming cottage, and gruff Commander Faintary, and Lucretia Tang, that magnificent dreamer, and those splendidly silly Racosku. All the while, Jim's calm, steady voice kept him from drifting so away entirely.

At long last, Jim announced: "We're almost there! I've got the strip in sight."

Sid peered ahead, and there, between the glowing forest and the shimmering waters, was the long, flat runway, the white shape of the tiny plane Lucretia and Jeremiah had brought shining like a seashell from its right side. It looked so far away, yet so close. *I've got no depth perception*, Sid knew.

And putting his plane down would be no walk in the park.

"Put your flaps down," Jim instructed. "All the way."

Sid pushed the lever all the way down, and VZ803 lurched as she slowed, nosing forward slightly. He fumbled for the throttle, but the lever seemed to elude his grasp.

"Easy now," Jim said, his voice like a balm to Sid's racing mind. "It's the lever that feels like a screwdriver head. Just nudge it ahead a little, and try not to hit the high-pressure cock."

As if guided there by Jim's words, Sid's fingers curled around the throttle lever, inching it forward. The Wyvern's nose came up with a little back pressure on the control stick. Sid couldn't read his airspeed indicator, but the plane felt slow. Was he stalling?

"You're good, mate," Jim assured him, as if he could read Sid's fear. "Just stay with me. I'm gonna take you all the way down. Just follow my lead."

Sid drew a deep breath. His hands were trembling. His knees shook like the stones of a fortress under bombardment. Every breath was strained, fitful, and wrought with choking pain.

As the strip grew bigger in Sid's windscreen, his vision began blurring. *I'm not going to make it. No, I have to make it. I have to.*

"Moose? You still with me?"

"Yes, sir," Sid whispered.

"What's that, mate? I can't hear you. Listen, you're a little too far to the right. Bank left."

But the words didn't register. The strip was coming closer... closer...closer...

"Left, Sid!" Jim yelled. "Left, left, *left*..."

The wheels hit the soft ground hard, but VZ803 didn't bounce. There was a cracking sound coming from the right, and a slight jolt in that direction. He'd hit something. Sid chopped his throttle and applied the brakes, and the aircraft groaned to a halt.

With one last effort, Sid powered down the engine. He collapsed in his seat, the sound of Jim Wellington's voice morphing into wordless noise in his ears, and the last thing he saw before passing out was Gene Faintary running toward his aircraft.

CHAPTER XVI

IT WAS A good dream. The kind Lucretia never wanted to wake from.

She was in a fantastical world, surrounded by strange and beautiful creatures beyond count, dancing beneath an ever-purple sky and twinkling stars. The trees and ferns glowed like lanterns, and she was a respected scientist—nah, scratch that, she was a princess, an elf-maiden with pointy ears and dragonfly wings—and everyone loved her.

For a while, Lucretia and Chao-Xing were one and the same.

But every dream was marred by its awakening, and this one came at a hand forcefully shaking her shoulder. She blinked the moisture from her eyes, and there was Jim Wellington, his countenance grave.

"Jim?" she said groggily. "What is it? Where's Sidney?"

"He's hurt, ma'am."

Lucretia blasted from her hammock, her heart racing. "What happened?"

"Bird strike. He's awake now; the skipper's tending to him down in the laboratory. If you'll come with me—"

Lucretia was out the door and halfway down the ramp before Jim could finish his sentence. When she reached the lab, Sidney Daventry was lying on the ground, the left side of his head wrapped in a bandage that must've come from the first aid kit that Eugene Faintary was holding. The commander was kneeling over his man, holding his hand.

"Hey, pretty lady," Sidney said with a strained smile as his one good eye beheld Lucretia.

She forced herself to chuckle. "You look like hell."

"Been worse. Thought I lost my eye; turns out it's just scratched."

"Clearly," Eugene said with a roll of his eyes, "the lieutenant's gravest wound is to his ego. Anyway, I've dressed his bandage with some of that soil. If my wound is any indication, he'll be all right."

"Yeah," Lucretia said, "but look how long that took to heal. Do you think he'll be ready to fly back? We only have, like, three hours before the wormholes open."

"He'll be able to fly," Eugene assured her, offering a smile of admiration to Sidney. "This man doesn't go down without a fight. I think some of his wife's Irish stubbornness rubbed off on him, because he certainly doesn't give up."

At that moment, Jim and Jeremiah burst into the lab, both relieved to see Sidney sitting up with Eugene's help. From the periphery, Brain and Violet watched intently.

Eugene clasped Lucretia's shoulder. "I'd like for you to stay with Lieutenant Daventry. Lieutenant Wellington and I need to tend to our aircraft."

"I'm fine, sir," Sidney said. "Besides, she needs to get her stuff. If nothing else, us flying so slow on the way back should mean that less of it got blown off." He gestured to the Racosku. "These fellows are here; I'll be in good hands. Or…good tentacles!"

"I could grab the samples," Jeremiah offered.

"Actually," Jim said, "we could really use your help, mate. The skipper and I have to take the windshield off Willie Love and put it on Eight-Oh-Three. There's no way we're making it through that storm with a busted canopy. Then, we've got to clean all the bird guts off the instrument panel. With what little time we've got, we could use an extra set of hands."

"The second part sounds lovely," Jeremiah grumbled.

Lucretia looked at Sidney, clearly in pain even though he tried to hide it. She wanted to stay, if only so that he wasn't alone, for she knew that there was nothing worse than suffering alone. But he was right, she needed those samples.

"I won't be long," she said, taking Sidney's hand in hers. Then she turned to Jeremiah. "Go help them, you big strong bull. Show them what you're made of."

Jim bit his lip as he turned a bashful gaze upon Lucretia. "There's one more thing, ma'am. When Lieutenant Daventry made his landing, he…well, ma'am, his wing struck your aeroplane."

Lucretia's heart sank. "Oh. Uh…that sucks."

"Aye, clipped a piece off the tail. No damage to the Wyvern, but yours is looking the worse for wear. I just wanted you to know."

She exhaled, looking at a deflated Jeremiah. *Well, isn't that just splendid?*

The damage to the Velis wasn't as bad as Lucretia had expected. Two inches chopped cleanly off the rudder. The remaining piece was lying on the ground fifty feet from the plane. *Nothing a little duct tape can't fix, at least long enough to get back to Galveston.* The fixed part of the vertical stabilizer hadn't been damaged, or else it'd have been unflyable, since the tailplane was set atop the fin. Hell, it could probably fly the way it was, without mending the rudder; yaw control would be tricky, but for one flight? By the way Jim Wellington had been talking, she'd expected to find the entire empennage lying in tatters halfway across the beach.

That was one problem solved. Jim, Eugene, and Jeremiah were with the wrecked Wyvern, well into the process of removing the forward portion of its canopy to replace that of the *other* wrecked Wyvern. Pinky and Ramen had pitched in to help carry the part, which Lucretia assumed wasn't exactly light as a feather. She chuckled as she remembered Sidney telling her about the maintenance manual Eugene kept in his plane, which the commander now had before him, along with a tool kit that he'd obviously brought with him too. *There's a man prepared for anything.* Jeremiah, for his part, was doing as he was instructed without complaint, and even seemed to be enjoying making himself useful.

Collecting the last of the significant amount of anemone poop plastered to VZ803, she trudged up the hill, approaching the working men. "You guys need a hand? I can come right back after I set this up."

"We're good," Jeremiah shot back, exhaustion rippling aloft his voice.

"No need to get your hands dirty, do...*Doctor*," Jim said.

Lucretia shook her head. "You know, just because I'm a woman doesn't mean I'm completely useless. I'm pretty good with my hands when I want to be."

"I assure you, Dr. Tang," Eugene said, "no one in their right mind would underestimate you. But we've got sufficient hands and...other appendages. You focus on your science, and see to Lieutenant Daventry."

Lucretia shrugged, gathering her samples and making for the laboratory. In truth, she was perfectly content with them not wanting her help, especially since she was pretty sure they'd assign her the task of cleaning the snarge out of the cockpit.

When she arrived, Sidney was on his feet, his head still bandaged. He was standing beside Lucretia's workstation, next to Brain, the two of them seeming to marvel at it.

"Clear the road, boys," she said, donning her lab gear and sliding the first dish under the microscope.

Once again, Brain couldn't help but prod at her hairnet.

She rolled her eyes, turning to Sidney. "Brain thinks it's trying to eat my hair."

THAT IS INCORRECT, the words on the wall panel read. YOU APPEAR INACCURATE WITH THAT COVERING YOUR FOLLICLES.

Lucretia screwed up her face. "Is that its way of telling me I look funny?" she asked Sidney.

The pilot shrugged. "I think Brain just likes you better without it. You do have very beautiful hair."

"Why, thank you! But I'd rather not have my samples contaminated with human DNA." She shot an icy glower at Brain. "Got that, pistil-face?"

I SHALL NO LONGER INTERFERE WITH YOUR EXPERIMENTATION, HAMMOCK-HEAD.

Lucretia drew back, mouth agape, her head cocked like a confused puppy's.

"It does look like the stuff they use to make their hammocks," Sidney said. "If you look at it a certain way, I mean."

"Right." She gestured to the projector screen, then leaned back. "Now, we wait."

"For what?"

"Their computer will analyze the sample you took from the

lake against the one the DNA sequence they have on file. If they match, it worked."

Sure enough, within five minutes, the sequence appeared on the screen next to the one from the files. Brain noodled the clear panel, and a green line appeared on the wall, growing longer. *Like a status bar.*

Then, the two parallel sequences flashed green.

Lucretia gasped. "Does…that mean what I think it does?"

Brain prodded at the panel, and the words kindled in Lucretia's heart a hope and a joy that she hadn't known since she was a child. Tears welled in her eyes.

THE SEQUENCES ARE IDENTICAL.

"Does that mean we did it?" Sidney asked.

Lucretia drew a deep breath to calm herself. "Let's not declare victory just yet. Let me run the other samples."

But with each analysis, the screen flashed green, again and again and again.

The knockout had worked.

The toxin was neutralized.

The Racosku were saved.

"We did it!" Lucretia squealed like she was a little girl. She threw her arms around Sidney, holding him tight. "Thank you, thank you, *thank you!*"

He looked into her eyes, beaming that averagely perfect smile, and even bandaged and broken, his joy shone through. "It was the honor of my life, Lucretia Tang. I've always wanted to be part of something bigger than myself. I told myself that's why I joined the Navy, but that was always for me first and foremost. Now, thanks to you, I truly have been."

Lucretia took his hands in hers. "You're a good man, Sidney. Your family is lucky to have you."

Before he could reply, Lucretia felt a softness curling around her arm. When she turned around, Brain was standing before her. It pulled her arm to its head, pressing the palm to the featureless surface, and it needed no words on a screen to communicate with her this time. The faint vibrations under the surface evinced all the creature's emotions, as clearly as if it had spoken them. Gratitude. Relief. Admiration. Bliss.

Love.

She wrapped her arms around the strange creature, awkwardly, and tears fell from her eyes. "Whatever god or fate brought me here, I'm grateful to it."

Brain held her hand to its face once more, and this time she read a new emotion, a plea of sorts. A plea for her not to leave.

She smiled at the creature, and nodded.

Just then, Jeremiah entered the lab, Eugene, Jim, and the other Racosku close behind. Lucretia bolted across the room, throwing herself into her brother's arms, kissing his cheek. "We did it, Jay!" she said, and the room erupted in cheers, handshakes, high fives, and pats on the back.

And for the next hour, they all celebrated—human and Racosku alike.

CHAPTER XVII

THE WALK TO the beach was sullen, even amid the undimmed beauty all around Lucretia. Her job was finished; the pollinators had survived the lake and would live on to give life to the next generation of Racosku. The light of this world would burn on. That, at least, soothed some of the sting.

But as she traipsed toward those magnificent Westland Wyverns, the kind she'd thought she'd never see but in photographs and the odd YouTube video, her heart sulked behind her. This was goodbye, to Sidney, to Eugene, to Jim.

And then, the hardest goodbye of all.

Jeremiah nudged her shoulder. "You have your duct tape, right?"

She nodded.

"Should be an easy fix, right? Think it'll hold until we get home?"

She couldn't put off the inevitable any longer. Grasping her brother's hand, she announced her decision: "I'm not going back, Jay."

He spun around, raising his eyebrow. "What? What are you talking about?"

"I mean I'm staying here. They invited me to stay. So, I'm staying."

Jeremiah's eyes rolled. "Don't be ridiculous, Lu. We had our fun. Now, it's time to get back to the real world."

"What is there for me to go back to? My job? You know that, as soon as some university or big tech company buys our lab out, I'm out the door. That world doesn't want me."

"Maybe not, but it *needs* you. Quit pissing around. You're not staying here. Now, help me fix the plane."

She shook her head. "I'll help you, but I meant what I said. I'm not going back. I'm sorry, Jay. I'm tired of living in a world that hates me."

"Oh, I'm sorry," he sneered. "I thought you cared about changing the world, doing the right thing because it's right, no matter what people thought of you. I thought that was your life's work."

"That world doesn't want to change, and no matter how hard you or I try, it won't let us change it. But here, I can make a difference. I could find a way to help Violet back to full health. Who knows what perils they'll encounter down the road." She sniffled back a tear. "Jay, I'm *happy* here. The kind of happiness that I forgot ever existed. What am I leaving behind? Nothing. I mean, yeah, I'll feel kinda bad for Clete, having to run the canoe business alone, but he does it himself most of the time anyway, and he hardly knows me. He'll barely notice I'm gone." She exhaled. "You know, I used to think you were right, that our world needed me. But it doesn't. There are plenty of other scientists back home, most of them smarter than me. Don't you see, Jay? I've finally found the world that *does* need me."

Jeremiah uttered a pitiful chortle. "Yeah, there's nothing back home for you, right? Not even your own brother."

She clasped his hands, swallowing the pain. "Jeremiah, listen to me. There is nothing I could say or do to express the gratitude I have for all you've done for me. That's why I want you to go. You've done so much for me; now it's time for you to let me go. Live your life the way you want. It hurts like hell to leave you." Tears streaked down her face. "But, Jay, I'm doing this because I love you. I don't want to be an anchor anymore. That's not right, and it's not fair to you." She produced the duct tape from her bag, holding it out to him. "Go on. Live your dream; don't abandon it for mine."

Jeremiah's nostrils flared, his face hardening. He ripped the roll of tape from her hand, spinning around in a black flash, storming off toward the plane.

"Jay!" Lucretia wailed. "Don't leave me like this! Don't you dare leave me in anger!"

Jeremiah halted halfway to the plane, dropping the duct tape onto the ground, a yellow ring glowing around it. He turned around, grinning. "I just remembered something, Lu. I can't fly. I'm not a pilot. I guess I'm stuck here."

"Jay, don't be silly. You can do it. You got it down. It's easy; just remember the stuff I taught you."

"No, you don't understand, Lu. If you're not going, then neither am I."

"Come on, Jay, stop arguing with me. You're almost out of time. You've got to get back. Your meds—"

"I've been checking my sugars religiously, Lu. They're better than they've ever been. Whatever's in that soil is working miracles. Quit making excuses. I'm staying."

She grasped her brother's hands. "Jay, I'm giving you a chance to be free of me, to shed that burden. It's a burden you shouldn't have had to bear, and one you've borne long enough. I know it'll hurt for a while, but you'll have your life."

Jeremiah's mouth twisted as if wrought by the ache inside him. "Fuck you, Lucretia. Did it never once occur to you that I stood by you because I *wanted* to? Not because I felt like I had to, but because you mean the world to me?"

Lucretia gasped like she'd taken a knife to the heart. "Jay—"

"You're my family, Lu. And that matters to me. That's *all* that matters to me. And, if Mom and Dad could agree on one thing, it's that family sticks together. I'm not giving up on that. So, if you want me gone, if you want me out of your life, then just say it."

"I *don't* want you gone, Jay!" she cried, holding her brother tight. "I'm so sorry, Jay. So, so sorry!"

He pulled away, pinching her cheek. "You'd better be sorry, thinking you could get rid of me that easily." He jerked his head at the Velis. "Besides, you might need it. Once we get it fixed up, that is."

Lucretia smiled, taking her brother's hand. Through thick and thin, they'd always had each other. And now, they always would.

"Come now," Jeremiah said in the absolute worst English accent Lucretia had ever heard. "Let us bid the blokes a fond farewell."

"How the hell is this going to work?" Jim Wellington wondered as he stared at VZ803, looking quite resplendent with her new unbroken windshield.

Sid had been wondering the same thing ever since Commander Faintary had expressed the idea of putting two men to a cockpit. He'd thought Fanny was joking at first. The Wyvern's cockpit was spacious enough, but that was with one man in it, one man whose helmet came only inches from bumping the canopy hood if he was of average height. At the very least, they'd have to fly with the hood open, limiting their airspeed and risking the hood somehow shutting on the second man's neck. And that was to say nothing of the lack of visibility, or that one man would be flying in a high-performance warplane through a storm without a harness.

There was no response from Gene Faintary. The commander stood with his lips pursed, his hands behind his back, his eyes downcast. Never before had Sid beheld such despondency in the man before.

"It's not going to work, is it?" Sid prodded. "It was never going to work."

Faintary shook his head. "Not even under the most fortuitous of circumstances. God, how I have been dreading this moment."

Jim gasped. "You mean...one of us has to stay behind?"

"I'm afraid so."

"But, sir—"

"It's okay, Jim," Sid said, swallowing the sickness and despair rising in his throat. "I guess it ought to be me. I've got one eye, and I'm the reason we've only got two planes left."

"No, Moose, you've got a family to go back to."

Sid smiled. "So do you."

"Then how do we decide?" Jim cried out.

"The decision has been made," Commander Faintary said. He stood erect, face pinched to conceal his emotions, then saluted with the utmost precision. "Gentlemen, it has been my great honor serving as your commanding officer."

Sid gasped aloud. "Sir! You...you can't!"

"I can," Faintary said with resolve. "I leave nothing behind, Lieutenant. I have nothing to go back to, no one, only the Service. I have done my duty. My mission is complete. But you men still have your mission, your duties—the most important duties of your lives. You have families. You have people who depend on you. That is one mission you must not fail. And I know you will not."

"But, sir," Jim protested, "we can't just leave you—"

"Enough, Mr. Wellington!" The commander's voice crumbled as tears welled in his eyes. "You *will* get in those aeroplanes. You will go back home, and you will be the finest of husbands, the finest of fathers, the finest of men. That's an order!"

Jim gave a firm salute. "You have my word, sir."

"I know." Faintary shook Jim's hand, then Sid's.

"They'll know you were a hero, Commander," Sid promised.

Faintary shook his head. "They will know nothing, Lieutenant. No one will believe you if you tell them what transpired here, or that this place even exists. You'll be mocked and ridiculed. You must tell them that Spoke Flight was lost in inclement weather, nothing more. They will hear that I died an unremarkable death, even that I led my pilots into harm's way. They will remember me as a failure, if they remember me at all."

No, Sid thought. *That's a lie, and I am not a liar.* He opened his mouth to speak...

The commander clasped his shoulder, and Jim's. "It matters none to me what others think. And you mustn't let it matter to you. You know what we did here. I've come to realize, gentlemen, that medals, mentions in dispatches, accolades, the praise of others...none of that is important. Pure vanity, that's all it is. What matters is being a good man. Nothing else. You have done that, both of you. And for that, I can proudly say that you are two of the finest naval officers I have ever had the pleasure of serving with."

"The pleasure was mine, sir," Jim said.

"And mine," Sid added.

Faintary nodded kindly, then gazed at the two Wyverns, as if looking at a lover he knew he'd never see again. "You know, gentlemen, if more of us did the things that we knew were right rather than the things that we thought would cement our legacies, we might actually live our lives as to be worthy of remembrance."

You'll be remembered, Sid wanted to say. *At least two men will know your quality, and through us, and our children, your legacy will live forever.*

⤴

The loneliness was the thing Lucretia had feared most. Barring some interstellar travelers falling through a wormhole at a later time, she'd be the only human on the planet. That was going to be the worst part.

And now, not only would she not be alone, but she'd have the person she loved the most, *plus* an eligible bachelor to boot! Was there potential there? After all, he was only six years older than she, and certainly handsome, and it wasn't as if there was any competition. She didn't get the vibe that Eugene Faintary was gay, and he surely wasn't into human-alien relations. He was hers to lose. Sure, the commander could be abrasive at times—he was a *commander*, after all—but those types had their own charm. She'd been as shocked as his subordinates that he'd chosen to be the one to stay behind, but at the same time, she wasn't. He'd been right; those men had families. The old world still needed them.

Lucretia, Eugene, Jeremiah, and all the Racosku they knew save Violet, plus a bunch more she'd need to think up names for, gathered at the beach to bid farewell to Sidney Daventry and James Wellington. She'd expected there to be more tears at their parting, but instead, it all felt like the end of a story, a good story. The kind where she'd get to watch the heroes ride off into the sunset upon their noble steeds, even if those steeds were oddly proportioned and absurdly noisy warplanes and there wasn't actually a sun to set.

"Are you gonna be all right to fly?" she asked Sidney. His head was still bandaged, his right eye still covered, but the scars and swelling had mostly receded.

"As good as can be," Sidney said with a smile. "I just hope no one's shooting at me when we get back. I think I've already earned the dubious distinction of having wrecked more Westland Wyverns than any man alive. Not sure I want to add to the tally."

Brain ambled forward, holding in its foreleg a pouch made from material Lucretia had cut from her travel bag. The reddish Racosku extended its foreleg to Sidney.

"It's for your eye," Lucretia said. "Some of the soil to take back with you, just in case."

Sidney took the pouch reverently, then touched Brain's foreleg. "Thank you. Thank you all."

"They're very grateful," Lucretia said, taking Sidney's hand. "And so am I."

Sidney took both of her hands, dressing them in a chivalrous kiss. "Goodbye, Tang Chao-Xing. Don't you ever stop dreaming."

Lucretia smiled. "You take care of those girls, you hear? Teach them to dream too."

"You have my word on that." He touched her cheek, then shook Jeremiah's hand and said his goodbyes.

"Watch out for that one," Jim said to Lucretia, gesturing at Eugene. "He's a sly old fox, he is!"

"Oh, don't worry, I can handle him!" She embraced the young executive officer.

The men said nothing to Eugene; they had already said their farewells. Only stoic nods and rigid salutes, that silly British salute with the palm facing outward. Then, as the minutes wound down, as clouds appeared on either horizon, they got into their Wyverns. The engines screamed to life, the propeller blades churning like their own little maelstroms.

The clouds began to swirl as the Wyverns taxied to the far end of the strip and turned around. They would take off in the direction of the vortex. Lucretia reached for her phone, holding it out in front and activating the video camera. To hell with temporal paradoxes and all that sci-fi shit. This was a moment worth capturing.

Jim Wellington's Wyvern leaped into the air, climbing and banking toward the descending wormhole, maintaining discipline and decorum throughout the pattern. Sidney Daventry followed close behind but couldn't resist a nice big barrel roll right as he disappeared into the tempest of cloud.

And then, they were gone. The storm vanished, and all was tranquil again, and the forest's serenade danced in Lucretia's ears.

Only to be disturbed by Eugene's grumble. "Such disregard for regulations."

Lucretia spun around, only to find the commander giggling like a schoolboy. His mirth quickly infected Lucretia and Jeremiah.

"Well," Lucretia said, gazing out at the glittering river, the glowing forest, the serene purple heavens, the majesty that was her new home, "it's all over now. We saved the world."

She took a moment to let that sink in. *We saved the freaking world! Damn, that's awesome.*

And not just one of them. All of them. Whether it'd been divine intervention, or fate, or mere chance, the right people had been brought to that one place, at that one time. It seemed too perfect to be chance, but...maybe nature *did* find a way. Without Jeremiah's knowledge, Lucretia wouldn't have been able to engineer the compounds that saved the pollinators. Without the Wyverns and their rockets, without the noble men who flew them and Eugene's steadfast leadership to guide them, there'd have been no way to get the compounds where they needed to go. And, who knew, perhaps without Tom Wickler's moment of insanity, Eugene may never have had his epiphany.

Sometimes, things just worked out for the best.

"So," Eugene said after a moment of peace, "what shall we do now?"

"We enjoy ourselves, I guess." Lucretia looked at Jeremiah, his face afflicted with a puerile smirk. *Oh, no. I know what he's thinking.* "Anything but *Sharknado*!"

CHAPTER XVIII

THE STORM HAD been much less violent than Sid had remembered from the first time. So it had seemed; maybe he had simply been prepared for it this time.

Almost in the blink of his one good eye, the storm was gone, and azure daylight was all around Sid's canopy. The cloudless sun seared his eye. His temples hurt as if being stabbed by a screwdriver.

He glanced around the sky. The storm was gone; not a wisp of cloud remained.

And he couldn't see WP335.

"Spoke One, come in?" he said frantically.

"Beneath you, mate," Jim's carefree reply came a second later. "No need to fret."

Sid rolled slightly left, peering over his wing at the Wyvern about a thousand feet below, almost directly under him. Breathing a sigh of relief, he took another look around. Nothing there but a gradient of blue. Blue sky, blue sea.

No sign of the coastline.

"Shit," Sid muttered into his radio, looking down at his compass and noting that they were heading north, away from Port Said. "Where the hell are we?"

"Check your eleven!" Jim yelped like a boy who'd just kissed the girl of his dreams for the first time.

Sid looked through his windscreen's left panel, noting several white lines gashing the deep blue of the Mediterranean. Ships' wakes. "Are they ours? Can you see?"

"Are they ever, mate! That's *Eagle* down there!"

Damned if he wasn't right.

Suddenly, Sid's heart was dancing. *Hello, beautiful!* Even from afar, Sid could make out the big gray hulk with the flat top, a behemoth amid the smattering of smaller escort vessels. His mind pictured the angled lines on the deck, calling him home, and the big white J painted on her bow. Was it real? Were his eyes deceiving him?

No, even with one eye, he could see just fine. They were almost home.

"All right," Jim said, "let me call them, make sure they're heading into the wind for us."

"Hold on, sir." He eyed the ship, and he knew damned well that trying to land on a moving, pitching carrier deck without his depth perception would be like driving a car without a steering wheel. "I might be best just punching out and letting the whirlybird come get me. There's no way I'm catching that wire with one eye."

"I thought you weren't keen on wrecking any more Wyverns, mate. Besides, you eject and you risk further injury. What about that magic dirt the lads gave you?"

Of course! Sid reached into his pocket, where he'd placed the pouch next to Marie's cross. He opened it, kneading the soil through his fingers. The yellow light had all but gone out, as if whatever gave it its luster had lost its power the farther it was from its source, but some lingered, like the last embers of a waning fire. Sid lifted his bandage, rubbing the soil over his eye.

He blinked. Nothing.

He blinked again.

Slowly, the red glaze drew back, and he could see, clearer than ever before. "It worked!" he squealed. "All right, Spoke One. Let's go home!"

"Best idea you've had all day, mate!"

As Sid watched HMS *Eagle* turning slightly to the right, he maneuvered his aircraft half a mile behind Jim's, banking gently to the right to keep the view of the ship from being obstructed by the Wyvern's huge nose. At one hundred seventy knots, he lowered the flaps the first notch. The plane jolted more than it had back on the alien world. As the carrier grew larger and larger in his windscreen, he went through the final checks. *Brakes off, sufficient pressure. Air brakes closed. Arrester hook down. Wheels down and locked. Tail wheel unlocked*—that was the proper procedure for deck landings. *Flaps down. Harness locked.*

As Jim approached the deck, Sid could see a helicopter landing on *Eagle*'s forward deck. *Lucky bastards*, he thought; they didn't have to worry about which way the wind was blowing. He turned his attention back to his leader, just passing over the ship's rear deck.

Perfect landing.

The pressure was on Sid now. He dropped his airspeed to one hundred knots, eyes fixed on the myriad lights of the optical landing system, specifically the red one floating this way and that—the meatball, in aviator parlance; the one that relayed his position relative to the flight deck—working the control column and throttle to get that red light right in the middle where it belonged.

He leveled off just behind the deck, shoving the throttle forward as his wheels slapped the armored steel surface. The Wyvern jolted to a halt that would've thrown Sid straight out of the cockpit were it not for that magnificent harness. Exhaling, he quickly raised the tailhook, folded the wings, and followed the deckhand's instructions to his parking space beside Jim's ship. He quickly ran through his shutdown checklist, securing his electronics and ejection seat, and opened his canopy hood for what he hoped would be the last time.

The noise of turbines and rotors and rushing wind and displaced water and men shouting assaulted his ears as he got down from his plane. As he followed Jim to the ship's island, he saw a man running at them from the direction of the helicopter.

It was D.B. Barluck.

After embracing the soaked, shivering young pilot, Jim led him and Sid into the island, where they'd at least be out of the wind and be able to talk without shouting.

"It's good to see you up and breathing, Lieutenant," Jim said to Barluck.

"You too, sir," the tall, stout man said. He turned to Sid. "And you, Daventry."

"Are you well?" Sid asked.

Barluck nodded. "They want me in the sick bay to get checked out, but I had to see my mates!" His rosy mien quickly turned pensive. "Where's the skipper?"

Sid nodded to Jim.

Jim bowed his head. "Commander Faintary and Lieutenant Wickler were lost in inclement weather. It's only by the commander's actions that Lieutenant Daventry and I were able to return."

"Damn," Barluck sniffled. "Such a shame, especially now."

"What do you mean?" Sid asked.

"Haven't you heard? The fighting's over. We're going home!"

❧

Home. The word danced in Sid's thoughts as his clear eyes beheld the letter, written in Marie's elegant hand. *Home. The place I belong.*

Now more than ever.

Four days into the journey back to England, the memory of what had happened on that alien world had faded, almost as if it had been a dream, a good dream. Lucretia Tang, and jolly Jeremiah, and those incredible Racosku, and even Gene Faintary were characters in that dream, characters in a story that took on a life of its own, and he would remember them, but he'd shed no tear for them, for they were always with him, if only in memory. But memory had a life of its own, a life that endured through space, through time, even through death. That chapter was over; he would reread it, relive it in his dreams, but now it was time to turn the page, for, as he pored over the joyous words before him, he knew that a new chapter was indeed ready to be written. The pen had already been put to the paper.

A knock on his bunk's railing startled him. Jim Wellington was standing beside him, holding a duffel bag.

"I'm gathering up Wickler's things to send to Susannah," Jim said. "Is there anything you'd like to send? A note of condolences, maybe? You were his section leader."

Sid exhaled. "Sure, give me a minute. I'll write something. I guess I owe Hags that much. Just a quick 'Sorry for your loss,' eh?"

"Aye, mate."

Sid put down Marie's letter, gathering a pen and paper from the drawer beside his bed. But as he pressed the tip to the sheet, he halted. "No. I'm going to write a proper letter. I'm going to tell her that he was a fine and dutiful naval officer. I know Tom had his vices—the arrogance, the bigotry, the zealotry—but who am I to say that those were the only things that defined him? Maybe I'm wrong to lie, but Susannah needn't know what happened. After all, there's a little baby inside her right now. That child will never know its father. No harm in letting them grow up believing their father was a good man. Maybe then they'll grow to be the person that Tom never was."

Jim nodded. "What about you?"

Sid exhaled. "I think I'm done with this life, Jim. I've had enough of war. I'm proud to have done my duty, but after what we've just been through? It just…gave me a new perspective, I think. I keep hearing about those companies out west flying old bombers and Cansos to fight forest fires. I'm sure they're looking for pilots. Besides, Marie always wanted to see the mountains." He slapped the letter. "And we're going to need more space; our little house is about to become very crowded!"

Jim's face lit up. "You're having another baby, mate?"

Sid nodded proudly.

"Well, congratulations, Sidney!" Jim shot him a sly wink, giving him a firm pat on the back. "Think it'll be another girl?"

"Oh, Lord have mercy! Well, if it is, I like the name Lucretia. I think Marie will agree."

"That's a good name, mate. And if it's a boy?"

Sid didn't need a moment to think. *He'll be named after the finest man I've ever known. The one I swore to remember, to honor.* "Eugene."

❧

The last lyrics of "Sleeping Sun" by Nightwish trailed away, yielding to the music of the forest seeping into the laboratory through the arched doorway. That had always been Lucretia's favorite song. How it swept her away, took her to another world, a world of endless twilight and enchanted forests. A world of her dreams. And now, she was there in that world, and her most blissful nighttime would indeed last a lifetime.

"Splendid tune," Eugene said. He was in the corner playing checkers with Violet—though, unlike Jeremiah, he wasn't taking it easy on the poor creature.

"Sure is." Lucretia sat down next to him. "We're gonna need more games."

"Oh, I disagree. This chap's getting quite good at draughts." He offered an admiring nod to the Racosku.

Draughts? Oh, yeah, that's what they call checkers in England. "We're going to need new clothes, too. These ones won't last forever. I mean, I guess we could all just run naked through the forest. No one's gonna see us. But I really don't want to look at my brother's naked body."

"What are you talking about?" Jeremiah boasted, tearing off his shirt. "You've got Adonis in the flesh over here."

Lucretia cringed. "Well, there's certainly plenty of flesh." She shook her head to expunge that ghastly vision. "Yeah, living here is going to take some getting used to. We've got a lot to figure out."

"Well," Eugene said, "we can't say as we're pressed for time."

Jeremiah chimed in: "What if we fixed our plane, flew through the next wormhole, went shopping for clothes and movies and maybe some snacks—I mean, my diabetes is cured, so I can eat whatever I want now without you lecturing me—and then flew right back?"

"Are you insane?" Lucretia barked. "Who knows where we'd end up if we tried something like that? I mean, we could end up in the time of Genghis Khan!"

"Or in China during the Tang Dynasty," Jeremiah suggested. "I mean, we're Tangs, right? We ought to be treated like royalty!"

"Yeah, right. Our luck, they'd make me a concubine and you into a eunuch. And who's to say we'd even end up on Earth, and not some distant planet full of poisonous gases and evil aliens and temperatures hotter than our old sun?"

Jeremiah bit his lip. "Yeah, that's probably a bad idea. I guess we'll have to make do with what we have."

"What we have will do. And what we don't have, we'll make." Suddenly, she pinched her eyes shut. "Okay, we definitely need the clothes. Because there's no magic in this world that could heal the scars in my psyche if I have to see you running through the forest with your junk dangling."

Eugene buried his face in his hands, grumbling.

Suddenly, Violet stirred, as if to get up and scurry to the window, drawn by something happening outside, forgetting its brokenness for a moment. Lucretia smiled at the creature, pity giving way to resolve. *I'll fix you, I promise. You will run with your friends again.*

Lucretia got up, following Jeremiah and Eugene to the door. The Racosku—hundreds of them—were moving in a herd toward the beach. Brain was at the van leading them. The procession was slow and solemn, yet the air around the creatures carried a savory scent, and the mood was one not of mourning but of something like reverence, like devotion. Like a religious ritual.

The three humans followed the creatures until they stopped, not at the beach but by the wreckage of WL891. The Racosku gathered around the aircraft, swaying on their tentacles, rubbing the hairs on their forelegs together.

Lucretia raised an eyebrow. "Are they…worshipping it?"

"It's the symbol of their salvation," Eugene said, and his arm curled around Lucretia's shoulder, the other around Jeremiah's. "That aeroplane was made to be a weapon of war, an instrument of death. But only through the wickedness of men was that task made manifest. Here, they know it only as something that gave life, that brought hope. The things we make are just that: things. They have no souls, no free will. How many of our greatest inventions that we use for ill, that we wield with envy and greed and hatred, could make the kind of difference that Willie Love did if we only wielded them with hands of kindness?"

Lucretia nodded, smiling. How true that was for so many things. How often did humans blame their problems on inanimate objects, objects that only did what the sentient hands upon them, the very hands that made them, guided them to do? How often did they chide the things they created for causing them to sin when, with just a little willpower, those very same things could have been used for virtuous deeds?

"And what about the humans who used that plane to bring their salvation?" Jeremiah sneered. "No love for them?"

"That's not true, Jay," Lucretia said. "You know that. Why do you think they invited us to live in their world?"

"Our lives are fleeting," Eugene added. "That's why we build monuments and shrines, why we take photographs and paint portraits. So that we'll live on through them long after we return to dust. Willie Love will endure long after we've gone, broken, rusted and faded maybe, but a monument to you and me and James and Sidney. After all, we are all of us flawed, and all too often we falter. Better, then, that they should revere the vehicle of our successes rather than the vessels of our weaknesses."

With a warm smile, Lucretia took Eugene's hand, and he did not shun her.

Jeremiah shrugged in agreement. "You realize, though, that we've basically created a cult, right?"

Lucretia chortled. "A cult of the Wyvern!"

EPILOGUE

Present Day

WHEN GARETH OGDEN took a job as research assistant to the famed author and aviation historian Nigel Allcock, he thought he'd landed the gig of a lifetime. After all, Nigel was a star, least-wise as much of one as anyone in his profession could be. He'd act as a consultant for Hollywood films, having champagne and caviar with the hottest celebrities; he'd travel to exotic places and stay in fancy hotels; his long, saggy face was on every aircraft-re-lated documentary on the airwaves.

Gareth's first hint should've been the job description. Scratch that—the job title itself: *research assistant.* For which the primary responsibility was *research.* Digging through musty old archives, scouring the internet in a dark room, sorting through lists and records and logbooks, so far from the glitz and glamour that Nigel so often found himself surrounded by that he might as well have been on the other side of the universe.

It was a beautiful autumn day and they were in London,

deep in the bowels of the National Archives, looking for records Nigel could use to finish his book about the Suez Crisis of 1956. Gareth didn't know what the old man had hoped to find; the conflict had been written about exhaustively. What new could even a writer of Nigel's caliber bring to the subject?

And why couldn't they just have done a web search from home?

Of course, Gareth told himself, *Nige does everything the old-fashioned way, as if it makes him a better writer. Prick.*

After rooting through drawers full of logbooks for endless hours, expecting to come up empty-handed, Gareth found a volume, a private journal written by the captain of the aircraft carrier HMS *Eagle*. He browsed the stained pages, struggling to read the sloppily handwritten notes.

Then, he stopped.

"Hey, Nige! I think I've got something!"

Nigel's head poked above the desk like a meerkat peeping out of its den. "Keep it down, boy! Other people are working here too, you know."

Are they? I don't see any. Gareth shrugged, got up, and walked the journal to Nigel. "Look," he said, pointing to the page that had caught his attention. "It says that a flight of five Westland Wyverns from Number 1776 Naval Air Squadron took off on sixth November and were never heard from again. Look here, the page is torn at the bottom, but I make out something about a 'strange weather phenomenon.' It seems the planes just disappeared."

Nigel screwed up his jowly face. "Bollocks. Only one Wyvern squadron was operational during Operation Musketeer, and each of their aircraft and sorties is accounted for. We know that two were downed by anti-aircraft fire: Whiskey November Three-Three-Zero while striking the Gamil Bridge on third November, and the senior pilot in Whiskey November Three-Two-Eight two days later. Both crewmen ejected and were rescued, and those were the only Wyvern losses in the conflict. This is hogwash."

Sometimes, Gareth envied Nigel's encyclopedic knowledge of aircraft; others, he wanted nothing more than to beat it out of the old man to make room for some sensibility. "But, Nige, this is the ship's captain writing this! Aren't you curious about what happened to those planes and their pilots?"

Nigel looked over the journal, an extended, sonorous "Hmm" gurgling from his gut and hanging in the musty air like the groan of a rutting stag.

At last, Nigel closed the journal, shrugging as he placed it back in Gareth's hands, and voiced his professional conclusion:

"Must've been aliens."

AUTHOR'S NOTE

For a book that started out as little more than a play on a running joke on #avgeek social media, I have to say I'm rather pleased with how this one turned out!

The Westland Wyvern is something of a cult favorite among a certain cadre of aviation enthusiasts—hence the title of, and inspiration for, this book. The type led a quite troubled history, though this is often the case when pioneering so much new technology. Think of the more contemporary V-22 Osprey tiltrotor, much maligned in the media and public spheres due to some teething problems early in its development that unfortunately resulted in several fatal mishaps, but now that the kinks have been ironed out, an extremely good and reliable aircraft. Alas, the Wyvern never had the chance to fully exorcise its demons in the same way, as it was withdrawn from service in the spring of 1958 after a protracted development cycle and an operational career of just under five years. In that short time, thirty-nine airframes were lost in accidents, out of sixty-eight total mishaps, with thirteen tragic fatalities.

Number 1776 Naval Air Squadron is a fictitious unit— surely, no one in Her Majesty's Royal Navy would countenance the crass indignity of designating an elite flying squadron after the year we filthy Colonials shunned the King's good graces and rashly declared our independence! The actual Wyvern outfit that saw combat during Operation Musketeer was No. 830 NAS, whose nine aircraft flew seventy-nine sorties from HMS *Eagle* between 1 and 6 November 1956.

Astute observers will surely notice that I've taken some liberties with the identification of the aircraft in this tale. The serial numbers I've assigned to the Wyverns in this nonexistent squadron are also fictitious, and, per my research, have never been assigned to any UK military aircraft, though they are in sequence with serial numbers assigned to actual Westland Wyverns. By this logic, Sid's original ship, VW888, would have actually been a very early Wyvern built as the TF2 (Torpedo Fighter, Mark Two) variant, later converted to the ultimate S4 (Strike, Mark Four) standard. (In reality, this sequence stopped at VW886.) The short monograph *A History of the Westland Wyvern*, published in 1973 by the Blackbushe Aviation Research Group and an indispensable resource in the writing of this novel, offers a brief but detailed history of each of the 127 Wyverns produced.

Sid's underwater ejection at the end of Chapter 3 is based on an actual occurrence, in which the Westland Wyvern indeed claimed the dubious honor of being the first aircraft from which its pilot ejected while submerged. The incident happened on 13 November 1954 in the Mediterranean Sea, as Lt. B.D. Macfarlane attempted a routine launch from HMS *Albion* but suffered an engine failure due to fuel starvation from the force of the catapult acceleration. (The issue of the fuel pump's failure was eventually rectified, but the Wyvern never shook its reputation for being accident-prone.) It was a harrowing experience for the lieutenant, but he indeed lived to tell the tale, and that's what's important.

The story of Lt. Cdr. Eugene Esmonde and the sacrifice of No. 825 Naval Air Squadron in February 1942 is true. The attack was a disaster, with all six Swordfish shot down before they could launch their torpedoes, but the bravery of those men did not go unnoticed, with even the German admiral making reverent mention of them in his reports. Hopefully, by my mention of it in this book, you will be inspired to learn more about this tragic act of selflessness, that it shall always be remembered, like so many such acts amid the horror and inhumanity of war.

A big thank-you to Mirna Gilman and Sabrina Broderick, my beta readers; and to Eliza Dee, my editor of four books now. Without yinz, this would verily be a lesser book. I'd also like to tip my cap to the anonymous chap on eBay who sold me the Westland Wyvern pilot's manual that was so invaluable in providing the technical details. Of course, as always, my deepest gratitude goes to **<your name here>** for sharing this adventure with me. It's truly a privilege, and a pleasure, to write for you.

Stay tuned for the next installment in this series of an American author writing outrageous tales featuring obscure British military aircraft: *Saved by the Blackburn Blackburn!*

(I'm kidding. Or...am I?)